THE VIKING'S CURSED BRIDE

MAIRIBETH MACMILLAN

CLOTA
PRESS

THE VIKING'S CURSED BRIDE

Brothers of Thunder Book One

Mairibeth MacMillan

First edition

Author Copyright 2019 Mairibeth MacMillan

Editor: Lucy Felthouse

Proofreader: Sharon Pickrel

Second Edition

Author Copyright 2021 Mairibeth MacMillan

Cover Design Copyright 2019 Cora Graphics www.coragraphics.it

To Euan, James, Eilidh and Marissa.
All my love.
Always.

Acknowledgments

With many thanks to everyone who has helped me and supported me during the past few years, especially my family. It wouldn't have been possible without any of you.

There are too many to mention everyone individually, but an extra special thanks goes to my two writing groups, one past, one present, and particularly Julie Bissell for her unending support and helpful suggestions (I would not have finished this book without you!).

To Sara Israelsson for her insightful contributions and patience during our many conversations on all things Norse, and also to my editor, Lucy Felthouse, whose patience while I fixed a hundred things I knew better than to do in the first place is much appreciated.

And lastly to Marguerite Kaye for all her support and many, many cups of coffee looking out onto the Firth of Clyde where the story is set!

The Viking's Cursed Bride

Rejected by her own people, despite saving them all from the Norse raid on Alt Clut two years ago, Aoife's father forces her to marry one of the Kingdom of Strathclyde's Norse invaders. While this rids her family of a cursed daughter, and rescues her from a miserable existence as a nun, she may be in more danger among the enemy if they discover her secret.

Jarl Tormod intends to settle on the River Clut and a high-born bride from amongst the Britons ought to ensure the safety and prosperity of the Norse settlement. But when relentless attacks on the settlement threaten their future on the shores of the Clyde, Tormod realises the Britons have deceived him and must consider extreme measures to exact revenge. But is his new wife to blame?

All Aoife wants is a place to belong, but traitors are everywhere, and finding those responsible might mean losing those they hold most dear.

.

PROLOGUE

*A*LT *CLUT, KINGDOM OF Alt Clut, 870 CE*

"Smile," Aoife's stepmother, Ula, hissed at her. "You don't want King Artgal to think you are ungrateful you were invited, do you? He has been known to punish even his most loyal subjects for less. And for one such as you..." Ula's cruel laughter made Aoife want to run far from here. Not that she had anywhere truly safe to go. She glanced towards the dais and managed to force her lips into some semblance of a smile, then returned her attention to the plateful in front of her.

All around her, the families of the richest, most important nobles of the kingdom of Alt Clut feasted. Every one of the long wooden tables was full, and the room was too warm for the fire burning in the grate, more to demonstrate the wealth of the king than from necessity on a summer night such as this one. The gathered nobles were richly dressed in heavy woollen kirtles, and with the excessive heat, the stench of their sweat only grew stronger as the feast wore on, making Aoife's stomach churn. Not even the smell of roasted meats and vegetables could mask it.

Aoife pulled at the neck of her dress. She'd grown over the past winter and Ula had not yet instructed the servants to make a new summer dress for her. Ula's four natural-born daughters always came first. There was also the fact she knew Ula did not wish her to look too attractive tonight — at least not in comparison to her half-sisters. Any suitor found at a gathering such as this one was of a higher status than Ula would ever allow Aoife to marry.

"Eat," demanded Ula, nudging her elbow and smiling beatifically towards the king.

Aoife lifted a mouthful to her lips. Obediently, she chewed and choked it down as fast as possible under her stepmother's wrathful glare. It tasted like ashes. The noise of the surrounding revelry was giving her a headache. The smoke from the fire stung her eyes and the heat made her queasy. The room swayed around her. She closed her eyes, then felt a sharp elbow in her ribs. Her eyes flew open.

"If you bring dishonour to our family..." her stepmother whispered urgently, her cold expression and hands clasped as if in prayer making it clear where Aoife would be headed. A prisoner forever behind the bare stone walls of the abbey, with no family, no hope for a home, nor a husband and children.

Not that she was sure why she yearned for those things. Her own childhood had been far from idyllic. And there was little chance of any of them before Ula had secured decent marriages for Aoife's half-sisters. But she wished for them, nonetheless.

Across the room, a gentleman caught her eye and inclined his head towards her. She thought she recognised him but couldn't remember his name. She nodded at him.

"Keep your eyes down," Ula said. "And if you have any ideas in your head about Lord Cadwgan, then forget them. He will not be for you."

"And what if I am *his* choice?" Aoife replied before she could stop herself. Sometimes she found it hard not to answer her stepmother back, despite knowing it only ever made her life more difficult.

"Your father will send him away," Ula promised, hatred etched on her features. "Your father always does what I tell him."

It was true and becoming more true as each year passed. Ula's influence over her father's decisions was not a good thing. Not for the first time, she wished her own mother was still alive to care for her and protect her. What Aoife would have given for her to have lived through her brother's birth. But they had both died, and her father, Lord Cadell, had remarried. And now she had Ula as a stepmother. Most of Cadell's people had been happy to see him marry another Briton rather than a Pict. Aoife had often regretted that her father had not sent her back to her mother's family in Pictland, but Cadell wasn't willing to give up anything belonging to him – even an unwanted daughter.

Aoife picked up her cup of wine and took a sip. A wave of dizziness swept through her. The cup clattered onto the table, wine spilling like blood and seeping into the wood. She clutched at the edge, as if doing so would help her remain conscious. Then she glared at her stepmother. Had the woman finally poisoned her, hoping she could blame another?

"What are you doing?" Ula demanded, talon-like fingers gripping Aoife's elbow. "Stop this at once."

But Aoife's eyes no longer saw the woman, nor the room, nor the walls of the hall at Alt Clut. At first, she didn't understand what she saw. She smelt the salt tang of the sea and heard the whoosh of waves and the cry of gulls. It was night, dark out on the water, and yet in front of her were the heads of hundreds of serpents. They approached Alt Clut in the darkness just before the dawn and swept onto the land, slithering up the walls of the rock and on into the fort. Above them, two ravens circled, watching the progress of the serpents, their frantic screeching encouraging the invaders. Blood-curdling screams sounded, and she realised they were her own.

"They're coming! The sea serpents are coming!"

A slap from her stepmother was hard enough to jar her neck and her head hit the back of the wooden chair, sending her down into darkness.

CHAPTER ONE

Tormod glanced from Lord Cadell to his wife, Lady Ula, and couldn't help but grin. From the giveaway turn of Cadell's head towards his wife at every question posed to the man, it took little to guess it was Lady Ula who controlled the decisions in this household. And what a bitter household that must make it.

"So, an alliance between us," Tormod stated. "Sealed with the hand of one of your daughters and my word that my men will seek no more of your land for their own as long as our agreement remains in place."

"An alliance," confirmed Lord Cadell, raising his tankard of ale after only the slightest of glances at his wife. The woman's expression was hard to read. He'd have expected regret at giving one of her daughters to a barbarian such as himself, but instead, it was more like... glee.

For a moment he wondered if there was some trickery in their agreement, but having a high-status Briton in his village could only help with trade negotiations and reduce the likelihood of attacks from these people. As long as the daughter was capable of warming his bed and bearing his sons, he cared for little else from her. Beauty was certainly not a prerequisite.

His first wife had been the most beautiful woman he'd ever seen, but her heart had been black and deceitful. He would give his heart to no other in this lifetime. That way led only to betrayal and despair. It had been a hasty marriage, which had accomplished nothing more than to prove he was a fool.

He straightened. The past was the past. He had grown and learned since then and would not be taken for a fool by a woman again.

He caught Lady Ula's smirk and wondered if it would be best to see this girl before the final agreement was made, but Lord Cadell pushed himself to his feet.

"Lady Aoife is not within the walls of Car Cadell at present. She will need to be sent for," Cadell announced. "I will also need to gather together the other items we have agreed to... exchange."

Tormod smiled inwardly at the man's reluctance to admit to having no other choice than to agree to Tormod's demands. The siege and capture of Alt Clut two years previously had reduced the power of the Britons in Alt Clut and Norse settlers were pushing their advantage, forming settlements and trading posts all along the coasts of the great river. Under Artgal's son, Rhun, the power centre had moved further up the great river to Gorfaen, where Doomster Hill now signified the centre of government of the new kingdom of Strath Clut—the successor to the kingdom of Alt Clut which had fallen after the siege.

Tormod himself had liberated a substantial peninsular area near the mouth of the firth from Lord Cadell. Liberated may be too strong a word — by the time his men had made landfall, the inhabitants had fled.

Their new settlement was nearly built and as jarl he was determined to make it more prosperous than anything the previous owners had accomplished. The extra tools, seeds and animals from Lord Cadell would contribute to the success of the growing village, and a wife and sons for Tormod would ensure his future as jarl.

"Two mornings hence, then. When the sun has risen to its full height, at Ffos-y-Lan where our lands meet." Tormod smiled again, amused by Cadell's frown. Tormod had usurped some of Cadell's land, abandoned or not. But with no resistance, why should Tormod feel even the slightest twinge of guilt? If these Britons were not strong enough to hold their lands, then they didn't deserve them and this alliance with Cadell was only a means to a more peaceful future. Many of Tormod's people were tired of raiding — after all, what good were riches if you didn't get to enjoy them? But he and his men would hold the land by force if need be.

The most worrying thing about this alliance was that Lord Cadell had few friends. He had few friends left amongst his fellow Britons. Perhaps because he was the only nobleman present at King Artgal's banquet who had escaped the siege. It had taken the Norsemen four months—the entire summer—to capture Alt Clut, but Lord Cadell and his family were rumoured to have simply left as the longships were sailing up the river. Had someone warned them? Rumours abounded amongst the Britons that Cadell had been in league with the Norsemen, but Tormod knew of no Norseman who trusted the man. King Artgal's son Rhun had not been present at the banquet either, but the finger of suspicion never seemed to rest on him for long before Cadell was named.

Despite this, the man was still a wealthy man with substantial lands. Tormod's life would be far more peaceful if he were not fighting with his nearest neighbour constantly, although he suspected that, despite any alliance, Cadell would seize any opportunity to recover the land. But Tormod would be watchful, and surely, with their daughter as his wife, Cadell would hesitate to attack.

"Do you wish to stay here tonight, my lord?" Lady Ula asked. "Appropriate lodgings can be found for you and your... men." The look she gave him confirmed she saw the Norsemen as barbarians, far beneath her own civilised status.

Tormod's hand clenched on the hilt of his sword, and he felt Björn tense beside him. He was grateful he stood here with three of his cousins at his back. Cousins by blood, but they regarded each other as brothers. The brothers of thunder. He knew none of them would ever let him down in the face of an enemy—even if one had every right to doubt him.

"Our best rooms, of course," Lady Ula assured them, smiling sweetly after a nudge from her husband.

"Our thanks, my lady," replied Tormod. "But we have been too long from home already and it is not more than a few hours' ride. Until noon two days hence then, Lord Cadell, and the penalty for failing to honour our agreement will be... violent."

Tormod swept from the room, followed by his men. He'd brought only a small group of those he trusted most. No one spoke until they were clear of the fort's palisades.

"Well?" asked Björn. "Do you think he will abide by the agreement?"

"If not, then we will return," said Tormod. "And our lands will grow."

His men laughed—all except Ulf.

"There's something about the daughter," Ulf said. "I don't know what it is, but I sensed no reluctance in either of them to part with her. And why was she not within these walls?"

"Ulf," said Tormod. "We will find out two days from now. But my needs when it comes to a wife are simple enough."

Ulf merely nodded at him, and Tormod was relieved he did not mention Ingrid by name. Yet Tormod rode the rest of the way home, disturbed by thoughts of what could possibly be wrong with Cadell's daughter and realising it mattered to him more than he would have cared to admit.

CHAPTER TWO

AOIFE SHIFTED SLIGHTLY FROM one knee to the other, desperate for morning prayers to be over. She had barely slept, her dreams filled with the rumbling of thunder as they had been now for weeks. The low booming echoed around every part of her body and from the depths of the sound came a vision — the same every time — a bear and a wolf walked side by side on the land while a hawk flew high above them. Three creatures were all she had seen, but there was a fourth. She was sure of it. Someone she'd been running from, but the faster she ran, the closer he got. One whom she could not see, could simply feel his presence in the thunder. It was as if the thunder itself was a living being, intent on consuming her.

A raven croaked and her eyes shot open, her gaze drawn towards the window where weak sunlight trickled in. Her lips curved into a smile, which then faded. What she wouldn't give to be outside this morning, or any morning. She missed walking by the loch with her maid, Rhiannon, and the sounds of the fort. Even the smells. The food here was plentiful but basic, and she missed the excitement of the men returning from the hunt, followed by the smell of roasting meat.

It had been almost two years now and she couldn't bear the thought of another summer stuck behind these dreary stone walls, where any hint of comfort was soon taken from her. She'd thought living under her father's roof had been miserable until she'd been sent here. At least there she'd had pretty clothes and jewellery and games to play with her sisters. Here, she had nothing. Nothing but time to think. At summer's end, she would be expected to take her vows as a nun—something which every part of her rebelled against. She knew she had no vocation, and she didn't want to spend the rest of her life imprisoned here.

Two ravens fluttered down to sit on the window ledge and stared directly at her. Then they tilted their heads, exchanged a glance, and took off. She bowed her head in prayer once more, trying not to think about the freedom enjoyed by the birds but denied to her. The ravens were also a reminder of Alt Clut.

Despite her attempts to ignore the memories, the sights and sounds of the attack on Alt Clut assailed her. Despite opening her eyes, she could still see the past. As dawn had broken, they had looked across their lands to the firth only to see hundreds of ships heading towards Alt Clut. Wooden ships with dragons carved at the prows, the square sails of Norse raiders striking terror into all their hearts.

"We must warn them," Ula had said.

Cadell closed his hands over his wife's and stared at her. His skin was pale, fear etched on his face. "Aoife already did. They didn't want to listen. There is nothing more we can do. We should return home and prepare for an attack."

The boats had moved swiftly, cutting easily through the deep water of the river towards the rock on which Alt Clut stood. The warriors flooded onto the land at its base while others surrounded the rock in their boats, cutting the inhabitants off from any source of supplies.

They had turned back along the road through the hills, the sounds of battle carrying through the still air behind them. The clatter of swords and shields and axes and the screams of the dying. Tears slid down Aoife's face. If they had only listened to her... But they hadn't.

As they rode away, an old beggar man emerged from the bushes. His long, grey hair was partially covered by a misshapen hat pulled tight onto his head, almost managing to conceal a lost eye.

"Alms for those less fortunate," he begged.

Her father shook his head. As they passed the old man, two ravens screeched high above them, then came to rest on the old man's arm. One tilted its head and stared straight at her. It was just like one of the ravens in her vision. But then, didn't all ravens look alike? She reached for a crust of bread that lay wrapped in a pouch beside her sisters and threw it.

The raven took off and swept in to catch the crust, then carried it straight back to his master.

"Aoife."

It was little more than a whisper. She couldn't swear she'd heard it. How could the old man have known her name?

When she had turned back to her family, her stepmother was staring at her, hatred and fear colouring her features. For a moment, she had thought Ula was going to kill her. It had taken her months to realise the only thing stopping Ula was the fear that even in death, Aoife might strike her down.

In the end, it had taken four long months of a siege before King Artgal surrendered due to lack of water. Aoife had heard rumours of most of those captured in the fort being taken as prisoners to Ath Cliath and sold as slaves. Artgal had been amongst them, and it was rumoured that Causantin of the Picts had effectively signed Artgal's death warrant. Now Eithne, Causantin's daughter, ruled the new kingdom of Strath Clut with her husband Rhun ap Artgal, son of the deceased king. Their son, Eochaid, now heir to both thrones. Aoife had always wondered exactly who had betrayed whom.

The amen sounded in the small chapel, bringing Aoife back to the present. She repeated it, not having heard a single word of the prayers. *So let it be*. She sighed. It was hard to believe that the God they spoke of was a loving one. But he was just like her father, absent and uncaring about the punishments inflicted on her in his name. She stood as the priest made his way along the row of nuns, followed by one of the monks. She repeated the necessary words and accepted the body and blood of Christ with as much humility as she could muster, but her gaze was drawn to the window and the ravens once more. They were watching her.

As the sisters filed out of the chapel towards the building housing their living quarters—more of a prison than a home in Aoife's opinion—they heard the sound of hoof beats. No one was allowed to speak, but they exchanged worried glances. Still, horses were better than the raiders who appeared first from the sea in their dragon boats.

Brother Pasgen headed for the gates and greeted the new arrivals. Aoife was shocked when they entered the courtyard and she recognised them as her father's men. What business could they have here? Brother Pasgen hurried over to her and took her arm, then led her towards her father's steward, Rhydderch. He handed her up into the small cart driven by her father's priest, Father Bricius. He gestured for her to sit, careful not to touch her or sit too close. She was almost grateful for the fact he feared her.

Sister Ninniaw handed her a small, familiar pouch. Aoife's only belongings, confiscated upon her arrival last year. Not that they were much, but she smiled to see them. Aoife rifled through it, disappointed to note the amethyst cross, given to her by her mother, was not amongst the meagre items inside. She remembered Father Bricius taking the pouch from her to hand to the nuns when he had brought her here. Had he taken the cross? Her stepmother had always coveted it. He was watching her, and his slight smirk made her think she was correct. She held tight to the pouch, placing it at the side of her, furthest from him.

Rhydderch headed out and onto the road. Bricius took up the reins, turned the cart and followed. So that was it? She'd been handed from one person to another. If her father had sent for her, she had no doubt it was not to improve her situation for her own sake. He must have found a different way for her to be of use to him.

"Where are we going?" she asked Father Bricius as soon as the cart passed out of the confines of the abbey. Rhydderch rode beside them.

"Your father has decided you are to be married," Father Bricius replied, then turned away from her as if there was nothing more to say.

"To whom?" Aoife asked tentatively. Many of her father's friends had been killed or taken as slaves during the raid on Alt Clut, and the others regarded him with suspicion. None of them would have seen her as any kind of prize. They would have wanted one of Ula's daughters as a bride, not her.

"A Norseman now holds the peninsula on the western edge of your father's lands," Rhydderch said. "You are to be married to him. The fool thinks it will seal an alliance with your father." His mocking laughter made her cringe.

A Norseman? One of the enemy? Why would her father... of course, Ula. Her stepmother would never offer any of her daughters to a Norseman, but it would be no sacrifice to marry Aoife to one. Then another, more chilling thought struck her. If her stepmother didn't care whether Aoife lived or died...

"Does... does my father plan to go back on his word?" She didn't expect an answer, certainly not a truthful one, but neither could she simply sit in silence.

"It is not a sin to break your word to a barbarian," Father Bricius stated, signalling an end to the discussion.

Was her father planning to reclaim his lands? What would happen to her then? When the Norsemen realised they had been tricked. She shuddered. They were not a people rumoured to be kind to those they conquered. Artgal was proof of that. Would her father send his men to rescue her? She looked at Rhydderch and doubted it. Then she turned to stare at the priest. Father Bricius refused to meet her eye. How could a man of God allow her to be treated like this? However, Aoife knew for a generous donation to the Church, these holy men would turn a blind eye to many things. She drew her cloak tightly around her and shifted as far away from the man as the seat would allow.

Aoife tried to make sense of it all as the cart trundled along. If this man, this Norseman, thought she was part of an alliance, what would happen when he found out how little her family cared for her? Perhaps if she told him before they were wed, he would understand and send her back. Did she want to go back, though? And to where? The abbey? There was nothing for her either there or at her father's home. She would just have to ensure the Norseman didn't find out the truth and try to make the best of her new life. Aoife was determined to survive this, as she had survived in the past.

CHAPTER THREE

BROTHERS OF THUNDER

T ORMOD STRODE BACKWARDS AND forwards across the pass. The sun had reached its height some time before. Tormod had not expected Cadell to be on time and had been proven correct.

"The Britons are late," Björn muttered beside him.

Tormod's fists clenched at the thought he'd been betrayed again. Not that Cadell would live to regret it. Tormod had noted many weaknesses in the man's defences when they'd visited the fort the day before yesterday—the most unforgivable of which, in Tormod's opinion, was Cadell's overconfidence.

Steep hills rose around the loch-side plain at Ffos-y-Lan, making it easily defensible for warriors such as his own. Eventually, all this land would be theirs, the land and all the riches that lay within them. This was the westernmost edge of the kingdom of Strath Clut, north of the firth. Dal Riata lay to the north, and the borders were often contested by the Britons in the south and the Gaels in the north. Occasionally the Picts invaded from the east, although now there was an ever-strengthening alliance between Pictland and Dal Riata which currently shared a king. He had as much right to claim it as any of the others, and for as long as he could hold it, then it was rightly his. The Norse controlled the rivers and seas far more successfully than these Britons had ever done.

Tormod's men spoke in low voices as they ate freshly caught fish by the fire. He knew they were aware of their surroundings and watched as carefully as he himself did. Armed with swords and shields as well as their axes, they were more than a match for the Britons, despite their heavier armour. The Britons' heavier chain made it awkward for them to move, never mind fight. Tormod preferred his more flexible chain over leather, giving him greater freedom of movement. Rarely did these Britons get close enough for him to need the armour, anyway.

He'd heard the rumours about Cadell's escape from the attack on Alt Clut two years ago, led by Ivarr the Boneless and Olaf the White. Cadell and his family had left mere hours before the Norse fleet had sailed up the Clut. The Britons suspected he'd been in league with the Norsemen. If it were true, however, he'd yet to find a Norseman who would admit to it. Most seemed as ignorant as the Britons about what had caused Lord Cadell to leave when he did. The only explanation seemed to centre around talk of demons, which Tormod was apt to dismiss. The Britons often blamed anything they didn't understand on demons when most likely it had been the actions of a coward unwilling to fight and die with his people.

The looks exchanged between Cadell and his wife still nagged at him, though. Was there something wrong with the girl? Surely, after everything that had happened here, Cadell would not be foolish enough to risk his wrath. The man had few allies to support him in a fight against the Norse.

"Jarl Tormod!" A young lad came running from further up the pass. "Cadell's men approach. Ten carts carrying the tools and grains agreed upon. There are many guards with them."

"Very well," said Tormod. "Most of our men should remain hidden while we greet our guests. Attack if there is any sign of treachery."

"Yes, *herre*."

"My bride...?" Tormod stopped himself from asking what she looked like. Her appearance was irrelevant. Provided she was capable of bearing him strong, healthy sons, he cared not whether Cadell thought he was cheating him in any other way.

"She is in the first of the carts," the boy replied. "With a holy man."

Tormod dismissed the boy, who ran off to spread the word.

Less than half an hour later, the procession of carts trundled into the pass.

"Lord Cadell?" Tormod called to the group.

"Lord Cadell sends his deepest regrets." A tall man, whom Tormod recognised as Cadell's steward, rode towards them. "I am his steward, Rhydderch—Lord Cadell has sent me in his stead."

When Tormod didn't react, Rhydderch halted his horse and inclined his head towards Tormod in a show of some respect, although Tormod suspected it was not heartfelt.

"I bring everything that was agreed," Rhydderch assured him. "Lord Cadell's presence was not promised in the agreement."

"Bring forward my bride," Tormod demanded, signalling to his men to check the items in the carts.

"Lady Aoife!" Rhydderch called.

Tormod saw a figure in a pale dress stand up. She climbed down from a cart, followed by a man dressed in dark robes. One of the Christian priests, no doubt sent to marry them. He waited, forcing them to come to him, noticing the priest didn't touch or help the girl, even though she was clearly exhausted and frightened. Had they travelled all night without allowing her to rest? She was dressed all in white, her hair covered by a veil. She looked like one of the Christian God's followers. Weren't those women forbidden from marrying and kept from men all their lives? Was this the joke Cadell and Lady Ula had shared?

Tormod couldn't quite work out at whose expense the joke had been played. An untouched woman, kept from other men, was not a disadvantage as far as he was concerned. Although, he had heard rumours that sometimes women were sent to the church as a result of their indiscretions. He would need to ensure she was not going to lumber him with another man's child. He needed an heir — his own son, this time — and if he found this to be the case, he would return her to her father.

At any rate, his worries about his bride having some kind of affliction were at least appeased. When he got close enough to see her face, he smiled. Despite her pallor and the slenderness of her figure, she seemed hale and whole. Her eyes were a strange shade of blue and a few wisps of red hair curled around the sides of her face. She was pretty. He would grant her that—maybe not beautiful, but certainly not the hideous troll he had begun to imagine.

When her gaze came to rest on him, her eyes widened and she drew in a sharp breath, then it slid to the ground. Her hands trembled, and he fought an urge to reassure her. He would show no weakness in front of Cadell's men. Besides, he had made a terrible mistake before, when he had allowed his feelings for a woman to cloud his judgment. He had sworn to himself he would not do that again.

"My lord." The priest gestured for Tormod to move forward, which he did.

Tormod stretched one hand out towards the girl, but she merely stared at him. Then, at a word from the priest, she let him take her hands and lift them to his lips. Her hands were cold, and she was shivering. He waited for her to meet his gaze. When she did, he saw fear in her eyes. He smiled at her. Her fear would soon pass when she came to understand the status and riches he was offering her.

Keeping his gaze on hers, he kissed her fingers. "I am Tormod, jarl of the Norse settlers here. I am pleased to welcome you as my bride." When she smiled shyly at him and nodded, he turned to the priest. "We are ready."

The priest hurried through what seemed to pass for a marriage ceremony, then scurried back to where his cart stood and took up his seat again.

"Everything is there, *herre*," one of his men reported.

"Very well," said Tormod. "Send our carters forward."

Within a few minutes, Tormod's carters were seated in all but the first of the carts. The holy man was seated in that one and it had turned to face back towards Cadell's lands, ready to return.

Rhydderch nodded at Tormod, then all the Britons turned and left, the holy man's cart trundling along behind the mounted guards, the remaining carters walking at the rear. No one even spared a backward glance at the girl. Was no one here concerned for her well-being? His sense of distrust returned. Was she really Lord Cadell's daughter? He examined her while her gaze remained fixed on the disappearing carts. Yes, he thought so. The set of her jaw and the line of her nose were certainly similar enough, although her eyes... her eyes were unlike any he'd seen before. He squeezed her hands. She turned to him, appearing no less frightened than she'd been a moment ago, and her steps were hesitant as he led her across to his own cart. He lifted her into it, ignoring her look of surprise, and settled himself beside her.

"We will be home soon," he promised her. "And there will be a proper wedding tonight. You may rest beforehand."

He had meant the comment to cheer her; instead, it made her recoil from him. At least it seemed likely she was a virgin, nervous about what would happen after the wedding. Unless... And now he let his own fears colour his thinking. Was she already planning to betray him? No, that was unfair. Not all women were as treacherous as his first wife, and this time he would be watching for signs of deception. His traitorous heart would not hide the truth from him again.

Chapter Four

A OIFE GLANCED OVER AT the man she'd been given to. Her new husband. A sliver of fear crept down her spine. Everything about him was different from the men of her previous acquaintance. He wore a helmet, as did all his men, so she couldn't see his face properly. He was taller, tanned from time spent outdoors. His blond hair was long and braided tightly down his back, his beard braided as well. His ruggedness contrasted directly with the more pampered nobles she knew, who often expected their men to do their fighting for them. This man was clearly a warrior, broad-shouldered and strong. He'd lifted her easily into the cart and had many scars on his face and hands, presumably from battle.

She'd only ever seen men of his people. What were their women like? Would she be accepted as his wife, or even more ostracised than she had been in the past? Would she even live long enough to find out?

She couldn't stop shaking and her gut churned with an odd mix of fear and anger at being married off to a man she'd never met. A man whose people had attacked their lands for years, killing indiscriminately and sacking the monasteries over and over. How could her father have agreed to this?

She clenched her fists and frowned. A marriage arranged to suit her father's purposes was only to be expected. However, until now, she'd always assumed she would have the option of refusing a suitor. And to be sent to live amongst the Norsemen? These men were strangers to her country. Men who had killed so many of her fellow Britons, including their king, and kept others as slaves, people whose language she didn't even know. What would become of her?

He must have felt her gaze on him, because he turned to look at her. And smiled. She glanced away and then back. It had been a pleasant smile. Perhaps he didn't intend to kill her immediately.

She sighed. She couldn't remember the last time anyone had simply smiled at her. As the daughter of a lord, she should have expected more from her life. However, fate had never been on her side. Not since her mother had died. Hesitantly, she smiled back at him. He reached for her hand and took it in his own. Their eyes met, and she found herself unable to look away.

"I look forward to showing you your new home, introducing you to our people," he said. He spoke in her own language of Brythonic, strangely accented but understandable. The knot of worry in her chest loosened slightly.

"Thank you," she said. She swallowed, trying to quell her fears. He knew her language. It was a small comfort, one which gave her hope for her future with this man.

The cart reached the crest of the hill and passed by a clump of trees. On one of the branches, two ravens sat staring at her. One of them tilted its head to one side and croaked. Were these the same birds she had seen at the abbey? Were they following her?

Both creatures took flight and soared above her. Hope flared again within her. Maybe this was her fate. She looked again at the wild-looking, heavily armed war band around the cart and sighed again. If it wasn't, there was certainly going to be no escape, anyway.

Strangely, she felt safer with them than with her father's men—not least because none had cast a single lecherous nor fearful glance toward her. Curious stares now and again, however, all had averted their eyes when she looked at them. Of course, none of them knew about her curse—her father would hardly have mentioned *that*.

She got the distinct feeling they believed she had some value, undoubtedly tied to the fact they thought her father cared enough about her to not want her dead. Would they feel differently when they discovered this was not the case? Not that she was going to be the one to tell them. She was certain these were not men who were afraid of killing anyone. She would have to simply hope and pray her father honoured the alliance.

One man stood out from the rest due to his scars. Deep wounds covered all the skin visible on his face and hands. She shivered when she looked at them. What pain he must have suffered. And how strong must he be to have survived?

"Aoife?" She jumped at the sound of her name, although her husband spoke gently. "We are nearly home. I hope it will be to your liking."

"Would it matter if it wasn't?" she said, regretting the comment as soon as it had passed her lips. She steeled herself for a blow or harsh words. None came.

"I would have my wife happy," he replied after a pause, his expression revealing nothing.

She opened her mouth to speak but could form no words.

"Is that not a husband's duty?" Tormod asked her.

"Makes for an easier life," the man who rode alongside them said loudly and laughed. "And Tormod is known for his ability to make women very happy."

"Björn!" Tormod chided him, but the other man grinned. "My cousin has no manners."

Aoife looked ahead, her cheeks heating.

"But if he keeps you happy, it will mean an easier life for us too," Björn continued. "If your father keeps his word."

Aoife glanced sharply at him. Her father keep his word? Unlikely, especially if her stepmother wanted something different. "What did my father promise you?"

Björn laughed loudly.

Tormod gave her an appraising look, as if trying to judge whether it was worthwhile answering her or not. "You, for a start."

She stared at him for a moment. The tone of the laughter from both him and the others suggested it was simply a joke — not any kind of threat. He reached out a hand as if to cup her face, but let it fall back to his side when she involuntarily recoiled.

"We are allies and he has promised not to contest my ownership of this land," Tormod said. "And to help us defend it if necessary. After all, what father would risk his daughter's safety?"

Aoife wasn't sure she wanted to answer the question. She could only pray he was right. "So, I am a sort of hostage?"

He shook his head. "No. Whatever else you are, you will be a jarl's wife, with all the status and responsibilities that entails. You are still a free woman. You have choices. Even the choice of divorcing me. Although that seems a bit extreme already."

"Divorce?" The Church never allowed such a thing. And what did he mean about being free? Married women were the property of their husbands.

"I think we should at least try being married first," he said, grinning. "You may even enjoy it."

The warriors around them laughed.

"But..." She couldn't believe he was amused by the notion rather than anything else, and the knowledge she still had a choice made her feel better. Still, they were married now. Bricius had performed the ceremony, albeit the shortest version Aoife had ever witnessed. Her father had decided she was to marry this Norseman and there was no alternative. Besides, no Briton would want a woman who had been married to a Norseman. Not that any of them had wanted her in the first place, not after Alt Clut. She could only pray Tormod was right about her father not wanting her dead.

A thought occurred to her—if her father was going to help them defend their land...

"You plan to stay here?" she asked.

"We do. Our village is nearly complete and there are many farms in the surrounding area."

For a moment, only the footsteps of the men and horses and the trundle of the carts broke the silence.

"You do not intend to sail back to... the north?" She realised her ignorance about anything concerning these men. Where had they really come from?

"Perhaps one day," Tormod replied. "But my father has many sons, too many to share his lands in the north, so I have lands here now. And this is where I will make my home. A native wife will help."

"You are sure?"

"You can teach the others your language, share what you know about foodstuffs, herbs and animal rearing. Help us to make a successful living here. As the daughter of a lord, I expect you have been trained in the running of a large household."

Aoife nodded, her hopes for the future leaping at his words. She could do those things. She was going to be needed here, would have a role to play, and may in time come to be accepted by his people. Perhaps it wouldn't be so different from the life she might have led had her mother lived and arranged a marriage for her to a Briton or even a Pict. Unless... She would have to make sure they didn't discover her presence, did not assure them the safety they expected. Or maybe she should tell them now, so they were better prepared. She realised Tormod was looking at her.

"If you are worried I cannot provide for you, then let me assure you I am a richer man than your father. And my men are loyal... unlike your father."

"What do you mean?" Shock ran through her. He thought her father disloyal?

"Your father abandoned his king, right before we attacked. Is that not true?"

"Yes..." Her heart raced. Her father's misfortunes may, in fact, all stem from her if what this man said was true. "He wasn't fleeing because of that." She frowned, remembering the beating she'd received—even after her family knew her vision had saved their lives. Her stepmother had used it as an excuse to send her away. She'd had visions at the abbey and been beaten every time—far worse than her stepmother had done. The most recent only a few days hence. Brother Pasgen had claimed he was beating the demons from her, and her penance had been long hours spent on her knees, praying.

How would these men, known for their violence, react to finding out what had happened, what she had seen? What she was?

If civilised people beat her, then how much worse would the punishment be from these barbarians? Except so far, their treatment of her was better than anything in her past, even if it had only been a matter of hours.

Perhaps as a wife, she would have more status. And later as a mother. She pursed her lips. She was no naïve innocent. She was aware of what happened between a man and his wife.

Her new husband tilted his head from side to side, then pulled off his helmet. As he turned to face her, her breath caught. His appearance, the jut of his nose and chin, the expression on his face, and his eyes—it was all so familiar. She'd seen his face before. In one of her visions. She felt the rumble of the thunder from her dreams echo through her body and heard the croak of a raven.

Yes, this was indeed her fate, for better or for worse.

Chapter Five

BROTHERS
OF
THUNDER

T ORMOD WAS CONVINCED THERE was something Aoife wasn't telling him. However, he was pleased with the arrangement in other ways. She was pretty. Perhaps a little too delicate, and he suspected childbearing might be hard on her, however, given the imaginings he'd had the past two days, she was, indeed, a very pleasant alternative to those. After his first marriage, however, he had to make sure that there was no doubt in anyone's mind that any child she birthed was definitely his.

"So," he said, pushing aside the lustful thoughts that crowded into his mind with her proximity. "You were to be a holy woman?"

"That was what my father had decided, yes." She smoothed her hands down the fabric of her robes. Everything she wore was white, bar her cloak, and most of her hair was veiled. He smiled at the thought of running his hands through it later.

"Sometimes your people send girls to the Church when they have... been indiscreet." She gasped and glared at him. His grin widened. "No indiscretions. Then why?"

She turned away from him again and reached for the small cross hanging around her neck, then let her hands fall into her lap. "Does it matter?"

He nearly didn't hear her, the words were whispered so quietly. However, he picked up the tremor in her voice and saw that her hands, now clasped in her lap, shook with more than just the motion of the cart. He looked around at the men he had brought with him. All armed with swords and axes, their shields carried beside them or hung from their saddles, helmets covering most of their faces, and leather armour making their already broad chests look even larger. In contrast, she was only a girl, alone. Her family had not even had the grace to send a maid with her, although Tormod had seen the simple lives the holy men and women led and realised she had probably been without that luxury for however long she'd been at the abbey.

"Björn!" he called and indicated he should give them more space. His cousin grinned at him, then shouted the order and all the men distanced themselves from the cart.

He placed his hand over her clasped ones. She tensed and started to pull away.

"I'm not going to hurt you," he said, closing his hand around both of hers. They were still cold, almost icy, and so much smaller and softer than his own battle-hardened ones. After a moment, she seemed to accept his touch and relaxed. She turned her head slowly to look at him. He took in the paleness of her skin, the smattering of freckles across her cheeks, the intense blue of her eyes, and then his gaze centred on her lips. They were pale pink, thin like the rest of her, and when he jerked his hand, she gasped and her lips parted.

He meant only to comfort her, but instead, his lips touched hers gently before he lifted his head. She said nothing; just watched him. She was his wife—he had all the time in the world to spend teaching her how to please him and accept the pleasure he could give her. Tonight there would be no rushed coupling, but he would not be fool enough to lose his heart to this woman. That would not stop them from enjoying meeting their physical needs together.

Her throat moved as she swallowed, and he admired the fact she didn't pull away from him this time. She was afraid, this daughter of a lord, but she knew her duty. She would submit to him as the

Christians taught their wives should. However, that was not what he wanted. That was not enough. Nor was this about love, not at all. It was simply the desire to have her submit to him through choice — how much of a victory would it be to have Cadell's daughter willingly sharing his bed and not forced there by either her father or her husband? He smiled at the thought.

"May I kiss you again?" he asked, pleased when she nodded. This time he lingered, running his tongue along the join of her lips. When she opened her mouth, he touched his tongue to hers. She made a tiny sound deep in her throat. He ran a hand down the back of her head, pulled her in towards him, and kissed her deeply. Then, deciding to retreat while he was ahead, he set her back from him and cupped her cheek. She stared at him, a look of wonder on her face. Then her eyes clouded, and she lowered her head.

He turned to see Björn watching them, a grin on his face. Tormod pulled Aoife close and frowned at Björn over her head. Let Björn grin. Tormod was not displeased with his new wife and was sure with some patience, she would become a willing bedmate. He was not without some skill in that area.

But then doubts came crowding back, and he wondered if her demureness was an act. She had responded eagerly for a few moments. Was it simply a case of her forgetting herself and enjoying his touch, or was it more sinister than that? Was she already planning how to betray him?

They reached the abandoned church at Nevyth where they would turn westwards away from the water's edge and cross the peninsula through a pass that cut through the hills running down its length. As they approached the settlement at Kirkjaster, they would be able to see down the firth of the great river Clut to the islands lying in its waters. The waters stretching north from Kirkjaster were known as the *Skipasfjorddr* in his own tongue, or Loch Long here — both meant ship loch. North of the shieling lands lay Tairmbert, a village sitting on an isthmus, where those ships could portage into the freshwater loch upon which Car Cadell stood. With friends to the north and his new father-in-law owning all the land to the east, he felt confident he could keep his people safe here for now.

As they crossed the open fields by the shore, he noticed Aoife looking around. Was she expecting an attack? Had this whole thing been a ruse? Did her father plan to rescue her at the water's edge? After all, his lands lay only a short distance across the sea-loch at this point.

"What is it you seek?"

She jumped when he spoke, a guilty expression on her face. "Nothing... my lord." Her eyes moved rapidly. She was lying.

He gripped her wrist tightly and wouldn't let her pull away from him. He scanned their surroundings and could see nothing out of place, nothing to draw his suspicions. Maybe she didn't know when help would arrive. Maybe she was waiting for a sign. Maybe...

"Tormod," he said, letting go. "My wife is allowed to call me by my given name."

A small, dark shape flew overhead and landed on the back of the cart. Tormod turned to stare at it, then faced forward again. He sensed Aoife was stopping herself from looking. Was it just the bird she had been watching?

"It's just a raven," he said.

Her eyes met his and widened. "I know." She twisted around, then watched as it flew away again before landing in a tree a distance in front of them.

"Is that what you were watching?"

Her eyes widened as she nodded. "Yes, the ravens. Both of them. I have seen them many times since..." She didn't finish the sentence and he assumed she had perhaps seen many ravens on her journey from the abbey. Perhaps this was a good omen.

"When we are at sea, we use ravens to tell us if we are far from shore," he said. A second raven flew overhead, then landed near the first. "And Lord Odin is said to travel with two ravens."

"Odin is the leader of your gods?" she asked.

He wondered who had been teaching her about Norse beliefs. "The most important of our gods," Tormod said after some thought. "He often travels the earth as an old man with only one eye, accompanied by his two ravens, Huginn and Muninn."

"An old man with one eye?" She frowned in confusion when he agreed. There was a long pause before she continued, "With ravens?"

"The ravens fly all around the whole world, every day, then return and whisper in their master's ear everything they have seen. Odin seeks knowledge, and knowledge is power. He sacrificed one of his human eyes for the gift of knowledge. Some even say he can change the path of destiny."

"And can he?" She stared at him.

Tormod laughed. He had seen the priests of her religion praying to their god for things to change. He'd never seen it work. The holy men and women seemed to believe they were invulnerable, that their god, rather than strong weapons, would save them, and so they knelt and prayed—and more often than not, they died. His own gods took a more active role — as did his men.

"It is not enough to simply wish for things to change or even to pray for them. Our destinies are already carved in the Well of Urd. Odin learned to read runes," he explained. "And when he could read the runes, he could read from Yggdrasil, the tree of life, to find out what destiny awaited. Then he was able to change destiny, although..."

"What?"

"*Seidr*—using the runes to change destinies—is a pastime usually for women. It is an odd choice for a man, even a powerful god. Seeing the future is not always something to be wished for."

Her curious expression turned to one of fear.

Chapter Six

A OIFE COULD NOT GET the image of the one-eyed old man she had seen as she travelled home from Alt Clut out of her head. It couldn't have been Odin, and yet the thought would not leave her. There was also Tormod's comment about seeing the future to ponder. Her visions did not always show the future. Sometimes they showed the immediate past, at others the present in another place. Rarely did she see anything in time for any changes to be made. But at least he did not sound horrified by the prospect. Was there a chance then he would not regard her as being cursed? She daren't ask, at least not yet.

"You have people amongst you who can see the future?" she asked, trying to keep her tone light.

"Those who claim to at any rate," Tormod replied. "I always consult a seer if I can before I make a decision or leave on a raid. There was to be one in the village. Sadly, she did not survive the journey here. That was not something she foretold, of course." He laughed.

"Oh." Aoife swallowed. Would a seer know the truth about her? Would a seer know she was cursed and her family had sent her away because of this? She was relieved she would not have to deal with the prospect immediately. Although... If they truly were gifted, then proximity was not a prerequisite for knowledge, as she well knew.

She shifted her attention back to Tormod as he reached out and touched her white veil. "Why were you at the abbey? What made your mother and father send you there? Were you there to pray for a different future? Your family has had problems these last two years."

Aoife said nothing. Should she trust him with the truth? Would her curse make him hate her or afraid of her? Not that she thought this man was afraid of very much. Perhaps she should tell Tormod now and throw herself on his mercy. But what could she say to him? Had the old man she'd seen been Odin? She shook her head. Those gods were not real. The church teachings were clear.

"Why were you at the abbey?" he asked again.

"It was... My father thought he'd never find a suitable husband for me."

Tormod put his fingers on her chin and turned her to face him. "Why not?" His eyes narrowed with suspicion. He raked his gaze up and down her body. "It doesn't look like there's anything wrong with you. And you're pretty."

She gaped at him. He thought she was pretty? It shouldn't have concerned her, although somehow it did. She felt a tiny spark of hope deep inside that perhaps with this man as her husband, she would finally have a place she belonged. Someone who might come to care about her and see her as more than just a burden. She smiled. He thought she was pretty.

"So, what is wrong with you?" And with that, her dreams crashed around her once more. "Your mother seemed almost anxious to be rid of you. In fact, from her reaction, I had expected some kind of troll. You are indeed a pleasant surprise."

Aoife pulled away from his touch and gazed out over the side of the cart. He didn't really think she was pretty — it was just that he had been expecting something worse. Ula had probably made sure to give as bad an impression of her beforehand as possible. "She's not my mother. She's my stepmother."

"Ah," Tormod said, then laughed so loudly Björn turned to see what the matter was. "So, all this time, I have been worried about treachery, when the truth is far simpler. The jealousy of one woman for the daughter of her husband's first wife. And this is why you were sent to the abbey?" He turned back to her. "But you really are your father's daughter?"

"Yes," she said, grateful he'd asked a question she could answer entirely honestly.

"I had suspected worse trickery." He lapsed into a thoughtful silence.

Aoife's gut churned. Her new husband had indeed been deceived, and she wasn't willing to risk his wrath and perhaps even her life by admitting to it. Maybe when her position was more secure here, she could warn him. Although surely her father did not hate her enough to attack her new home and put her at risk? Surely he still had some love for her, despite her stepmother's hatred? So much was happening so fast and she was struggling to know what to say and do simply to keep herself alive. Exhausted from the stress and from travelling through the night, she let her eyes drift shut, hoping she was safe for now.

The rocking of the cart must have caused her to doze because she was roused by shouts in the distance. She gripped onto the closest thing to her, which she discovered was Tormod's thigh when she opened her eyes and looked up to see him grinning down at her.

"Are you so eager to touch me?" he said. She blushed and turned away from him. "I'm not complaining."

His presence beside her was comforting, while at the same time unsettling. Would he be rushing her off to his bed? Maybe it would be best if he did, then at least it would be over with. The anticipation was unnerving.

As they trundled into the village, she distracted herself by observing it closely. It was different from the settlements she was familiar with, although there were many similarities. Most structures were built of wood rather than stone, rectangular rather than circular, and were arranged in a semicircle, with the focus being on the sea rather than the largest of the buildings. There was also no building that might be a fort, raised above the height of the others, and no surrounding wall or palisade. Perhaps they planned to build these in the future. Now they had rounded the curve and entered the semicircle of buildings, she could see this one was far larger than any of the others. A large fire burned in the centre outside it and she guessed it must contain their hall. Villagers stood around it, talking and working. She could hear the clank of metal being worked and the sound of wood being chopped from other buildings. The smell of the two large beasts slowly roasting over the fire made her clutch at her stomach. She hoped Tormod could not hear it grumbling.

The cart rolled to a halt before they passed the first of the houses, almost all of which had smoke coming from a central chimney. Villagers started to appear from the doorways and, while she couldn't understand their language, it was clear they were pleased to see Tormod and his men. When they merely stared at her, it made her realise just how much she would like to feel at home, and here was as good a place as any.

Tormod climbed down from the cart, and the villagers began to draw closer. Many of the men who had accompanied them were being greeted by wives and children, although some of the others, Björn and the scarred man included, were not. They headed straight for the largest building together. Tormod greeted some of the villagers, then turned to help her down from the cart. Although help was not quite the right description. He slid an arm under her legs, put the other under her arms, and lifted her as if she weighed nothing.

Her heart began to race. Was he taking her straight to his bed? What would happen if she didn't or couldn't please him? And not just to her. What about her family? Would he kill her, then mount a war party and...

"You have nothing to fear from us," he said as he stood her carefully down on the ground beside him.

She hadn't been expecting him to set her down, so she wobbled a little and grabbed onto him for support. There was laughter from those who witnessed it, however, it seemed good-natured and certainly Tormod was grinning. Her heart slowed a little. Tormod didn't seem to be dragging her anywhere, and she was grateful he hadn't let her fall on her face in front of the villagers. She also appreciated his support when surrounded by so many strangers whose language she could not understand. She had, however, caught a couple of words similar to the language of the Northumbrians. The accent was different, but yes, she definitely recognised some of the words. She had a basic knowledge of that language. Perhaps she could use it to learn this one.

Tormod kept his arm around her shoulders as he steered her towards the door of the main hall. They were followed by a gathering crowd. She felt a tug on her cloak and looked down to see a small boy touching the white robe she wore beneath her cloak. A woman ran forward and grabbed the child. From the gestures and tone, she guessed the woman was apologising, although she, too, stared at the fabric.

Looking around, Aoife saw few of the garments here were bleached. Most were dyed in neutral tones with occasional items in brighter hues. The most noticeable difference was women's heads were covered with scarves rather than veils, and were dressed in two layers — a long dress topped with a more colourful apron embroidered with colourful and intricate designs. All had keys and other pouches tied to their belts and paired brooches fastening their aprons. Her own clothing, novice's robes, seemed plain and dowdy in comparison.

As they entered the main hall, she wondered if this was just a general meeting place or Tormod's residence. When many of the crowd followed them inside, she decided on the former. Inside, the hall was large, with a fire pit in the centre. Benches lined every wall on which Björn and many of the other men who had accompanied her here were already settling themselves with platefuls of food.

Tormod called across the room to an older woman who had been standing close to Björn. As she moved towards them, she gestured for two other women to accompany her. Both of these other women wore wide, metal collars and Aoife assumed they were thralls. She'd heard the Norsemen kept a lot of thralls, many of them from her own people, although these two had the dark hair and blue eyes of the Dal Riatans—perhaps they had been purchased in Ath Cliath or captured on the islands north of here.

The woman looked her up and down, then nodded approvingly at Tormod. She took her arm and led her through a door in the back of the hall into a short corridor. The thralls followed a short distance behind.

Aoife tried to look back to see Tormod, but he was now surrounded by the villagers and the woman was guiding her onwards. The room they stepped into was smaller than the hall, although spacious enough to prove her husband was a man of status. She shivered, despite the wooden walls and thatched roof making the space much warmer than the bleak stone walls of either her father's fort or the abbey had ever seemed.

"You will see him soon enough," the woman said. Aoife smiled at the sound of her own language. She was surprised the woman spoke Brythonic so well. "You did not expect me to know your language?"

"No. I know nothing of yours," Aoife confessed. "Although I have heard a few words that sounded like Northumbrian. I know a little of that language."

"Then I will have someone teach you. It is only right the jarl's wife can speak to her people. What is your name?"

"Aoife."

"Aoife." The woman repeated it a few times, then nodded as if satisfied she had got it right. "And I am Ragna. Björn, Arne and Ulf are my sons. Tormod, my nephew. Everyone refers to the four as the brothers of thunder."

"Why?"

"The four of them are inseparable, and Tormod is their leader," Ragna explained. "He is named after the thunder god."

"I see. I have met Björn."

"Ulf and Arne were there as well to accompany you here. You will get to know them soon enough. Björn will be a loyal friend to you as long as you and your husband get along together. The others... they may take some time to accept you. Arne is the scarred man."

The way in which the woman spoke made her think there was more significance to this than she was currently grasping.

"We will feast later to celebrate the wedding of our jarl. Before then, you will bathe and we will find you nicer clothes." Ragna let go of her arm and stepped back to look at her carefully. "Why are you dressed like a holy woman? I thought they were not allowed to marry?"

"These are novice's robes. My stepmother sent me to the abbey, but I had not yet taken my vows," Aoife explained. "My mother died when I was young, birthing my brother."

A sly grin spread across Ragna's face. "Ah, so it was your stepmother who sent you to the Church? And married you to a Norseman?"

"Sort of, yes." It seemed like an easier explanation, and it wasn't as if it was completely untrue.

"That explains much. Well, you will not need those clothes again," she said, gesturing for the two thralls to assist her. "Now we will get you ready for your wedding."

Aoife froze for a second. Surely Ragna wasn't expecting her to undress in front of them? Ragna clapped her hands and the two thralls began to help loosen her cloak and then her robes, ignoring all her attempts at covering herself.

"We are not afraid of our own bodies here," Ragna said, smiling at her in amusement. "Now step into the water and let us wash you after your journey. You Britons do not wash nearly enough—and you have the cheek to call us barbarians. The bathhouse is not yet finished, so this will have to suffice for now."

Aoife hid a smile. She had noticed that very thing about Tormod as they'd travelled here. He lacked the stench of so many of her father's men and even some of the monks.

She was urged to climb into a large half-barrel and found herself standing in warm, soothing water. Once she was clean and her hair washed, she did, indeed, feel much better.

Ragna busied herself laying out new clothes and undergarments and removed the brooch from Aoife's cloak before casting it into the pile of unwanted robes. When she turned to look at Aoife, her hands flew to her mouth.

Too late, Aoife realised that, although the pain had now gone, her skin still bore the marks of her latest beating. She'd been at Mass when she'd had a vision of a burning field, the stench of the smoke strong enough it had made her sick to her stomach. Brother Pasgen had not been amused.

"You have been beaten," Ragna said. She spoke to the thralls and one of them hurried out of the room while Ragna walked in front of her and gasped.

Aoife glanced down and saw the dark blue-black bruising on her knees.

"Why was this done?" Ragna touched one of the bruises, causing Aoife to wince. She didn't feel she could refuse Ragna's demand to explain, and neither she could she tell them the truth, not yet. Maybe when she became a wife, the curse would leave her? She hoped so.

"I became unwell during Mass... and it angered the priest." That was true, just not the whole story. "And my knees are bruised from praying."

Ragna regarded her for a long moment, then tsked. "If Tormod gets his hands on the man who did this to you... He would never treat a free woman this way, nor allow it in his village."

"Truly?" Aoife asked before she had thought it through.

Ragna's eyes narrowed. "For being unwell? Of course not. Our punishments fit our crimes here. And Tormod is a fair man. It would not befit his position as jarl to mistreat his wife. Welcome him to your bed and give him strong sons and you will not displease him."

"What if I displease him?" Aoife wasn't sure why she asked. This woman was Tormod's aunt and more likely to side with Tormod than with herself. However, in the absence of any other support Ragna's advice was all she had. "I'm not sure what to do."

Ragna smiled and put a hand on her shoulder, then gave it a gentle squeeze. "Don't worry," she said. "Tormod does. He will be gentle with you."

Aoife couldn't express the feeling of relief sweeping over her at Ragna's words. One of her concerns about her marriage had been laid to rest even as she still worried what welcoming him to her bed would be like.

By the time she was clean and dressed in an ankle-length dress, sitting by the fire with Ragna combing out her long hair, she felt better than she had in years, even if her gut was churning with anxiety about her wedding night. The thrall had brought ointment for her bruises, which had helped with the pain. These people were showing her more care than she had experienced before and she felt safer now than she ever had in her father's fort since her mother's death, and far, far safer than at the abbey.

"Now," Ragna said. "You must rest before the wedding feast begins." She indicated the furs piled thickly on the bench at the side of the room. "I will return later and help you dress."

Aoife didn't think she'd be able to sleep. However, as soon as she lay down and pulled the furs around her, warmth and exhaustion overtook her.

CHAPTER SEVEN

TORMOD LOOKED ACROSS THE table at his friends. He'd eaten well and then fallen asleep on the benches in the main hall — something he hadn't done since his own rooms had been completed. He hoped this was not an indication of how his marriage would be, however, Ragna had insisted on him giving Aoife the use of his room to prepare for the ceremony.

Now it was evening and Ulf and Björn had woken him earlier to go and bathe and dress in his finest clothing. Now that he was ready, he noticed them exchange glances more than once and wondered what they had planned. Nothing about the day was as it should really be. He was so far from home. Too far to follow many of the wedding traditions, but at least the most important aspect was in place—he had a bride. A bride who had given him an ally in this strange place and would, in time, give him sons.

His mouth curved. Aoife had not shrunk from his touch in the cart. Nor had she encouraged him, exactly. However, he knew he could make her crave his touch and was patient enough to take his time. After all, he had a lifetime in which to do so. However long that might turn out to be. No matter how the Britons saw him, he was not a barbarian. And he had seen them treat their own women in ways no Norse woman would tolerate. He drained his horn of mead before covering it with a hand when a thrall scurried over to refill it.

"Don't want to risk not being at your best tonight?" Björn said, slapping him on the back and grinning lewdly.

Tormod rolled his eyes. Just then, Arne entered the hall through the main doors. The sight of his scars stirred the usual feelings of guilt in Tormod. Ulf nodded over at him, and Björn stood.

"Come," said Björn. "Let the celebrations begin. You must claim the sword of your ancestors."

"But..." Tormod began.

"You think we wouldn't ensure our jarl was wed with all proper tradition?" Ulf said. "Ragna brought our grandfather's sword with her from home and we have done our best, even if the gravesite does not contain any of your ancestors."

Tormod was pleased Ulf seemed to be coming round to the idea of this marriage. Until Ulf added, "Even if the fact your wife's family are not here worries some."

"There are reasons for that."

"I hope they are genuine, *herre*."

"Ulf..." Tormod warned. It always disturbed him when any of his cousins addressed him as "*herre*." It was a term of great respect amongst their people, used to address a superior. They had always been friends, equals, and although Tormod had aspired to become more, he knew his cousins were all different. Björn, the oldest, was a warrior at heart, not a leader. At least he was not a rival. Tormod would not want to risk their friendship for anything. They had been through too much together in their lives already.

Ulf, however, was a different story. Tormod knew if any of his friends ever challenged him, it would be Ulf—even though he was the youngest of his cousins.

And Arne... Now, Arne was a different story altogether. Tormod pushed away the guilt that accompanied thoughts of Arne.

Tormod followed the three of them out of the hall. So, he would get to claim the sword of his ancestors. He swallowed, not wanting to let his cousins see how much the gesture affected him.

According to Christian rites, he and Aoife were already married, but the villagers would enjoy a proper Norse wedding. It would be as much a celebration of their new village as anything else, so that was what Tormod was determined to give them.

He knew the others were right to be suspicious of Lord Cadell's motivations — he, himself, was — and although it startled him to admit it, he was not suspicious of Aoife's. Yes, he felt she was holding something back and was determined to discover what it was. At the same time, he was sure she was exactly what she appeared to be — a young, scared bride, sent away to live amongst strangers for her family's gain. It was a common enough situation in every society and she seemed to want to make the best of it. A wish he was happy to accommodate, within reason.

The four of them marched down the street to the edge of the village. There they stopped at a mound of fresh earth. Tormod looked questioningly at Björn, who shrugged.

"We had to improvise a little," Björn said, handing him a spade.

"You didn't bury anyone in here, did you?" Tormod asked as he dug the spade into the mound.

"No," Björn said as Ulf and Arne chuckled. "Although..."

Arne elbowed him in the ribs and shook his head.

"What?" asked Tormod.

"Nothing," said Björn. "Just something my mother mentioned. You can deal with it later. Go on."

Tormod glared at him for a moment. He could tell from Björn's expression the conversation was over, so he started to dig. After only three or four shovelfuls, metal clinked against metal. As soon as the hilt was uncovered, Tormod knelt and drew the sword. He stared at the careful construction and ornate decoration, which made it a valuable piece as well as an effective weapon.

"I had the blacksmith sharpen it," said Björn, not taking his eyes from it as Tormod stood and raised it, watching as the sunlight glistened off the blade.

"Thank you," he said to his cousins.

Ragna came towards them, smiling. "Your bride is ready, *herre*. And all are eager to begin the celebrations." She looked at her sons.

"What is the matter?"

The three of them glanced at each other.

"We are concerned her family is not here," Ragna eventually said. "Surely any parent wants to see their daughter wed, especially to a powerful man, and yet..."

"Ah," said Tormod, then placed a hand on Ragna's shoulder. "Is that your only worry, you and all the rest of the village?" He glanced at his cousins. "The dowry has been paid in full. And their own priest and Cadell's steward witnessed the Christian rites."

"Yes, although her family did not even accompany her then. How can you be sure she is, indeed, Cadell's daughter? That this alliance will protect us?"

Tormod frowned. "Cadell has paid the dowry. My bride is here and hale." He stepped closer and hugged Ragna. "There is enough resemblance to Cadell that I believe she is his daughter. I think her stepmother does not care for her as she should. Her father looked to his wife for permission in all matters when we were there. We should not blame Aoife—she has had little say in the matter, I suspect. And it shows they are afraid of us—something that is surely not a bad thing."

"No, it is no bad thing," Ragna said. The tension in her shoulders eased, and she smiled. "She told me about her stepmother. And it explains... Well, you'll see. Now, let us begin. The villagers have worked hard these past months building the hall, their homes and their farms. It is time for a celebration—and what better way to celebrate than with the wedding of our jarl? It is a new beginning for all of us who chose to follow you." With that, she hurried back in the direction of the hall.

"Very well," Tormod said, cleaning the sword with a cloth Ragna had handed him. Then he slid it into his belt as he heard the noise of cups and pots being banged and the villagers began to come out of their homes. Ragna hurried back to the main hall, followed by the women, while the men made their way to stand with Tormod. There was much laughter and a sense of joy in the air.

Although he sensed an element of caution, he smiled to see his people so happy. And swore to himself he would make this marriage work, use it to ensure the village remained a safe and peaceful place. They would work hard and prosper here — an alliance with Aoife's father would ensure a safe border, and it would give them access to trade and knowledge—things his people relied on for survival as much as farming. And if Cadell could not exist peacefully alongside them, then Tormod would pursue a different approach.

The banging grew louder. The village women appeared, Aoife in their midst. He stared at her, now dressed in a traditional Norse wedding gown, embroidery down both arms, and thick rows of decoration along the hem. Her hair was both uncovered and loose. A jolt of lust ran through him. She was a striking woman. Her hair was red, an unusual shade the Gaels called *ruadh* and which he'd mostly seen on Gaels and Picts. If his new wife had ties to either of those peoples, then perhaps she was even more valuable than he'd thought. And yet a tiny, nagging voice of suspicion sounded in his ear. Why would her father have parted with her so willingly if she was so valuable? Mind you, after the raid on Alt Clut two years ago, the reputation the Norse had in this region was formidable. Perhaps her father appreciated that value, even if her stepmother didn't.

Now he saw her dressed in Norse clothing and smiling, it made him feel something he didn't want to examine too closely. He pushed the feeling away. This was a business transaction, albeit one with pleasurable consequences, however, it remained purely business. He had no reason to love his bride, none at all.

Aoife's eyes met his own. Then her gaze slid modestly downward. Whether her family were here or not, he had her dowry, he had her father's promise of an alliance, and most of all, he had Cadell's daughter.

As Tormod strode towards the hall, Björn, Ulf and Arne at his side, Ragna led Aoife around all the houses in the village, followed by a growing crowd. Those inside the houses came out and greeted her, giving her small gifts or flowers and then joining the group. Soon the whole village was involved in the noisy procession and the mood was one of jubilation.

Tormod could smell the meat roasting on the spits in the hall and outside. His people had worked so hard, it was good they had this wedding feast to celebrate not only his marriage but the completion of the village.

The procession turned onto the main street and Tormod found himself mesmerised by Aoife as she walked towards him. She was flushed and smiling, although her smile faltered every time she caught his gaze. He strode to meet her, the sword of his ancestors at his side, followed by Björn, Ulf and Arne.

CHAPTER EIGHT

RAGNA HALTED THE PROCESSION of women and urged Aoife to walk forward to meet Tormod, who stood with three men behind him. One was Björn, one was Arne—the scarred man—and she assumed the other was Ulf. As she started to move, she realised three warriors were following her. She turned to look at them and froze. All were armed, and one of them held a sword in front of himself, its tip pointing directly at her. Had she misunderstood? Was she a sacrifice rather than a bride? She turned to Tormod, who was also carrying a large sword. She gulped and took a step away from both men.

"Do not fear," said Tormod. "The warriors are there for your protection. Not to harm you. It is just a symbol—they are the bride's men. You are not in any danger." Tormod stepped towards her when she still hesitated and held out a hand. After a moment, she took it, wishing she had asked Ragna more questions about the ceremony and what she would be expected to do.

"Take the sword," Tormod said. He gestured to the man behind her, who was now holding the sword flat across his arms. She looked from the sword to Tormod and back again. The warrior held it out to her, and she lifted it. It was heavier than it appeared. Her knees buckled a little, and so the warrior steadied her and helped her to settle the weight. Her arms shook, not just with the weight of the sword, but with the worry that she would make a mistake.

"Give it to your husband," the warrior whispered to her.

She nodded at him, pleased there was another person who spoke her language. She turned to Tormod and handed him the sword. He took it and placed it in his belt, then knelt in front of her and presented his own sword to her. She noticed traces of dirt around the hilt and wondered if she, too, should have knelt, but it was too late now. She took the sword. This one was even heavier, but that was the least of her problems.

As her hands closed on the pommel, her vision blurred. Her curse was upon her. She shook her head, trying to subdue it. Not now. Not in front of all these people who might do anything to her once they found out about her visions. Despite Tormod telling her about their seer, she was worried. The tip of the sword thudded into the ground, and she leaned on it for balance as the familiar blackness dulled her earthly vision. A seer was one thing, someone who lived on the fringes of society. It would surely be different for a woman, the jarl's wife, to be cursed in such a way... there was no telling what they might do to her.

She blinked and looked cautiously at her new husband. Perhaps she could claim it was merely the heat, but it was not her husband's face she saw. Instead, a field burned in front of her. She could smell the thick, black smoke, feel it filling her lungs, stinging her eyes and making them water. The smoke gathered and formed into the hissing face of a wildcat. Claws came sweeping from the sky towards her and she gasped, inhaling the smoke deep into her lungs. She choked and jolted back to reality.

Slowly, her vision cleared, and there was nothing except darkness in front of her. Feeling returned first, and she knew Tormod held her. She rested against him for a moment, terrified that once she lifted her head, she would be beaten. He must have sensed she was awake again and set her back on her feet before holding firmly to her shoulders.

She lifted her gaze to his, unsure what she might see there. Only concern etched his features. Ragna was beside him. The woman placed a cool hand on her brow, then took her hand and squeezed it reassuringly.

"There is no need to be afraid," Tormod said.

Aoife swallowed and nodded, or at least tried to.

"Come," Ragna said for all to hear. "Let us finish the handfasting. Our jarl's new wife needs a good meal and a drink."

There was a moment of silence before Björn cheered. The villagers joined him and soon the knot of fear in her belly released. They thought she was just nervous about her wedding. That was a relief. She tried to smile while one of her hands was bound with Tormod's and then each of them promised to be faithful during their marriage. Tormod smiled at her as they placed the rings on their own fingers, then hand in hand they walked together to the door of the hall, where Tormod carried her over the threshold. There was a great cheer from outside. He led her to a seat in the centre of the dais as the villagers followed them in and settled down, ready for the feast.

As they watched, thralls carved the meat from the hog roast over the central fire. There were plenty of vegetables and fish. Aoife hadn't seen this much food since the feast at Alt Clut and her plate was refilled more than once, although she barely remembered eating any of it. She could still smell the acrid smoke, feel it burning her lungs.

Sitting beside Tormod on the dais, she observed all the villagers and tried to adjust to thinking of this as her new home. Everything had happened so quickly.

"Why so sad?" Tormod held out a horn filled with mead, which she took. "Drink," he urged her. "It will calm your nerves." He watched as she sipped at the sweet, potent liquid, then leaned forward to kiss her. Cheers sounded in the hall. As soon as his lips left hers, she pulled back and stared at her plate, unable now to eat another mouthful.

Someone, she thought it might have been Björn, started to sing, although she couldn't understand the words. They ate and drank, different people singing or telling stories as the evening wore on. Patiently, Tormod whispered to her what the stories were about, rarely letting go of her hand, and she began to calm down. He seemed to have no immediate plans to harm her, nor to rush her into his bed.

Eventually, the events of the past two days swept over her, and all her energy drained away. She shouldn't have drunk the mead. It had relaxed her, and the tension that had kept her going was fading.

Tormod said something to her. She just stared at him, unable to make sense of the words. He stood and pulled her up beside him, held her close. She leaned into his strength, grateful for his support, given how badly her legs were trembling. A thrall filled his horn with mead. The noise in the hall quieted as he spoke.

"I thank you for your attendance on my wedding day and for the welcome you have given my wife." There were cheers and some applause. "But I believe she is tired, so we will take our leave of you for tonight. Please, continue to eat, drink and enjoy yourselves."

Chapter Nine

BROTHERS
OF
THUNDER

T HE SHOUTS AND WHISTLES grew in volume as they made their way through the hall to the door leading to Tormod's room and many comments were hurled towards them. Most she couldn't understand, although she could guess at what they referred.

Aoife took a deep breath as they stepped through the door, hand in hand. The wedding celebrations were over and her duties as a wife were about to begin. She shivered. As her eyes swept the room, she noticed the barrel she'd bathed in had been emptied and there was no sign of her old robes. When her gaze came to rest on the large bed strewn with an assortment of furs, she took an involuntary step back.

Tormod took her arm before firmly walking her further into the room and kicking the door shut. She blushed at the sound of raucous whooping from the room behind them and pulled away from him. Studiously avoiding looking at him, she hurried across to where a knot in the wood had been pushed out and she could peer out. Dawn had already broken and the silvery sky tinged with peach was beautiful.

Was it only two mornings since she had looked out into such a pale morning light and heard the horsemen approach? Now that life was over and a new, strange one beginning, and yet the morning was just the same. The sound of the waves of the sea-loch lapping, the mountains rising jaggedly from the sea all along the coastline—all that was the same.

"It looks very much like my father's land," Tormod said, startling her. He'd moved to stand right beside her and she hadn't noticed. How could such a large man move so quietly, or had she blocked out his presence from her awareness on purpose? She couldn't do so anymore. Heat radiated out from him and the leather scent of his clothing reached her nostrils. Under that was her husband's own unique smell. She breathed it in, then closed her eyes, and yet still couldn't escape his presence.

"Help me," he said.

She opened her eyes and turned to see what he needed help with and froze as she realised he wanted her to help undress him. She stared at the fastenings on his clothing, unable to move. She tried to swallow, her mouth dry. She had some idea of what was about to happen, knew as a wife she couldn't refuse her husband. She was, however, afraid of the pain her stepmother had warned her about when cautioning her to remain chaste.

A single tear slid out the side of her eye. She tried to turn away from him, and he stopped her with a hand on her shoulder. The backs of his fingers gently brushed her face. "There is no need to weep," he said softly. "Tell me what you fear."

She was shocked he was asking, but touched that he even cared enough to ask. "This," she said, indicating the bed. "Will it hurt?"

He cupped her face and shrugged. "Perhaps a little, and only at first. I will try not to hurt you. It can be good, you know, between a man and his wife. Pleasurable. It shouldn't be a duty or something to be feared. I do not intend to hurt you or force you."

"My stepmother said even with my husband it would hurt, and I wasn't to cry out or you would beat me or cast me off. And the priests... They talk about sin and the evils of the flesh and..."

Tormod smiled, then slid his hand around to cradle the back of her head. He angled her face towards him, placed a gentle kiss on her lips, then drew back. "Do not listen to them."

After a long moment, he tipped her chin up with his finger and smiled. "What they have not been telling you is about the pleasure. It is a feeling like no other, and even your god does not disapprove of married couples bedding." He leaned in, kissed her again. This time his lips lingered on hers, moving gently and sensuously. His tongue parted her lips, and he groaned as he began to explore her mouth.

Slowly she began to respond, terrified of making a mistake, but this was more care and attention than she'd ever been shown before. She would be a fool not to respond to his gentleness.

He swept his hands down her shoulders and pulled her against him. As he deepened the kiss, she spread her hands across his chest, feeling the solid muscle underneath, the warmth of him. She found his belt and started to unfasten it.

He pulled back from her, smiling. She stilled. What was she doing, helping him with this? Her stepmother's warning came flooding back as Tormod let the belt fall to the ground, then pulled his kirtle and shirt over his head, leaving him dressed only in his breeks. His skin glowed with a golden tinge in the firelight.

Tormod loosened her belt, allowing it to drop onto the floor. He ran his hands up her sides and took a step closer. As he kissed her thoroughly, his hands moved to undo the brooches that fastened the heavily embroidered apron at each shoulder. Before she could grab hold of it, her apron slithered down her body onto the floor, leaving her only in her dress. He didn't try to remove that yet, though. Instead, he ran his hands through the length of her red hair. She shivered at the feeling.

"You didn't get this from your father," Tormod remarked, separating out a handful of strands and allowing them to flow over his palm.

"My mother was a Pict."

"It's beautiful. You're beautiful," he murmured. "This marriage can be more than just a political union. Your presence here will safeguard us from your father's men and his allies in Strath Clut, and maybe also from the Picts?"

She swallowed. Should she tell him now not to trust that her father would not attack the village just because of her presence here? No, she should wait until the marriage was consummated.

She realised the impact of the trick her father and stepmother had played. Not only had they rid themselves of an unwanted daughter, but they had also lulled the Norsemen into a false sense of security.

"Your mother's people?" he prompted. "They won't seek to harm you?"

"No," she managed to say. "My mother's people wish me no harm." That at least was true. As for the other... If she told him the truth, he might reject her and send her back to her father. Her punishment for failing in this would surely be far worse than being sent to the abbey. She'd never make it back home alive—murdered along the way, or even on her arrival—her death blamed on the Norsemen.

No, she would find a way to tell him, to warn him of the danger—but not now. Once her place here was more secure. If she did everything possible to make herself necessary, do everything he asked of her, then maybe, just maybe, she could have a value to him that wasn't built on her father's lies.

"I would like to kiss you again," he said.

For a moment she froze, then nodded. She tilted her head up to meet his. Their breath mingled and the heat of his body warmed her. His arms encircled her as their lips touched, and she gasped as he lifted her and carried her to the bed. Without taking his eyes off her face, he placed her carefully down and smoothed his hands down the length of her dress. She stared at the expanse of well-muscled chest beside her. The scars which crisscrossed it seemed to add to his masculinity rather than detract from his beauty. Could a man be beautiful? She'd never considered it before.

One scar across his heart was particularly deep, and she reached out, ran her fingers along it. "What happened?"

"My wife's brother challenged me."

She drew back, frowning. "You're already married?"

"Was married. She's dead." He took her fingers in his own and kissed the tips. "Loki was at work in that family, so Odin made me the victor."

His expression had turned fierce, and she hesitated to provoke him further. His hand went to the oddly shaped cross hanging around his neck on a leather thong. He flipped it over and she realised it wasn't a cross at all, but a hammer.

"Thor was with me when we fought." He smiled. "Your priests prefer it when it seems as if we believe the stories of their Christian god. And they seem also to have an unquenchable lust for gold."

"You do not believe?" Aoife felt for the wooden cross around her neck. She wished once more her own silver one set with amethysts had been with her things from the abbey. Her life for the past two years had centred around her faith exclusively, although much of her treatment had far from endeared her to Christian charity. Still, there was a part of her which believed.

He shrugged. "I have seen little evidence to prove their stories. And his protection seems to be worth little."

"But—"

"Shh, we will speak no more of this. You may believe what you wish, worship as you wish. As long as you fulfil your duties as my wife, I will not interfere. Together, we will build a strong village here. For everyone."

"And if I cannot fulfil my duties as a wife?" She glanced away from him. What if she couldn't have children? What if, like her own mother and stepmother, she bore only daughters?

He smirked. "I think you will find my needs surprisingly simple."

"But—"

He placed a finger on her mouth and shook his head, then reached for the ties holding her dress closed. Without taking his eyes from her face, he loosened them. He tugged on the cloth, pulling it from her shoulders, then slowly down her arms, baring her to his gaze.

She closed her eyes and bit her lip, then realised he had stopped. Had she displeased him in some way? Did he not like what he saw?

Fear crept into her thoughts once more, despite the warmth and comfort his touch provided. She opened her eyes and saw anger on his face.

"Who did this to you?" he asked, his voice tight.

"One of the brothers, at the abbey." Her voice trembled as she spoke. What if he questioned her in more detail? Could she lie to him?

"Why?"

"I was... I was unwell."

"If I see the man who did this to you, tell me, and I will kill him," he promised.

"They thought they were helping me, beating the demons from my body. My family requested it when they sent me to the abbey."

He stared at her so intently she couldn't look away, no matter how much she wanted to. "Demons?"

Her breath caught in her throat. Why had she said that? She should have stuck to her story about being sick. Although neither was a lie, she feared what he would do to her if he discovered why her family worried about demons in her.

"My family thought... thought that the sickness was caused by demons."

"The demons lie in those who would do this. This is how you treat a slave, not a free woman, the daughter of a lord. This will not be allowed to happen again — I promise you."

"Thank you," she whispered.

After a pause, he kissed her. His mouth was gentle and moved slowly over her own. His tongue prised open her lips and swept inside. After her initial surprise faded, she began to return his movements and found every touch, every stroke, was sending delicious shivers throughout her body. This must be the start of the pleasure which he had told her about. She sighed and moved closer to him, surrendering herself to the sensations and trying to block out her fears.

He cupped her breast. The rough skin of his fingers rubbed across her nipple and she gasped. When he pulled her dress lower, set his mouth there and suckled, her fears about their coupling began to slip away.

CHAPTER TEN

BROTHERS
OF
THUNDER

T ORMOD WOKE TO FIND a warm body beside him. His wife. He smiled at the memory of the night before. Then he saw again the reminders of her beating. His fists clenched and the dark anger that had been kindled last night as she told him her story flared back to life. If he saw any of the holy men from the abbey, they would answer for what they had done to Aoife. For whatever reason.

Although, he had sensed that her story... There was something missing. He didn't think she had lied—she had been too fearful for an outright lie—but like so much about the situation, he believed he was being shown only the surface. The truth would out, eventually. It always did. He only hoped it would work in his favour this time.

He smiled grimly, then focused again on the woman in front of him. He traced the marks on her back and she muttered under her breath. He frowned when he caught the words for fire and field.

He prayed to the gods that she was nothing like his first wife. He ran his hand through her long hair and swept it to the side of her neck, then leaned over to kiss the skin he had bared. She stirred, sinuously stretching her back, then twisting out of his grasp when she awoke. She sat up, pulling the covers up around herself, but not before he noticed a little blood beneath her. He reached for her, but she pulled away, staring straight ahead, breathing heavily.

"What is the matter?" he asked.

"The matter?"

"You are upset. You were talking in your sleep about fire and fields. I can see fear on your face."

"I'm sorry." As she pulled the furs more closely around her, he sat up and wrapped his arms around her, but she held herself rigid. "It was only a dream."

"You are safe here with me," he promised her.

For a while, they remained like that. Gradually, her breathing slowed, and she relaxed into his arms. When she turned her face to his, he kissed her, gratified when she returned the favour. She let the furs slip a little and he took the chance to run his hands over her bare skin until she whimpered with pleasure.

"It is morning," she said. "We should get up."

"There is no rush. I doubt anyone will dare to disturb us."

He kissed her again, trying to ignore the spark of emotion that flitted through him when her kisses grew as ardent as they had last night. He slid one hand down between her legs and felt how ready she was for him. Still he moved slowly, stroking her with clever fingers until the only sounds from her throat were soft cries and her body bucked towards his.

He rolled her under him and slid inside her, watching her face as his body claimed hers. Her eyes were closed, but they opened when he was fully seated. As he pulled back and thrust forward again and again, their gazes held until the moment her head arched back and she tightened rhythmically around him. Her reaction triggered his own, and he withdrew from her body as he had night before. He had told her he wanted strong sons, but after Ingrid deception, there must be no doubt in the minds of the villagers that any child Aoife birthed belonged to him—even if he knew it to be true. And there was another worry—Ingrid had died giving birth to his son. If the same thing happened to Aoife, there would be no guarantee that Cadell would not turn on them and attack the settlement.

Selfishly, he also wanted some time for them to be alone together, to get to know one another, before their family grew. If he had taken more time to get to know Ingrid, he would not have put his whole village in danger, nor risked Arne's life as he had done.

Tormod looked into her eyes and saw confusion etched in them, so he turned her away from him and settled himself against her back. As they lay together, he closed his eyes. It had been hard these past years—surely, even as jarl, he deserved this honeymoon as time just for himself and his new wife?

He must have dozed because he was woken by the sound of loud knocking on the door. Aoife pulled the furs around herself and pushed to the top of the bed, while he padded naked to the door and yanked it open, ready to yell at whoever dared disturb them.

Before he could draw breath, Ragna pushed past him with a tray full of food, leaving him facing Björn at the door. Tormod moved to block Björn's view of the room and his cousin grinned at him.

"What is so important you risk my wrath the morning after my wedding, Björn?"

"Morning? Why, cousin, it is already mid-afternoon, and it is only after great debate we dared to interrupt your... celebrations." Björn raised his eyebrows. "I trust the night went well and you are not disappointed in your new bride?"

Even though he knew Aoife could not understand all Björn was saying, Tormod pushed his cousin away from the doorway. He thrust his legs into his breeks, then grabbed his kirtle and pulled it on as he followed Björn through to the main hall. The day was dull and overcast, with a hint of rain in the air, and as Tormod took a deep breath, he detected the acrid smell of smoke. He frowned at Björn.

"Something has happened," Björn stated. "One of the fields burned last night."

"Where?" Tormod remembered Aoife muttering the words fire and field. Had she known this would happen? He looked back towards the door to his room and his heart hardened.

"The farm near Nevyth. They most likely came by boat across Loch Garw. At low-tide the spit near there can be forded."

Björn wasn't stating the obvious, but Tormod understood the implication. The land on the opposite shore of Loch Garw belonged to Lord Cadell.

"There are guards watching the spit," Tormod said. "By boat further north is more likely." If the fire-raisers had come by sea, then they had not necessarily sailed straight across Loch Garw. They had guards stationed around the coast at all times, but a small craft, sailing in the dark, could perhaps have slipped past their watch in the darkest hours of the night. Not to mention drink had been flowing freely in celebration of his wedding and the guards may have been joining in the celebrations. Even so, to cross Loch Garw unseen during such short hours of darkness implied a certain familiarity with the territory. Lord Cadell's people, without doubt.

"How much of the field did we lose?" Tormod asked and was relieved when Björn smiled in response.

"Remarkably little," he said. "It began to rain and Håkon returned from the celebrations in time to see it and raise the alarm. It only took a few men to beat out what the rain didn't quench. We were lucky this time and we shall keep a better watch in the future."

"I trust you will ensure that."

"I will," answered Björn, then frowned. It seemed as if he were about to say something, then stopped.

"What?"

Björn stared at him, clearly uncomfortable. "Should we challenge Lord Cadell?"

"No," Tormod said after some thought. "For now, let us pretend these actions have had little effect upon us. I will speak to my wife, see if she has any knowledge of these attacks. Our marriage was hasty—perhaps Cadell has merely not had time to inform all his men of our alliance."

"Or he is choosing to dishonour it already," Björn retorted. "There were no attacks of this type before on our eastern shore."

Tormod placed a hand on Björn's shoulder. "Go and search the area. Mount a better watch. Let us give Cadell some time. However, if I find out he was behind this..."

Björn nodded. Tormod knew that while he was a good friend, he was an even more formidable enemy. "And your wife?"

Tormod stiffened, then relaxed, slapping Björn's shoulder before he chuckled. "One thing I know for sure is she was not the who was out there setting the fire. I know exactly where she was. All night. And it is where she will stay." He met his friend's gaze straight on and held it. "Aoife is my wife now."

"But she is still Cadell's daughter."

"Then we must make sure she feels this is her home," Tormod said frostily. "She is one of us now."

Björn glanced away, then met Tormod's gaze. "And if she acts otherwise? Ulf—"

"Ulf is suspicious of everyone and everything. He may be right in this case, although he may not. If he is, then I will deal with her the way I would deal with any traitor." Tormod found it easier to say than he'd expected. The sight of the marks on her body flickered through his memory. Surely they proved Aoife owed little loyalty to her father's family, so he hoped it was a promise he would never have to keep.

"I thought you might have reason to confront her father now anyway," Björn said. "Once you had seen her bruises."

"You know she was beaten?"

"Yes, my mother told me. It reassures me she may well have no great loyalty to her father. No matter what Ulf says."

"You seem to underestimate my own charms," Tormod said.

Björn shook his head and laughed.

Tormod grinned and put a hand on his cousin's shoulder. "If the opportunity arises, I will punish him for allowing someone to hurt her. And if we ever pass by the abbey..."

Björn slapped him on the back, then strode outside.

Tormod returned to his room to find the half-barrel had been filled and Ragna was helping Aoife to wash. His wife squealed and covered herself when he let the door bang shut behind him. Ragna looked at him as if expecting him to take the hint and leave, but he wanted to be in his own room just now to give himself time to think. He shook his head and sat down on the far side of the bed. Ragna knew better than to argue with him.

Fresh clothing for both himself and Aoife was laid out. As soon as his wife got out of the bath, he'd wash and dress. He grinned, thinking that the amount of time he would stay dressed would depend only on how fast he was able to persuade his wife back into bed. The words she had uttered when asleep still niggled at him. Although, no matter what, she had not set the fire. Someone else was to blame for that.

CHAPTER ELEVEN

Aoife was relieved Ragna was in the room when Tormod returned. She'd never been so intimate with anyone before and her stomach was in knots, wondering how she was now expected to behave towards him. The warm water she stood in had soothed most of the aches from the night before, however a deeper ache made her keenly aware she had changed, had been changed, by what they had done together.

She glanced towards the bed, only to find Tormod staring at her. His gaze was intense, and for a fleeting instant, she fancied that she could see deep into his very soul. Last night she had felt such a strong physical connection between them — a connection that left her hoping for more. She had been alone since her mother's death, both in her father's house and at the abbey. She yearned for something more from her life here. Her husband would not have changed physically the way she had, although still she searched his face for some evidence of a deeper connection between them, but there was nothing.

She was fooling herself. The only connection between them was physical. They barely knew each other, and he had made it clear last night he did not want to give her a child. She bit her lip. What did that mean? Perhaps he did not want to sully his bloodline with foreign blood. So why had he married her? If she wasn't to fulfil such an important role for a wife, then what did he want from her? Maybe she was destined to never truly belong anywhere and her curse would always set her apart.

Ragna picked that moment to tip a bucket full of water over her head and begin to rub her hair with soap. Gratefully, Aoife closed her eyes, forcing herself to keep breathing in and out, in and out. Hands scrubbed her hair and then more water was poured over her.

"Out you get now," said Ragna.

Aoife waited, her eyes still closed. A large cloth was wrapped around her, then two things happened. She heard the door click shut, and she was lifted off her feet into a pair of strong arms. She opened her eyes to find Tormod looking down at her as they moved towards the bed. He set her down on its edge and she pulled the cloth around herself more tightly. He stared at her for a moment and then took a comb from his belt and began to comb out her long hair.

"I...I can do that myself."

"I know," was all he said as he continued.

Gradually she relaxed and her eyes drifted shut as he combed through the long, wet lengths. For now, she could pretend that he might care for her — if not now, then perhaps in the future. A future she could only pray they would have. His other hand caressed her head and then stroked the back of her neck and around her shoulders. His lips touched her own just an instant after he stopped combing her hair. She opened her eyes, looking at this man who she barely knew and yet who knew her more intimately than any other person had ever known her.

He brushed her hair away from her neck and dropped a kiss at the spot where her jaw ended. A delicious shiver raced through her and she reached for him, uncaring that the cloth fell open.

A knock on the door made her pull back from him and gather the cloth tightly around herself once more. Tormod cursed, then marched to the door. He flung it open and stepped into the doorway. Aoife twisted her head to see who was there. Björn. Again. He made no attempt to come into the room, but she could hear every word.

"We caught the culprit," she heard Björn say. "A boy. A Briton."

"Where was he?"

"Håkon found him hiding in his byre," Björn said, then added, "He's asking for your wife."

"Håkon?"

"The boy."

The two men turned to stare at her. She realised they'd been talking in Brythonic. They looked at each other and then back at her.

"For me? Why? Who is he?" Aoife frowned. Why would a child be asking for her? Especially one who had done such a thing as set a field on fire.

Her breath caught as she remembered her dream.

"Well?" Tormod asked Björn.

"Well?" Björn frowned.

"Who is the boy?"

"Why does your wife not come and see for herself?"

"You didn't ask him his name?"

There was silence. Björn waited.

Aoife's heart sank. "You didn't... You haven't... Is he dead?" She stood and backed against the wall, pressing herself farther and farther into the corner. If they had killed a child... She felt sick.

"No," Björn said. "He is not dead. He will say nothing except 'Lady Aoife' over and over again."

"We will come and see him," said Tormod. "Go and make sure nothing happens to him in the meantime."

"It won't. Arne is making sure of that. What do you think we are?" Björn sounded angry, although she could see guilt etched on his features. Killing the child for his crime was a thought that had occurred to them. "I'll wait for you outside." Tormod pulled the door closed, leaving Björn in the corridor. After a short pause he heard his cousin leave.

Tormod turned to stare at her. She couldn't read his expression. "Will you come and see the boy?"

"Why?" Her heart started to beat faster.

"A field was burned last night, across Loch Garw from your father's lands."

The remnants of her dream crowded into her thoughts. She'd seen the flames leaping, felt the warmth on her cheeks, smelled the harsh smoke, felt it sting her eyes and cause them to water. "And... and you think this boy may have done it?"

"It is possible."

"And my father might have ordered this?"

"You may know who he is. Be able to tell us who it is that is attacking us. Or perhaps you will not recognise him and then we will know that this is nothing to do with your father."

She nodded, clinging desperately to the hope that Tormod might be right. "But the boy asked for me by name."

"That's what Björn said."

Aoife watched Tormod, trying to discern what he might be thinking, but she could not. All that she knew was that she didn't want him to think she was guilty of such a thing. Neither did she want her father to be guilty, although there was a sinking feeling in her heart that he was. She looked down at her hands, loosening her grip when she noticed that her knuckles were white, then back up at Tormod. "You think a child was sent to attack you?"

"It is not too difficult for a child to set a fire."

That was true, but what kind of enemy would send a lone child to attack an enemy as formidable as the Norsemen? "I don't know anything about this. It has been two years since I last saw my father or visited my home, although..." She sat down on the edge of the bed and she shivered, partly with cold and partly with... Not fear, more a profound sense of disappointment. She had hoped she might be accepted here, find a family, but already the fact she was an outsider meant her loyalties were being tested. A test she wasn't sure she could pass as she simply knew nothing. Did Tormod blame her for this? If he did, it was unfair of him, although... What if it was her fault? What if her father was, indeed, behind it?

She straightened. She would go and see the boy and hopefully be able to reassure both herself and Tormod that this was either a random attack or an attack by another Briton. After all, her father was not the only Briton who resented the presence of the Norsemen. She looked at her husband.

He was staring at her. "This morning, before you woke..." He broke off.

"What about it?"

"You were talking in your sleep."

"Oh?" She tried to keep her voice steady. What had she said?

"You spoke of fire and fields." Tormod's expression was blank. Her chest tightened, and she found it difficult to breathe. "A strange coincidence."

"It was just a dream."

Their gazes held. Aoife felt sure that if she dropped hers, then Tormod would see through her half-truth, but she couldn't tell him the whole of it. The risk was too great, and the truth was that she really had not known this attack would happen, so her dream wouldn't have helped anyone.

"Come, we will see this boy and decide his fate," Tormod stated. The earlier affection in his voice was gone.

It was a challenge to prove her loyalty. That should not be difficult to pass—she owed her father none. She glared at her husband. Perhaps she should tell him about her visions, the fact that she had seen the burning field more than once and... She stopped that train of thought. If she told him now, he would wonder why she had not warned them. There was no way to win in this situation. It was unfair of him to blame her for something not of her doing. She wished she could make him believe her, trust her. She sagged a little at the thought that that just might never be possible. No matter how much she wanted to fit in, she might always be regarded as the outsider here. People had a tendency to stick to their beliefs, regardless of how one tried to show that they were wrong. Still, she had to try.

"You are my husband," she said. "My loyalties are to you. Is that not the case for any wife bought and paid for by her husband?"

Tormod didn't move, didn't change his expression. She shouldn't have challenged him. They waited in silence. She feared he would cast her aside, send her back to her father or the abbey with no hope of any future. She held her breath.

Finally, Tormod shrugged. "The sentiment ought to be true, yes. For some, however, betrayal is as simple as breathing. And I did not pay for you. I did not have to. Your father paid for me to take you."

As hurtful as that was to hear, she could believe it to be true.

"I have not betrayed anyone," she said, turning away from him. She closed her eyes. Outside she could hear the village sounds, the animals, voices, the clink of harnesses and the clatter of carts. Not her world, although not so very different either.

"Why were you beaten?" Tormod's voice was soft. She opened her eyes to see him cross the room towards her and sit on the bed. He lifted her hands and kissed them. She stared at her hands as she tried to frame what she would say.

"Aoife?"

He placed a finger under her chin and forced her to look at him. She was not ready to explain to him why she had been beaten, but neither would she lie.

"I became unwell. Like I did at the wedding. That's all."

Tormod searched her face, as if trying to discern whether her words were the truth or not. Then he frowned, pulled away from her. It was clear that what she had said was not enough to reassure him, however, to say anything else was too much of a risk. To her. For her future. For her life.

Chapter Twelve

BROTHERS OF THUNDER

T ORMOD OPENED HIS MOUTH to speak just as someone banged on the door, shaking it in its frame. He crossed to it and flung it open once more.

"You must come now, *herre*," Björn said. "The boy is here. For his own safety. Some of the villagers are growing aggressive."

"I just need…" Tormod looked at Aoife and sighed. He wanted to know more about this sickness. There certainly didn't seem to be anything physically wrong with her. He needed to know what she had been about to say, how she had known about the fire. Had it been merely a dream? A coincidence? Or had she known that the attack was to take place and not told him? But then, why should she?

Shouting from the main hall could be heard, however, and he realised Björn was right.

"Ragna!" Tormod called.

He was relieved when his aunt appeared quickly. "Help my wife to dress. Please."

Ragna hurried into the bedroom and Tormod stepped outside, giving Aoife some privacy.

He spotted Ulf and Arne waiting close by and frowned. "You think I need protection in my own village?"

"No," said Björn. "We think your wife does."

"But…"

"And the boy." Björn gestured towards Ulf and Arne. A small figure crouched on the floor between the men, both of whom had their swords drawn, despite the boy's hands and feet being shackled. Neither of the men met his gaze.

"He is just a child," Tormod said. "He cannot be more than eight years old. Can he really have done such a thing?"

"Håkon has accused him. And the boy has not denied it. The only thing he has said is your wife's name," Björn said. "And his hands and clothes are burned which proves that he set the fire."

"No," said Tormod loudly. "It means only that he was there when the fire was burning, and that he wishes to speak to my wife. Nothing else."

Tormod hoped his words turned out to be true, although he wondered why. It would be no great loss to him if the child were killed, would it? And yet somehow he felt that he must save the boy if he ever wanted to earn his wife's trust.

The noise from the main hall grew louder and louder with every passing second. The doors to the hall banged closed at regular intervals, and it was clear that a large crowd awaited him. The sooner the matter was dealt with, the better, although he feared what the outcome of any trial might be. He could wait no longer for his wife to be ready.

"Ragna," he called through the door, "when my wife is ready, bring her to the *Thing*."

"Of course, *herre*."

A great lump of rock settled in the pit of Tormod's stomach. If both Björn and his aunt were calling him *herre*, then something was very wrong. Perhaps settling here was a mistake. Perhaps they should just go home. He set his teeth. No. They had won this land fairly. The Britons had abandoned it long before they arrived. They had no more right to it than he and his men.

At home, all he had to look forward to were scraps from his many older brothers. Or to remain in service to another as a warrior his whole life. That was not what he wanted. Learning that was the only positive thing to come from his first marriage. He was a good leader, he could make difficult decisions.

Tormod drew himself up to his full height as he strode out of the main hall, across the common land to where the Thing site sat on its small promontory. Arne waited at the stone causeway which led across the circular ditch and Tormod handed him his weapons, then he crossed the stone causeway, entering the circle with as much authority as he could muster. Many of the villagers were standing around the outer edge of the circle, on the far side of the ditch. Only himself, those who were giving evidence, and the accused would cross the causeway itself. As he looked around the shocked and angry faces of his villagers, who yesterday had been celebrating his wedding, he mentally ran through his options for dealing with the matter. None of them sat well with a child so young.

Björn had followed close behind him, and he watched as brought Ulf crossed the causeway, bringing the boy into the *Thing*. The eyes of every villager were on that small, lonely figure.

Tormod lifted his hand and everyone quieted instantly. He hoped this situation would not work out the way he feared. "Who accuses this boy?" he called out.

Håkon handed his weapons to Arne and crossed the causeway, coming to stand in front of Tormod.

"I do," Håkon stated. "Last night one of my fields burned, deliberately set on fire. This morning I found the boy hiding in the byre with the animals. He set that fire. He has burns on his hands and clothes which prove it."

The crowd shouted and yelled, all demanding justice.

Tormod raised his hand for order and turned to Håkon. "Did you see him do this thing?"

"No," replied Håkon, narrowing his eyes at Tormod. "But there was no one else there. And who else apart from the Britons would have wanted to burn my field?"

A general shout of agreement went around the circle. Clearly the man had not expected to be questioned and thought that a sentence would simply be handed out—but Tormod could not help seeing the boy as one of Aoife's people. That, coupled with the fact the boy was similar in age to his dead wife's son, and Tormod was struggling to believe a child had managed to do this alone. And for what reason? Why not run away? Why wait to be found? How had he got there in the first place?

Tormod held up a hand again, and the circle fell silent as the villagers waited for him to speak. "He's just a boy. Can one small child really have done so much damage all by himself? Where were our guards? And what does he have to say for himself?"

"Nothing, *herre*, save for the Briton's name." The distaste in Håkon's tone was clear. Tormod glared at him.

"My wife's name?" Tormod said. He caught and held Håkon's gaze until the farmer was forced either to look away or risk challenging Tormod.

Håkon looked down, his shoulders slumping as he realised he had angered his jarl. "Your wife's name, *herre*," he finally mumbled.

So, the situation was not just about burnt fields or captured boys. He had known his choice of wife might cause some concern, although he had hoped for some time for her to settle before facing an obstacle such as this. However, they couldn't possibly think she had anything to do with it. Especially on her wedding night.

"How can you be sure this child was responsible?" Tormod was careful to emphasise the word "child."

"His burns," Håkon said, quickly trying to re-establish himself. "And he is one of... them. A Briton."

"I see," Tormod replied, sitting down without taking his gaze from Håkon. "The boy is not even old enough for arm rings, and yet he was able to either cross the spit alone, unseen by any of our guards or else he sailed or rowed across Loch Garw and set fire to your field alone. He was not, however, capable of leaving the field before burning his arms. And where is his boat?"

"*Herre...*" Håkon scratched his head and frowned. "Who else would do it except for the Britons?"

"Who else indeed?" Tormod said. "But tell me, what is that I see on your arms?"

Håkon put his arms out in front of him and frowned at them. "Burns, *herre.*"

"Burns?"

"Yes," Håkon agreed.

"So, did you set the fire?"

"No, *herre*, I tried to beat the fire out."

Tormod stared at Håkon for a long moment, hoping the man would work out what he was getting at by himself. However, before that happened, Tormod heard a murmur grow around the circle. Tormod's heart sank. If only Aoife had taken a few minutes longer to arrive. Perhaps it was better to face up to the fact that his wife was a Briton and not allow feeling against her to fester. It would only grow worse with time.

As Aoife approached with Ragna, most of the villagers turned to stare at her. Tormod couldn't help but smile when she lifted her chin and walked straight towards him, and he was grateful that Björn and Ragna followed close behind her. When she reached the causeway, Arne indicated that she should cross it after a nod from Tormod. Then she noticed the boy.

"Elisedd!" she cried out and stood moved towards him, but Ulf stepped between them and Tormod took her hand and guided her to stand beside him, opposite the causeway.

The boy had raised his head and now sat up, reaching his bound arms towards Aoife. Tormod could see the nasty burns on the boy's hands and noted that someone had tended to them. Probably Håkon's wife, Magda. Tormod believed she would have cared for this boy, no matter what she thought he might have done.

"Lady Aoife," the boy sobbed. "I tried. I really tried."

It was all but an admission of guilt. Tormod thanked the gods that Håkon couldn't understand the language. There was more to this situation, he was sure of it. And the way the boy's hands and clothes had been burned made Tormod wonder at Håkon's version of the story.

Aoife looked at Tormod. "May I speak to him?" When he nodded, she turned to the boy. "Elisedd. Why are you here? What has happened to you?"

Elisedd opened his mouth to speak, then seemed to realise he was surrounded by enemies and cowered back down, shaking his head.

"The farmer, Håkon, found him hiding with animals near the burned field," Tormod explained. "They think he set the crops on fire. You can see the burns."

Aoife frowned at Tormod. "He is only a child. Why would he do such a thing?" She looked around at the other villagers, then at Elisedd. "What did you do? How did you get here?"

Elisedd said nothing, still shaking his head.

"You must tell us the truth, Elisedd. No one will hurt you," Aoife said, sending a pleading glance towards Tormod, who nodded.

The child shrank away from Ulf and, with his gaze fixed on Aoife, he began to talk. "I heard them talking about you last night, so I followed them. Hid in their boat. They were saying how you would be blamed for the fire and the Norsemen would kill you. When they left, I tried to put it out..." He stretched his arms out in front of him and winced.

Aoife took a step towards him, but Tormod placed a hand on her arm. She sighed. "They left in a boat?"

"Yes, my lady."

"Who was it?" Aoife asked. "Who gave the order for the field to be burned?"

At that question, the boy baulked and pulled back. "They said you would be blamed. I hid on the boat and crept out after we arrived on the shore. I couldn't stop them from lighting the fire, but I tried to put it out. It spread too quickly." The boy put his face in his hands and started to cry. "They said the Norsemen would kill you. I didn't want the Norsemen to hurt you. I only wanted to help."

"Elisedd, does your mother know where you are?"

He nodded at Aoife, tears running down his face. "I told her what I had heard. She sent me. She wanted me to find you, to keep you safe. My father is dead and..."

"What?" Her hands flew to her face. She turned to Tormod, who shrugged.

"I do not think my mother is safe there anymore. Without my father—"

"Elisedd. What happened to your father?"

"Car Cadell was attacked," Elisedd replied. "More than once since Alt Clut. My father was killed. There have been... a lot of deaths. With you gone, and without my father there to protect her, I fear for my mother's safety."

"My father will see that she comes to no harm. He has always protected his own people."

Elisedd stared at her. "Lord Cadell, he... Lady Ula makes most of the decisions now. Father Bricius advises her. And she knows of your friendship with my mother. She wishes to punish her for it, I think."

Aoife gasped, then turned away from Tormod. He tried not to be disappointed that she had not turned to him for help.

"Ulf! Unchain the boy," Tormod said, stepping forward. Ulf did so but stopped him from running towards Aoife.

Aoife looked at him, a pained expression on her face.

Then Tormod spoke in Norse to ensure all the villagers understood. "The boy did not set fire to the field, but he knows who did so and he tried to put it out. That is why he has burns on his arms–burns just like Håkon's. The Britons wish for you to turn on my wife. Are you going to give them their wish? Or shall we all work together and make the true culprits pay for their transgression rather than an innocent child?"

There was a lot of murmuring around the circle. None of the villagers sought to enter the circle challenge the judgement. Perhaps the first flush of anger was wearing off, and they were beginning to realise the unlikeliness of this one child having bested them and their defences.

"The boy walks free this day and none of you shall harm him. Do we all agree?"

There was a general, if unenthusiastic, shout of agreement.

"Do we all agree?" Tormod repeated loudly. He would brook no disagreement about this.

A louder shout was more reassuring.

"What will you do with the boy?" Aoife asked, looking down at Elisedd.

Tormod turned to the farmer. "Håkon, will you take the boy in?"

"Take the boy in?" Håkon glared at Tormod.

"There are not as many burns on your body as there are on this child. Perhaps you did not try as hard as the boy to put out the fire in your own field," Tormod said, relieved when there was a ripple of laughter from most of those gathered around the circle. "He did more to try to put out the fire than anyone else. And he will recognise these men if they return."

"And if he causes any more damage?"

"Then we will deal with him as we would any proven traitor." Tormod stated. "And when we find those who attacked us in this way, they will be dealt with. You have my oath on this!"

Around the circle was a general murmur of agreement.

Tormod hoped they would find out who had done this, and quickly. His people had to believe he had only their interests at heart. Which he did, but he also knew they could not survive here surrounded by enemies that they were only going to antagonise and not at least attempt to work beside. He could only hope that the attack had been a one off. Somehow, he doubted it.

Lord Cadell had lied. Or perhaps it was, as the boy claimed, that Lady Ula made most of the decisions there now.

"Björn, arrange a better watch on the eastern coast at night. Get the boy to tell you where he crossed Loch Garw and where he landed. Håkon, I take it you have searched and found no sign of a boat?"

There was a long pause and some shuffling of feet, then Håkon took a deep breath and sighed. "No, *herre*."

"So, there is no way that the boy acted alone."

"No, *herre*." There was silence for a moment, then Håkon continued. "*Herre*, if the boy proves to be a good worker, I will be happy to take him in."

Tormod nodded at the man. Inwardly, he breathed a sigh of relief. This could have been disastrous, however, it seemed there was a chance it would work out for them all.

"Swear this to me," Tormod ordered.

Håkon stepped forward and swore the oath to Tormod.

"Justice has been served!" Tormod shouted.

The other villagers nodded, not overjoyed, but satisfied.

"Håkon will take the boy in and give him a home in exchange for work," Tormod explained to her.

"Elisedd," Aoife said. "His name is Elisedd."

"Elisedd," Tormod addressed him in Brythonic. "Håkon will be your new master. He will take you in and take care of you, and in return you will help him work on and protect his farm."

"But..." the boy began, fear etched on his face as he looked at the farmer who had only recently been calling for his death.

Aoife knelt down and leaned towards Elisedd.

Tormod envied the easy affection visible between his wife and the boy. It reminded him of the way Ingrid had focused all her attention on her son, Einar, as she plotted to have Tormod killed. He had hoped that there would be some affection possible in this marriage, but with a child from amongst her own people to fuss over, would Tormod be an outsider in his own family once more? If he kept Aoife and Elisedd apart, would his marriage stand a better chance of success?

He tried to push the thought from his head. This was a good solution to the current problem for all concerned. It was not about him being selfish. He couldn't assume Aoife was anything like his first wife. He should try to trust her. He sighed. It was difficult. It would be difficult for any man, let alone one who had already suffered due to the lies of a woman.

"I will come and visit you," she said, then glanced at Tormod, a scared look in her eye. He forced himself to nod at her. He must try to be benevolent, and was gratified when she smiled. "I will visit you and make sure you are all right and we will make a new home here."

Elisedd bit his lower lip and tears filled his eyes as Håkon approached.

Aoife looked desperately at Tormod.

"No harm will come to you," Tormod assured the boy and glared at Håkon before repeating the statement in Norse.

Håkon agreed and put out a hand to Elisedd. When the boy did not react, Håkon knelt down and repeated the gesture.

"Go," said Aoife. "These people have been kind to me so far. We must learn to trust them."

Elisedd dashed the tears from his eyes, then took the offered hand and walked out of the circle with Håkon.

Tormod stared around at all the other villagers, meeting as many of their gazes as possible, hoping that none decided his judgment had been wrong. They seemed cautious but not averse to his decision, and Tormod took that as a positive. No one had challenged him before. He had to hope they would not start now.

Aoife was straining to watch the boy leave, so he led her across the causeway and back towards the hall. They waited until the boy and Håkon disappeared out of sight on the path over the hill. There had been no sign of Håkon mistreating the boy, and Tormod was sure he wouldn't. The man had no sons of his own—only daughters who were almost grown now—he may welcome the boy in the long term of his own accord. His wife, Magda, certainly would.

"Thank you," Aoife said.

"There is no need to thank me. I do not think the boy had done anything wrong. If I did, I would have acted differently. His burns had been tended," Tormod said by way of reassurance. "I believe Håkon's wife, Magda, will care for him well."

She stared at him, then nodded slowly. He paused, unsure how to broach the next subject. Then he decided to just ask what needed to be asked. "Could your father have been behind this? The agreement was we would live side by side in peace, and yet someone has attacked my lands."

Aoife pulled her hand from his and took a few steps away. He let her go and waited until most of the villagers had started to make their way back to their homes.

"Perhaps news of our wedding and of the alliance has not spread to everyone yet," she said. "I am sure once it does..." she trailed off, avoiding looking at him.

"Let us hope it is the case," Tormod said, unsure of what he would do if it turned out not to be the case. Aoife was clearly as unsure as he was himself.

Chapter Thirteen

BROTHERS
OF
THUNDER

AOIFE BELIEVED TORMOD WAS telling her the truth about Håkon and his wife, but she'd seen the faces of some of the villagers. They didn't trust Elisedd, didn't trust her. Her hope of finding a home here faded a little, although she forced herself to smile at her new husband. "I look forward to visiting him."

Tormod tensed beside her and stared after Håkon. "Why do you wish to visit him? I have assured you that he will be cared for. Do you not trust me?"

She drew in a deep breath. Why was he so suspicious? Elisedd was the only one of her countrymen she was likely to be able to see. Surely he must realise it was hard to believe Håkon would have changed his opinion of the boy so quickly. Only an hour ago he'd been demanding he be executed. "To... To make sure he is being cared for."

"Håkon has sworn he will care for him," Tormod stated, still not looking at her. "He is no oath breaker."

"And what of the others?" she asked tentatively. "It is not just Håkon who wished him to be punished."

Finally, Tormod looked at her. "A judgment has been made. There are none here who will go against a verdict reached at a *Thing*."

"A *Thing*?"

"The meeting we just had. It was an official judgment. The villagers will abide by it — all of them."

Aoife thought for a moment, hoping Tormod was right. She realised just how at the mercy of others she lived, and now Elisedd's safety rested in their hands as well. "I would just like to make sure he is all right... Sometimes."

Tormod moved to stand in front of her, his feet placed wide apart. She couldn't take her eyes off him.

"Is the boy of more concern to you than me, your husband?" he asked coldly.

Aoife hesitated before answering. "Of course not."

"And yet, you ask to see him when I have already assured you of his safety," he said. "Do you not trust my word?"

She drew in a breath, realised that she had hesitated too long when Tormod started to turn away from her.

"I'm sorry," she said, placing a hand on his shoulder. He stopped but made no effort to turn back.

"He is the son of my maid. Former maid. She was not allowed to accompany me to the abbey, of course." She stopped, tears threatening as she remembered the ugly scene when her father had sent her away.

Rhiannon had watched with tears in her eyes, knowing she was to serve Ula's youngest daughter from then on, a spoilt, difficult child who made life for everyone around her miserable.

Elisedd had chased after the cart that took her to the abbey, screaming her name over and over, until she'd had to cover her ears to block out the sound of his distress. A distress equal to her own.

"I am alone here," she said. "He is simply a reminder of home in better times." She grimaced. Those times may have been better than her time at the abbey, but they had been far from ideal. Still, Rhiannon's company had made her life more bearable in so many ways.

Tormod paused before he faced her once more. For a moment she thought that he understood, then his eyes narrowed. "You consider yourself alone here, despite our marriage? Has our marriage meant nothing to you?"

The question hit her with an almost physical force. Her head snapped up and her jaw dropped.

"Yes, it has."

This was not what she had meant. She frowned, struggling to understand why he was so suspicious of her motives to see Elisedd. Surely it was not a difficult thing to understand, to wish to spend time with someone you share a common past with.

"If this alliance is tested," he said. "How can I be sure you will stand with me as a wife should?"

"You can be sure," Aoife stated firmly. "I have made my vows; I will honour them."

They stared at each other.

Aoife's thoughts raced while a chill swept through her body. No matter what she did or said, her husband simply did not trust her, and she was powerless to change his mind. She had done everything asked of her so far, and yet it did not seem to be enough.

Feeling like she had little to lose, she stormed past him into the hall and headed straight back to their room. Once there, she closed the door firmly behind her and crossed to the missing knot in the wall which let her see a little of the outside world. Some villagers still stood around talking in small, huddled groups. Most were starting to drift apart and get on with their normal, everyday tasks.

Aoife closed her eyes and sighed. It was early days, but if even Tormod didn't trust her, then what chance did she have here? Would there ever be somewhere where she was not seen as different, an outsider? That she was trusted?

Maybe she should take Elisedd and return to her father. She leaned against the wall, wondering whether to run out, or to stay and try to sort this out. There would be many things to establish. Life was all about compromises and fitting in with the demands of others. She heard the door open and close and decided to ignore it.

She opened her eyes when Tormod's hand landed on her shoulder, and he turned her to face him. He didn't seem angry, just thoughtful.

"This morning," he began. "You were talking in your sleep. Of fields and fires. You said it was only a dream, and yet it happened, and Elisedd was there. The boy that you wish to spend so much time with, was there. Why?"

She nearly told him that it was not important and would have done had it not been for the anguish in his expression. For a man who appeared to be so sure of himself, her loyalty was clearly something that concerned him. Her treatment here might have been far, far different. She had not been threatened in any way. Maybe it was time to repay him for his kindness by telling the truth. Or a version of it.

"Sometimes I dream things. It is not something I control, not something I want. I played no part in this. Please, trust me. This is my home now. I owe my loyalty to you, and you only. It was naught but a dream."

They stared at each other, each trying to work the other out.

"Please," she said. "I would like to see Elisedd again. And if I see him alone, he may tell me more of what is happening with my father than he would share with any of your people. Perhaps he will tell me who was behind the attack. He knows, but was too afraid to tell me just now. If I know that, then I will tell you and it might help you, help the village."

"Very well," Tormod replied. "Tomorrow, I have promised to help Hákon clear up the damage and replant what we can. I will have Ragna bring you to us at the end of the afternoon and you can speak to the boy."

"Thank you." She sighed and sat down on the bed, staring at her hands. "Elisedd and I are outsiders here... however, if you are sure he will be all right, then I will believe you."

"You are not an outsider. You are my wife." He sounded angry, but Aoife knew she was right. Whatever Tormod said, not all of his people saw it that way.

"But still an outsider, the daughter of an enemy."

"A new ally," Tormod corrected.

She watched him for a moment. He really seemed to believe what he said. The thought that her stepmother would betray her in an instant and worse, persuade her father to do so also was something she could no longer put off telling him, but before she could, he closed the gap between them and put his arms around her.

Tormod ran his hand over her hair and cupped the back of her head. For a moment, he did nothing more, then he gently angled her towards him and closed his mouth over hers. His kiss was warm and passionate, and her eyes drifted shut as she kissed him back as hungrily as he kissed her. Without thought, she took a step towards him, their bodies colliding and moulding against one another. As long as he was kissing her, she felt safe. Sure of him and his need for her.

She allowed herself to get lost in the kiss, wishing it would never end, or if it did, hoping somehow it would have solved everything. Of course, that was simply not possible, and all too soon his mouth lifted from hers and he set them apart. Reluctantly, she opened her eyes.

"You must understand this is difficult for both of us," Tormod said. "I have a village whose safety I have to ensure. I cannot..." He turned away from her. "I cannot allow lust to cloud my judgment." He looked back at her, and she thought she saw guilt in his face—but why?

They stared at each other and her heart beat faster at the knowledge he did indeed feel lustful towards her. It was a long way from love, although perhaps it showed some level of connection between them. A connection that could be developed over time.

"Are you sure you can trust my father?" she asked. Perhaps it was foolish. Perhaps she should go on allowing him to believe it, but she couldn't. It may not make her own life any safer, but now there was Elisedd to think about, too. The Norsemen wouldn't hesitate to kill him if they thought they were being betrayed.

"No."

She blinked. "But..."

"I never trust anyone," he said shortly and left the room.

Stunned, she stared after him for a moment, and when the door banged shut, she rested her head in her hands. She didn't know whether his words were a relief or not. He already didn't trust her father and had still been kind to her.

She tried to puzzle out in her head just what had happened and what was going on. It turned out she needn't have worried about Tormod trusting her father. That really had been rather naïve. No one became jarl by blindly trusting everyone around them. She smiled to herself. This husband of hers was no fool.

A knock at the door indicated Ragna's arrival.

"If you are ready, I will take you through the hall and some of the village so you can meet the villagers properly and see how we do things here. There are some decisions that need to be made, and I have been putting them off," Ragna said.

"Should Tormod not be—"

"Decisions that should be made by the jarl's wife," Ragna clarified. "Not things that are of interest to the jarl."

"I was brought up knowing how to run a household." Aoife felt a sudden spark of hope that perhaps she really could prove her worth and her loyalty in much the same way as she would have done amongst her own people. "I'm sure there are differences and your ways…"

Ragna's warm smile made her feel much better. "I'm sure much of it will be the same, the basics at the very least, and I will be here to help you. And there are many things you can teach us, about some of the native plants and your seasons and the people who live here." Ragna stopped speaking and peered at her. "These were your father's lands, were they not?"

"Yes."

"Did you know the people who lived here?"

"What?" Aoife blinked, then racked her brains, trying to remember if she had. "Perhaps." She frowned. "I'm not sure. I had never visited here, only seen it from the far shore."

"It had been abandoned when we arrived. At first I thought that was a good thing, although now I am not so sure," Ragna confessed.

"Why do you say that?"

"Well, if we had won the land in battle, it would have been truly ours. As it is, the previous inhabitants may well be still close by and none too happy about our arrival."

Aoife didn't know what to say. Of course, Ragna was probably right. She struggled to remember what she knew, but she had spent so little time at her father's fort after the siege of Alt Clut that she wasn't sure she knew that information. And she had never ridden out with her father to visit their surrounding lands. That would have been for a son to do.

"My father's steward, Rhydderch, would know," Aoife said. "Whatever has happened in the last two years, I cannot help you with." Aoife left the fact that Rhydderch was unlikely to ever share that information unsaid.

"Now," said Ragna, "let us see what we can do this morning. Tormod tells me we are going to visit the boy at Håkon's farm tomorrow."

Aoife smiled at her, genuinely pleased her husband was honouring his word. "You think Håkon will be kind to him?"

"Yes, he has no sons of his own, only daughters who are all nearly grown. His wife Magda will love to have a son to care for."

"But earlier..."

Ragna sighed. "Earlier, everyone was upset. Angry. And Tormod ensured justice was done and that will be the end of it."

"You are sure?"

"He is the jarl. The village must obey his judgments when they take place in the Thing. It is our way."

"I will speak to Elisedd, find out if he knows who did this thing, as well as why and how he came to be here."

"And if the answers mean you will have to betray your family?"

Aoife regarded the other woman steadily. "Tormod is my husband. He is my family now."

Ragna considered her for a moment, then nodded. "Come, we have work to do, decisions to make for the future."

The two women headed outside together.

Chapter Fourteen

BROTHERS
OF
THUNDER

W HEN TORMOD ARRIVED AT Håkon's farm the next morning, he checked first on Elisedd. Although he was sure Håkon would not break his oath, he felt the need to prove to his wife that he had taken her concerns seriously. Elisedd came outside with Håkon as soon as Tormod arrived, carrying a spade to help them. Tormod saw the disappointment on the boy's face when he realised he had not brought Aoife with him, but he'd smiled when Tormod spoke to him in Brythonic and assured him that Aoife would visit later.

"It seems like the boy's story holds," Håkon said as they watched the boy trying to dig over a small patch of burnt ground. "Elisedd led me to the spot where the boat landed. There are marks on the beach where a boat had been pulled up."

"No sign of a boat?"

"No, and I have searched up and down the coast. Whoever started the fire most likely left in it once the blaze took hold." Håkon glanced at Tormod, then away. "I should have thought first, before I accused him. Elisedd did not try to run away when I found him. He only wanted to see your wife."

"No one will threaten my wife," Tormod stated, then put a hand on Håkon's shoulder. "But no one blames you for being suspicious, Håkon."

"No," the other man said. "But maybe they should. He's just a boy... and I wanted him dead for what he had done. What I thought he had done. And then it turns out he was trying to help me."

"A wise man never makes a decision in haste. It is why we have a *Thing*. You made the right choice in the end."

"Your wife..."

"She does not blame you. She just..." Tormod stopped and took a breath. He did indeed wonder exactly what Aoife thought and how she felt about the boy. Was it just as she had said, that he was her maid's child? Was it just because he was a familiar face amongst so many strangers? Or was there a bigger secret here? Had the boy been brought over intentionally? No, that didn't make sense. If he was being sent to Aoife, the fire would not have been started—and why not just send the boy with her in the first place? And what of his mother? Aoife was clearly worried about his mother's safety.

"We must work in the belief that this alliance will hold," Tormod eventually said. "Perhaps the news of it was slow to reach some quarters and this will be an end to it all." Tormod knew even as the words left his lips that he did not even believe them himself.

"Do you think the boy spoke the truth?" Håkon asked.

"Yes, although maybe he did not tell us the whole story."

"He is just a child. He may not have known all that was going on, may not have understood the relevance of what he was overhearing. I think he just came with the men whom he thought would take him to your wife. He hinted at there being trouble in Lord Cadell's household."

"You have spoken to him?"

"Magda has learnt some Brythonic. She was able to speak to the boy a little." Håkon bowed his head. "I... I should have asked her to speak to him before I assumed his guilt and dragged him to you for judgment."

"That's true. However, it is in the past now. Aoife will ask him later and we will make sure the village knows that neither my wife nor the boy is our enemy."

Håkon put a hand on Tormod's arm. "Perhaps you should let your wife spend some time with him. He will trust her."

Tormod hesitated, then realised what he felt was jealousy that Aoife wanted to spend time with the boy. How ridiculous. They were the only ones of their people here in the village, why should they not want to spend time together? Had he not felt the same when he had found himself in faraway marketplaces or even among the Norse living across the Kattegat?

"I believe the boy," Håkon said, distracting Tormod from his negative thoughts. "He showed me where the boat came ashore. I could not understand everything he said, but I think he was worried about your wife — I think he thought they meant to kill her. But why would her father want her dead?"

"I hope that is not the case," Tormod said, frowning.

Håkon walked into the burnt field and dug his fork in at the edge of the scorched earth.

"Come, we shall repair this damage and show that we will not be forced from this place. I will replant this field with another crop. It's not too late. Something fast growing," Håkon said. "I will make the best of this."

Elisedd watched Håkon carefully and copied what he did. He didn't yet have the strength to work effectively, but Tormod could tell he was trying.

"You will," Tormod said. "And for today, I will help you." But the comment about Aoife's father nagged at him.

"You must have other things to do." Håkon grinned. "You are a newly married man."

Tormod made a face at him and dug his spade into the ground.

"Ragna has many tasks for my wife today. I think my aunt is happy to pass many of her responsibilities over. Finding wives for my cousins is something I know she is now ready to see happen sooner rather than later. Besides, the physical work will be good for me," Tormod said. "Give me time to think and a task which has an end. It will be a relief from all the problems of starting a new life in a new land."

"We will succeed," Håkon assured him. "We always do. Have courage."

"I do," Tormod said. "Truly. Now let's get to work."

The three of them worked side by side as the sun grew hotter. Finally, Tormod pulled his kirtle and shirt off and relished the feel of the sun warming his bare skin. It was not a sensation he had felt often since coming to this land, where even the summers could be wet and miserable. Håkon's wife, Magda, brought them ale regularly, and soon the worst of the damage to the field had been dug over, the burnt crop now back to being a field ready for planting. The smell of smoke was still in the air, but less noticeable than it had been earlier.

At the end of the afternoon, Tormod couldn't wait to get back to the hall and bathe. He told Elisedd he had done enough, and the boy ran towards the water and jumped straight in to swim not appearing to mind the cold water. Tormod was going to arrange for some more men to work on the bathhouse. The weather had grown warmer these last few days, and it was now a priority. He'd tested the waters of the Loch Garw late morning and the cold had been breath-taking. Not that it had stopped him from bathing regularly—the bitter smell of the fire was best washed away as often as possible, although he yearned to soak in water that was not cold enough to shrivel his extremities.

"The gods have blessed us with a day fit for our purposes," Håkon said when they stopped. "It is a sign that we are where we ought to be."

"Yes, although we have much to learn." Tormod looked around, then across the sea-loch to where Cadell's land lay. He could see some planted fields, but it was mostly forested and there were also a few areas of pasture. No fences or boundaries surrounded the fields and the land uses were so very different. Livestock wandered on the beach, and Tormod wondered idly how they kept track of their beasts. He would be sure to ask his wife.

Håkon followed Tormod's gaze and laughed. "I think it may be that they have much to learn from us. They do not protect well enough what is theirs."

"Not in the way we do anyway," agreed Tormod. "But there may be other reasons. We will be sure to ask and to learn."

Håkon obviously caught the note of warning in his voice as he frowned before he nodded. "Yes, *herre*. And thank you, I am indebted—but if I could beg another favour? Both of which shall be repaid in full upon the harvest."

"Yes?" Tormod asked.

"My wife and daughters would like to learn the language of the Britons better. Their lands stretch from here all the way east up the River Clut and south from the firth all the way down the west coast. Many of our people trade with the Gaels and the Northumbrians on the east coast; far fewer here in the west. It is a good opportunity to reach a new market. As you know, Magda is a fine seamstress, as are my daughters, and they sell many of their wares. Plus, if the boy is going to stay with us... We will teach him Norse. It will be a show of friendship. Would your wife be willing to teach them Brythonic?"

"My wife?" Tormod had thought only of Aoife taking over some of Ragna's burdens, although maybe this was a good idea. "Allow me to think about it. And to ask her."

"It might be a good way of her showing that she wishes to help us..."

"Yes." Tormod turned to face Håkon. There was a line to be drawn here. "But I will decide how best she can do that."

"I'm sorry, *herre*, I meant no disrespect, it's just that—"

"I know what it is, Håkon. I am not a fool."

"No, that you are not." Håkon started to pull his kirtle back on. Their day of companionship was over. "But there are many—"

"I know," Tormod said. He was torn. He held suspicions of his own, but he would say nothing to anyone in case he made Aoife's position even more precarious. Wives, especially jarl's wives, were often outsiders to a village. But Aoife was not one of their people. She could not even speak their language.

A thought struck him. He'd intended to ask Ragna to teach Aoife Norse. "Your wife, Håkon."

"Magda? What of her?"

"In return, Magda can also teach Aoife Norse. Our wives can work together each day and it will allow Aoife to visit with Elisedd. Yes, I think that may work well for us all."

Håkon stared at him for a long moment. "Yes, that would be good. Magda is a quick learner, and the girls can take on more of the household tasks. It is time we found them good husbands now we are settled here. And then Magda can teach others. She will like that, *herre*. Thank you."

As Håkon walked towards his house, Tormod closed his eyes and enjoyed the sunshine warming him. Then he opened his eyes, picked up his drinking horn and filled it with ale from the jug, then drank it slowly, relishing the sensation against his parched throat. The cool waters of the sea-loch lay still in front of him, sunlight flashing off the surface and beckoning him to slide into their depths.

He had only taken a few steps towards where Elisedd sat on the shore when he sensed someone watching him. He turned, fully expecting it to be an animal or a bird, but smiled in surprise when he saw his wife standing near the edge of the field, her gaze on him. Ragna was beside her. However, he barely noticed his aunt as he picked up his kirtle and slung it over his shoulder before starting to walk towards Aoife. He may even have swaggered a little.

CHAPTER FIFTEEN

A OIFE COULD HAVE SIMPLY followed the smell of burnt grass and found the farm, but Ragna had insisted on accompanying her. Along the way she spoke to everyone she passed, doing her best to include Aoife in those conversations, despite how difficult it was as she was confined mainly to smiles and hand gestures. Although many of the people had some words of her language, she quickly realised they were limited to numbers and the names of the goods most commonly traded. Hardly topics of everyday conversation.

"Will you help me learn your language?" Aoife asked Ragna as they left yet another group of curious villagers. Aoife wished she was able to talk to them, ask them about their homes, their families, their lives. Show she cared about them and their needs, and would try to ensure her husband's decisions took into consideration the needs of the women and children living in the settlement as well as the men. She had seen the workings of her father's fort first hand and the problems that had often arisen between the needs and wants of the men, particularly the warriors and the other residents of the fort.

"Of course," Ragna replied. "It is good you have a few words already of Northumbrian. And it is important the villagers get to know you and trust you for yourself."

Aoife shook her head. "It is hard to believe they fear me," she admitted. "I am only one Briton, a woman, alone in the midst of so many Norse."

"Ah, but you are married to their jarl. They wonder about the power you may have over him, the ways in which you might betray him, or poison his thoughts against his own people," Ragna said.

"But..." Aoife had never considered such a thing.

Ragna smiled. "Don't worry, it will all work out. I have been telling them how good the two of you are together. And once children start to arrive, they will soon forget you are not one of their people, for your children will be Norse in their eyes."

Aoife bit her lower lip. It had only been a few days, but if Tormod continued the way he was, it was unlikely children would be coming along any time soon. He seemed to enjoy her body, but there would be no child if he continued to withdraw from her. Would that count against her in the eyes of the villagers? Maybe Tormod just needed some time. After all, surely every man—especially a jarl—needed sons eventually.

They rounded a final curve and the stench of burning grew greater.

"Looks like they have finished," said Ragna.

Aoife followed her gaze and her mouth went dry. There was Tormod. His kirtle was off and his chest glistened in the summer sunshine. She blushed when she heard Ragna chuckling beside her.

"You are not too displeased with your husband, then," Ragna said. Aoife wasn't sure what to say. "My nephew is a handsome man. And caring in his own way." Ragna slapped her on the back and they watched as Tormod approached.

Tormod kept his gaze on her as he drew nearer, but didn't smile or react in any way. Once he had reached them, they stood staring at one another. Aoife racked her brain for something to say, but could think of nothing. Her heart thumped in her chest and she worried that Ragna would tell Tormod of her reaction to him.

"You have nearly finished," was all Ragna said. Aoife breathed a sigh of relief.

"Yes," Tormod said. "And Elisedd has been a great help. He wishes to speak with you, my lady."

Aoife frowned at Tormod addressing her so formally, then nodded in agreement.

"I will return to the village," said Ragna. "Now that you are in the capable hands of your husband." The older woman headed back the way they had come, chuckling.

Aoife caught sight of Elisedd sitting at the water's edge and headed towards him. She had taken only a few steps when Tormod caught up to her and took her arm.

"I wish to come with you," he said.

Aoife glanced over at Elisedd. It certainly did not look like he had been punished in any way and Tormod was pleased with his work. "Why?"

"I wish to hear what he has to say."

"He may talk more freely if it is just me." She wasn't sure why she was pushing the matter. If Tormod wanted to hear what the two of them had to say then he would simply do it, although... she just wanted to feel he trusted her. If she felt that trust, then she would be happy to let him listen.

"And he may say something that means more to me than to you," Tormod said. "I have much more understanding of the way attacks are planned than you do. Or at least I presume I do."

Aoife wondered how much of that was true. Did he simply not trust her, or did he just not want to run the risk of her missing anything? She decided to hope for the best, even though inside she wanted it to be different. "Very well."

Together, they walked down to the beach. Elisedd turned at the sound of their feet on the shingle. His face broke into a bright smile at the sight of Aoife and only dimmed a little when he realised Tormod was there, too.

"Elisedd," Aoife said as the boy ran over to her and hugged her. "How you have grown. I nearly did not recognise you yesterday. Why did you come? What has happened at Car Cadell?"

"I thought I would never see you again," he said, holding her tightly. His voice broke with emotion and he hugged her tighter, then pulled back, putting on a brave face. "It has been so long. When I heard the men talking about you, I told my mother. She said I had to come with them and try to find you. Everything has changed since the siege at Alt Clut."

Elisedd refused to meet her gaze after he finished speaking.

"Do you know who did this? Or why?"

Elisedd looked at the ground and said nothing.

Behind her, Tormod scoffed and her stomach felt like it was full of the rocks that lay all along the beach.

"You heard them speak. You came across the sea-loch in a boat with these men. You must know who they are," Tormod said.

"I heard the men speak, but I was hiding and couldn't see their faces. They didn't know I was there." Elisedd looked at Aoife for support. "My mother told me to come here and warn you, to make sure that you did not get the blame again for something that was not your fault."

Aoife saw Tormod frown at those words and hurriedly questioned Elisedd about the details before Tormod could ask the boy what he meant.

"I hid under some sails on the deck."

"That was quite a risk to take," Tormod said, clearly not believing him.

"They would not use the sails that night. It was too calm. It was one of the reasons they had chosen it, as the wind would not spread the smoke and give you warning of the fire."

"Who was behind it?" Tormod asked, gently this time.

Elisedd looked up at Aoife and bit his lip. "I don't know who planned it, but the man in charge of the boat was Rhydderch's son."

"Your father's steward?" Tormod asked.

"Yes," Aoife said. It didn't surprise her. Rhydderch had always sided with her stepmother—even over her father. She had often worried about how loyal he was to her father. However, nothing she said had shaken Cadell's trust in Rhydderch. Aoife had never understood it.

"Rhydderch and Father Bricius do not want the Norsemen here. And there are other men who have visited the fort saying this. They want them to return to their lands in the north," Elisedd said, although it was clear something more was troubling him. "They hoped that either the burnt crops would force them to leave or that you would be blamed for the fire and sent back to them. So you see, I had to come. I promised my mother I would find you and look after you. It isn't fair that they blame you. It isn't fair at all. Just like at Alt Clut."

"Thank you for telling us this." Aoife wound her arms around the distraught boy and hugged him. He pushed away from her, obviously embarrassed by his outburst of emotion, and ran a short distance down the beach. She suspected Rhiannon feared for her son's life now that his father was dead and had thought he stood a better chance with Aoife than by staying at Car Cadell. How bad must the situation be for her to have sent her son to the unknown with no guarantee of safety?

Tormod grasped her arm and turned her to face him. "What is it they blame you for? Is Alt Clut the reason they sent you away?"

She wondered how much of the story should she tell him? What should she keep from him - for her own safety?

"Yes." She moved to stare across the loch towards her father's remaining lands. "My stepmother blames me for the attack on Alt Clut."

After a moment's silence, Tormod laughed. "She blames you?"

She nodded, frowning. For her, it was no laughing matter. "I... I became unwell at the feast and we had to leave. It was only a few hours before the attack. No one else escaped that night. Because I was ill, the others—both the survivors and the relatives of those who were captured or killed—they blamed me. They said I was cursed."

"Cursed?" Tormod said. "That sounds to me more like good fortune. Extremely good fortune. If you hadn't left then, you would have died during the siege or... My countrymen are not known for their delicate handling of prisoners."

"I'm sure King Artgal would agree," she said wryly. "If they had heeded my warning, then many more, including King Artgal, might still be alive. Instead, they blame me for the deaths. They think that my illness caused the events to occur."

"They blame you?" Tormod said. "How can they possibly blame you? Do you know how many months Ivarr and Olaf spent planning the attack? The number of men involved, the ships, the preparations..." He put a hand on each of her arms. "Your former king was foolish and ignored all threats. His army was unprepared, his decisions unwise. Alt Clut was an easy target for those who are not afraid of the sea and her moods. Only the strong survive. Your illness saved your family — it played no part in whether the raid happened or not. They should instead be searching for the Briton who told Ivarr and Olaf about the feast."

Her understanding of the situation shifted. Was Tormod right? Was none of this her fault, after all? She had warned her stepmother about the attack, nothing else. And if another Briton had been the one to betray them, then she was not to blame at all.

She smiled at Tormod. Her family owed their lives to her, and if Ula chose to consider that a disgrace, then there was nothing Aoife could do about it. She straightened. "You are right. I was not to blame. It was convenient for them to blame me. I don't know why they attacked you here last night. Other than as revenge. Maybe they oppose the agreement you made with my father. I cannot believe that my father would do this — not when it might endanger me."

Tormod shrugged. "Perhaps we should pay him a visit and ensure he informs all of his people that if they do not feel bound by it, then neither do I."

"I do not think that will help." Aoife panicked at the thought. What would happen to her if, in doing so, Tormod discovered that there was more to her story? That she was truly cursed and had no value to her family. What if he sent her back there?

She wanted more time to prove herself. To make herself part of this community and indispensable to Tormod despite him having made it clear that love was not what he was looking for. Love she could live without—she just wanted a place she could call home. Was that too much to ask?

If the Norsemen knew how much her family feared her, would they accept her more easily, or would it mean she had no value to them? It was hard to know.

"You do not wish to see your family?" Tormod asked.

Her head jerked up. That was not what she had expected him to ask. "It has been a long time, and I'm sure you have realised my stepmother does not wish to see me." She looked out across the water to where her childhood home lay just over the craggy mountains.

"I am sure your father will. After all, what father would not wish to see his daughter after her marriage and ensure she is well cared for?"

She continued gazing across the water, her mind racing. Was this a test? What would he say if she told him now? It might be for the best in the long run. She opened her mouth to speak, but she couldn't get the words out.

"You would not tell him that we had treated you ill?" Tormod said as the silence stretched.

"No!" she replied, stunned that he even thought to ask.

"Those bruises were from before you came here."

She drew in a breath. So, that was what concerned him. That she would lie? Or was it that he was concerned about her family judging him?

"I would never lie about who did that," she assured him. There was a long pause, and then he nodded. "And I expect your step-mother already knows who is responsible."

"I am sure she does," Aoife whispered.

"I have arranged for you to work with Magda, Håkon's wife."

"Oh?" She smiled. That would allow her to remain close to Elisedd.

"That pleases you?"

"Yes. I will be able to see Elisedd and..."

His smile faded. "The boy? You care a lot for him."

"Yes, I do. His mother was one of my only friends. Besides, the two of us are alone here and I am worried about her. And about the attacks on Car Cadell Elisedd spoke of."

Tormod moved away and frowned. "Alone? You are alone within an entire village of people? You are alone with me, your husband?"

"You know what I mean. He is my kinsman."

"I am your kinsman, now."

"Yes." She stopped. He was in no mood to listen and she must be careful when speaking of the boy. If Tormod turned against him, then he would have little hope for a life here, and if they were to send him home... She shuddered at the thought of what might happen if Rhydderch found out he had run away to the Norsemen. Then she realised what he had said and drew in a breath, searching his face for any kind of emotion, and finding none.

"You are my husband. This is my home," she agreed. How she wanted those words to be true. She looked at the ground, not allowing the tears prickling at her eyes to fall. She would not let him see how affected she was. And, in reality, she did not know whether the tears had come because he had declared her his kin, or because she was frustrated by his jealousy.

"Let us go back. It is time to eat."

They said goodbye to Håkon and Elisedd, then the two of them walked side by side in silence as they started along the path back to the village.

"You spoke of me working with Magda?" She hoped he would not now change his mind. Could he not see that the boy had only come here to be with her and save her from trouble? Why was he so against him?

"Yes. Håkon wishes to learn your language so that he may trade with your people. If you teach his wife, she will, in turn, teach him and then others. She will also teach you to speak Norse."

"But what about Ragna? I thought she would do that. She expects me to take over the day to day running of the village from her."

"And you will. After you have done this. I have decided, and Ragna will agree." He said it so abruptly that it made her realise for the first time he truly was the one in charge of the village. His word was law.

"Very well," she agreed. They had reached the crest of the hill and she turned to take one last look across the Loch Garw before they headed down towards where the village lay on the shore of Loch Long.

Chapter Sixteen

A FEW WEEKS LATER, Tormod oversaw the final work on the bathhouse. Long days of battle training meant that a place to relax and soak fatigued muscles in warm water and good company would be most welcome. The summer days were at their longest and, although it was not as warm as he was used to in summer at home, he was looking forward to the feast that night in celebration of Midsummer, and in the distance he could hear some of the young men finishing nailing together the *Midsommerstång*. The cross-like structure with two circles hanging below it was central to their celebrations of summer and, once constructed, it would be wound with greenery and erected outside the hall. The younger girls had been gathering greenery from the forest under the close supervision of some of his best warriors. The celebrations would help to ensure a good harvest later in the year.

There had been no further trouble from any of their neighbours since the field had been burned and Tormod hoped the fire had simply been a knee-jerk reaction from a few of Cadell's men. Lord Cadell himself had denied all knowledge when Tormod had sent Ulf and Arne to inform him of the incident, and reluctantly even Ulf had admitted that he believed him.

Håkon was pleased with Elisedd. The boy was learning Norse quickly, although he spoke to Magda often about his mother. Tormod had begun to wonder if he could buy the woman from

Cadell or trade for her when he visited. He didn't want to mention the idea to Aoife, though, in case it came to naught.

Just the day before, Aoife had returned from the farm in obvious distress and had said she was worried about Rhiannon. Elisedd had told her more and more about the situation at Car Cadell as the weeks passed. The boy was too young to understand the significance of all he had witnessed but both Aoife and Tormod were concerned. Tormod worried too remembered the meeting with Cadell and Ula, the influence the woman had exerted over her husband. Could he attribute it merely to Ula's desire to get rid of an unwanted stepdaughter, or was there a more sinister force behind it?

Cadell had not brought Aoife to meet Tormod as promised. Instead, it had been only his steward, Rhydderch. Was there a significance to that? The steward certainly had not seemed to hold his master in proper respect.

It was clear that he should visit Lord Cadell himself and demand answers. The sooner he understood what was happening at Car Cadell, the better. He would prefer to take Aoife with him so she could help him to understand what was normal for her people and what was not. On the other hand, though, he worried about her safety. Strange how he was now more concerned about her in her own father's fort than here in the Norse village. However, he would fight for her, if necessary, as would Björn, Ulf and Arne. He suspected there were few in her father's household who would be willing to do the same.

Tormod turned at the sound of cheering and clapping at the top of the slope. The *Midsommerstång* had been hauled upright into position and the villagers were excited about the dancing and feasting that would come later. He spotted Aoife and Ragna next to the fire pit, supervising the thralls preparing the food for that night and was impressed when he heard Aoife call out some simple orders in Norse. She must have felt his gaze on her, because she turned and smiled at him. His body reacted to the sight of her. He had almost forgotten what it was like to have a willing woman in his bed every night. Perhaps soon, he would consider the prospect of a child although recently the memory of Ingrid's death in childbirth haunted him more and more often.

"I know the bathhouse is ready, but I fancy a swim," said Björn coming up to stand beside him.

They had spent much of the morning training for combat and he could see the fatigue on his cousin's face as well as feel it in his own muscles. A swim would be pleasant. "I will join you," he replied, and they headed for the shore, undressing as they walked.

"Your wife pleases you, then?" Björn asked.

Tormod frowned. "Why do you ask?"

"You were watching her just now."

Tormod glanced sharply at his cousin. Was there an underlying suspicion in the question? Björn had every right to be concerned about how Tormod's loyalty to Aoife would affect the village. Tormod just didn't want to admit it. "Yes. She does."

"And her father?"

Tormod laughed. "He does not please me. But then I never expected him to."

"When do you plan to confront him?"

"Soon. And we will take my wife with us. Although we will need to protect her carefully. There is treachery in Lord Cadell's house, I am sure of it."

"I agree. He should not have sent his steward to the exchange. There was something not right about that. I would like to know exactly what."

"They will not interfere with our settling here."

"No." Björn surveyed the village, took a deep breath, and grinned. "I like it here. Come on, to the rocks and back — a race." With that, he ran into the water and dived. Tormod soon followed.

"Marriage has slowed you down, cousin," Björn crowed from the beach after he had soundly beaten Tormod in the race.

"The advantages outweigh winning a mere race," Tormod replied, grinning as he strode through the shallow water and sat beside Björn on the beach to dry.

"The advantages this time."

"Aoife is nothing like Ingrid," Tormod snapped.

"I hope not. For all our sakes."

Tormod glared at his cousin, although there was little he could say. Björn was right. He had made a terrible mistake in the past. One that had nearly proved fatal. Arne had suffered more than others as a result. He would not make the same mistake twice.

"One advantage of an arranged marriage," he said to Björn, "is that there is little to cloud one's judgment. No mistaken ideas of love, certainly." Seeing that his cousin meant to argue, he decided to change tack. "And when do you plan to settle down?"

"Never," answered Björn immediately.

"I think Ylva may have something to say about that."

"She can say whatever she likes," Björn retorted. "Marriage is not for me. It brings only sadness and misery. And besides, Ylva gets exactly what she wants from me already. Why would she need to marry me?"

Tormod raised his eyebrows. "And what if there is a child?"

Björn did not respond.

"What will you do if she marries someone else?"

"There are always other women," Björn replied, shrugging, the pause before he spoke enough to make Tormod grin, although he wondered at his cousin's apparent lack of ambition. He had never quite worked the other man out, no matter how close they were. He knew he could both trust and rely upon him, however, and for now that would be enough. He and his three cousins were getting older, their priorities changing, and he was sure Björn would soon settle down. If not through his own choice, then thanks to his mother's nagging. Ragna was nothing if not persuasive, and Tormod doubted that in a battle of wits with Ylva any man stood a chance of winning.

Tormod grinned again, then dressed before heading towards the village to find Aoife and join in the dancing.

CHAPTER SEVENTEEN

FROM HER SEAT ON the dais beside Tormod, Aoife spotted some of the villagers regarding her with suspicion or at best, curiosity, but their eyes lowered quickly when she caught their gaze. Others, however, seemed to have accepted her and she was beginning to get to know some of the unfamiliar names. Tormod had made sure to be very attentive towards her in public, more so than he was in private, and she was grateful.

His efforts to encourage his people to accept her made her feel more secure, although it still bothered her that she had not told him the whole truth. Every night before she fell asleep, she prayed she would not call out her dreams in her sleep and give away all of her secrets.

She should try not to worry so much. She was dreaming less, given how tired she was each night before she fell asleep. Her days were long with a list of chores that took up many hours and occupied her mind most of that time, even with Ragna's assistance. Learning a new language was also tiring and her head often ached at the end of each day. However, she was learning and she had even begun to dream in Norse.

Added to that was the fact her husband kept her occupied every night in bed and sometimes in the morning, too. At least his attentions made her believe that one day there might be a real connection between them, although he was still careful to make sure that he would not give her a child. That troubled her. As well as a child making her position here more secure, it would give her the chance of family she had always wanted. She had tried to ask him about it again, but he had simply said there would be time in the future for children and refused to speak any more of it.

They had been not been married long, she told herself. There was plenty of time. When the winter came, she would ask him again. She glanced sideways at her husband and smiled. Her husband. It was beginning to seem normal to her. This may not have been a marriage she would have chosen, but she was well aware it could have been so much worse. She remembered Rhiannon and the fear in her eyes when her husband's name was mentioned, the dark bruises on her arms. The brute had left her face alone and yet, knowing that he was dead, had Aoife even more concerned about her maid. Why had she sent her son here? Were things at her father's fort so bad?

She sighed. She noticed one of the thralls staring at her and realised most people had finished their food and the drink was starting to flow. She took a mouthful of food. The smell and taste of the hearty mutton made her smile. Then she felt lightheaded and caught at the side of the table. The mouthful of mutton suddenly tasted like ashes. The last time a vision had hit her quite like this had been at Alt Clut. As she raised her head, the hall and villagers faded away before her eyes, replaced by an image of the stone walls of her father's fort.

She heard the clang of swords on swords, of swords on stone. Smelled the coppery tang of blood. Heard the screams of the wounded and then the silence of the dead.

Was this going to happen there? When? Perhaps it already had. Her visions were not predictable in any way.

Then she felt an arm around her shoulders, a hand closing around her own. The noise and heat of the hall surrounded her once more, and she was left with a deep-seated worry for her father.

"Is everything all right?" Tormod whispered close to her ear.

His breath on her skin sent tingles down her spine. Unable to put her feelings, her worries, into words, she said, "I am just tired and ready for bed."

Tormod grinned. "You cannot wait to bed me again."

She rolled her eyes but couldn't help blushing at his statement. "Did I... did I say anything?"

"Just now?" Tormod asked. "No, apart from saying that you would rather be pleasuring me in our bed."

She pushed him away playfully, grinning. "That is not what I said at all." But he didn't seem perturbed, which was good.

Just then, Björn spoke from his other side and Tormod turned to answer him.

Aoife slumped in her chair, trying to gather her thoughts. Had Car Cadell been attacked already, or was what she had seen the result of Tormod's planned visit? It was frustrating to not see enough in her vision to know. Whatever it was, she suspected Ula was behind it and that death lay ahead. She could only pray it wasn't her own. Or her husband's.

At that moment, she knew she had no choice than to agree to visit with Tormod. While it may reveal the truth about her curse, she couldn't continue to live in such a state of uncertainty. She returned her attention to her food and found she had more appetite than she had thought. When she finished, a thrall hurried over and took the plate from in front of her and scurried back a few minutes later with a plateful of berries in a sweet, syrupy mead.

Tentatively, she tasted the first bite, then ate the rest as quickly as she deemed ladylike. Once she was done, she stared at the syrup left in the bowl. Tormod leaned in front of her and picked up the bowl, then held it to her lips for her to drink every last drop. Their eyes met, and he smiled, not taking his eyes from hers as she swallowed. He pulled the bowl away and immediately his thumb caught a drip at the edge of her mouth, which he then sucked off. She stared at him, mesmerised by the simple movement. Maybe the mead in the syrup was stronger than she'd realised.

"I can see it will not be long before you are greeting another son, Tormod," Björn said.

Aoife pursed her lips and dropped her gaze, her hand moving involuntarily over her stomach even though there was no hope of a child.

When she met her husband's gaze again, his expression was stony. "I am in no hurry." He turned to Björn, put his arm around her shoulder and pulled her to his side. "There is plenty to amuse ourselves with before we need to think about children." Tormod laughed, although it didn't sound happy.

She didn't resist his touch, but her stomach turned to lead. What was he waiting for?

Björn leaned around Tormod to talk to her. "You mustn't let him exhaust you. What with you walking to the farm every day to teach Magda Brythonic and taking over so many of my mother's tasks with running the village. She is grateful, you know. I have seen her smile more in the past few days than in the past year. Tormod works everyone to the bone. Thinks there are unlimited hours in each day. And night." He laughed and slapped Tormod on the back.

"I hardly think I need your advice on how to keep my wife happy," Tormod said. "Perhaps you should consider your own future instead of worrying about mine."

"You're right," Björn said. "But for me it's not about marriage or children. With that in mind, I will leave the two of you and go in search of some amusement and a willing woman to share my bed tonight, without the risk of ending up married and certainly not as a father." He drained his horn of mead and thumped it down on the table.

"Ylva is over there," Tormod pointed at one of the warrior women sitting at a table. Björn scowled at him, then stood and, a trifle unsteadily, made his way off the dais and into the main area of the hall where a game of chance was being set up.

Aoife watched Tormod stare at the couple as Björn put his arms around Ylva, kissed her neck. She felt a sudden twinge of jealousy. Was there a woman here with whom Tormod had spent time? How did she feel about Aoife's presence? Aoife turned her attention to Björn and the woman. The large man had his arms around her and together they were watching the game unfold. He leaned in and nuzzled the woman's neck.

Tormod suddenly shot to his feet and strode from the hall. Frowning, she looked back at Björn's woman. Was she someone who had been special to Tormod? Or was it Björn's mention of children that had disturbed him?

"Where is he off to now?"

Aoife jumped at Ragna's voice behind her. She really should pay more attention to her surroundings. She'd been so lost in thought the past few days that it seemed to have become easy to sneak up on her—even within a crowded room. She turned to greet at Ragna but found that she just couldn't make herself smile.

"What is the matter?" Ragna asked. Aoife shook her head, unable to speak for fear she would cry instead. "Whatever did those boys argue about now?"

Aoife shrugged, then frowned. "Björn was talking about us having children. I think Tormod took it badly." Something Björn said came back to her. *Another son.* Tormod would be welcoming *another son.* "Does Tormod already have children?"

Ragna pursed her lips and glanced away. "You will need to ask your husband about this, but yes, there is a child."

"A boy?"

"Yes."

"So he has no need of an heir?"

121

Ragna laughed. "No man needs only one heir, my dear. And it's not just the heirs but the getting of them that most men enjoy." She smiled. "Was that worrying you, that he would need no other child? Children die. Young men die in battle. And sometimes there are other things to consider."

"Like what?" Aoife asked, frowning.

Ragna glanced towards the door of the hall and froze. Aoife followed her gaze and saw Tormod standing in the open doorway, watching her.

"You must ask your husband that yourself. If not now, then wait until he is in a good mood. And if he will not tell you, don't take it to heart. Some things a man finds hard to admit. It may be wise not to push him."

Aoife stared at Ragna, even more confused than she had been earlier. She blinked, then looked towards the door that led outside. Tormod stood in the shadows, waiting for her. She swallowed. "All right. I will speak to my husband and hope for the best."

At least now she knew she wasn't the only one keeping a secret.

CHAPTER EIGHTEEN

BROTHERS
OF
THUNDER

T ORMOD WATCHED AOIFE APPROACH. The smoke and heat in the hall contrasted with the fresh chill of the night air behind him. It was very late; it must be after midnight as there were only a few hours of night at this time of year. The outline of the *Midsommerstång* could only just be seen against the darkness of the sky and the moonlight illuminating a trail over the water.

As she grew closer, he searched her face for any sign of censure or deception but saw none.

In front of him now, she asked, "Was what Björn said true?"

He knew he should simply tell her the story, however, then she would know he was not the great leader she thought he was. He realised he wanted her to trust and respect him more than he had thought.

"Do you have a son already?" she asked.

"What did Ragna tell you?"

"That I needed to speak to you."

Before he could begin to respond, one of the villagers staggered towards them, a horn of mead clutched in his hand, his red cheeks revealing how much he had already imbibed. "Jarl Tormod, the very man. As it is now midsummer, perhaps you will grant me a gift? The lands at the north of peninsula. The lands I have petitioned for more than once and have not yet been allocated. They go to wrack and ruin, *herre.*"

Tormod gritted his teeth and stepped between the man and Aoife. "You know the reasons why that land has not already been allocated, do you not?"

"Yes, although—"

"Then you know I am not going to simply allocate ownership of it without first discussing it at the Thing."

"Yes, Jarl Tormod." The man pulled at his collar, beads of sweat appearing on his forehead. "But I merely hoped that in the meantime..."

Tormod nearly laughed. "No, Erik, 'in the meantime' will simply become your claim for ownership, and I am not ready to hand that land to you and yours. Not without a proper discussion. Not after what happened to your farm back home. Now..."

"*Herre*, that was a misunderstanding—"

For a moment Tormod thought Erik wasn't going to let the matter drop, then his wife appeared in the doorway with a horn of mead and ushered her husband back indoors, apologising to Tormod as she did so.

Shaking his head, Tormod turned to speak to Aoife, but she was gone from his side. He wondered if she had returned to their room, but sensed that she had not. He started towards the shore and stopped short when he saw her. A pale figure crossing the shingle. He watched and listened, hearing more than seeing each step she took on the beach before she sat on a large rock by the water's edge. The way she was looking out across the water, she could have been waiting for someone or pining for her past life. Was she happy here? Did it matter to him? He stopped the train of thought, suddenly aware it mattered to him more than he wanted to admit.

Silently he crossed the green, grateful the sheep were too lazy to make a noise and announce his presence.

"Are you waiting for someone?"

She jumped and turned to face him.

Was she startled at his presence, or had she really been expecting someone else? He glanced around to see if there was anyone else there.

"I was just watching the moonrise," she said.

"It's beautiful," he replied, looking at the silvery trail shining across the water, then following it up to the bright circle high in the night sky.

She shivered, although he didn't think it was all that cold. "Perhaps we should go in."

"We can warm each other up," he said, smiling.

"I..." She stared at him. Again, he couldn't read her expression. She glanced behind her, out across the rocks, and his suspicions returned.

"Is there someone else here?"

"Shh." She reached out and pulled him close to her. For a moment, he thought she was going to kiss him. To distract him, perhaps? Instead, she whispered close to his ear, "I think there's someone on the water."

He took her hand and led her swiftly into a gap in the rocks, which offered them some protection. He held still for a minute or two, but neither heard nor saw anything. "Are you expecting someone?" he asked, attempting to pull away from her.

She held him tight and frowned. "Who would I be expecting? I don't know anyone."

"Elisedd?"

She laughed. "He will surely be in his bed. Most of the children are already in their beds, are they not?"

Tormod acknowledged that with a curt nod. "Someone else then."

"No, there is no one else." Her gaze had been drifting across the water, but now she turned sharply to him, as if she had just caught his implication. "Why do you think that? It was you who wanted me to leave the hall. How would anyone have known to meet me?

I left the hall with you, then you stopped to speak. I am here for you and no one else. Although we are not the only ones who are out here. Björn and—Shh, there is something else. Listen." There was fear on her face.

At first, the only sound he heard was another couple somewhere further along the beach where there were a few crannies a couple could meet and have some privacy. It was clear what they were up to and they were no threat to the settlement.

But then he heard it. Another sound. The regular splash and dip of oars and low voices out on the water.

Aoife must have had better hearing than he did because she jerked in his arms, trying to push away. "Can't you hear them? Can't you hear what they are saying? Why do they come?" The fear on her face was obvious. Enough to jolt him from his suspicions and consider that maybe she did speak the truth.

He strained to listen.

"... Cadell... field... missing..." Only a few individuals' words carried well enough to make out. One thing was clear, though—they were speaking Brythonic, not Norse.

"Do you know who they are?"

"No, I was waiting for you, and then I heard the sound of the oars. Please, you must believe me."

The assurances would, only a few years ago, have convinced him, but he'd learned since then that he was not a good judge of women. Ingrid had proved that.

He wondered where the watchman was. There should have been one at the far side of the rocks and one on the other side of the small bay, both tasked with ensuring the village remained safe from attacks by sea.

Unless these men out on the water had already disposed of the watchmen. There were many places a small boat could land around the coast—too many to be easily defended. It would have been more of a problem if the Britons' sea-skills were better than they were. The watchman to the north would not be able to see the boat yet, though Tormod had given specific orders for everyone to watch for attacks coming from the sea after the attack on Håkon's field.

Then the words "ready" and "attack" carried across the water and there was a clink of metal. A sword, most likely.

Tormod enclosed Aoife in his arms and held her tightly so that he could whisper in her ear. "Go to the hall. Raise the alarm, but tell the men to approach quietly and not be seen. Find Ulf or Arne as Björn is otherwise engaged—ask one of them to alert him—and then go to our room. Bar the door."

"But—"

"If you want to show your loyalty to me, then go, do this."

She looked straight into his eyes, kissed him quickly, then turned and swiftly made her way, keeping to the shadows of the rocks, back to the edge of the village. He watched as she reached the hall door and slipped inside.

Then he turned back to the water. The boat was closer now and not of Norse design.

Only the dip and swish of the oars could be heard as Tormod waited, his hand clasped around the pommel of his sword. He regretted that he did not have the comforting weight of his axe on his back, but he had not come out here with the intention of fighting. At least not with weapons. He listened for the sound of his men approaching, but heard nothing. A feeling of dread grew in his belly.

Where were his men? They should have been here by now. Had he been right to trust Aoife? Perhaps she had not done as he asked, but intended to simply escape and ensure her own safety. Had she betrayed him, just as Ingrid had? He shook off the thought. No, that made no real sense. She had been beaten at the abbey and her family had been only too happy to be rid of her. Where would she go?

He closed his eyes, trying for a moment to clear his mind and try to work out all the layers of betrayal. Why could life not be simple? His people had a lot to offer these Britons. They could give them access to markets far in the east that they did not even know existed, bring fine goods from there in return. Not to mention more and more of this large island was under Norse control. Soon even Paris would be theirs and all the riches that great city had to offer.

He heard a tiny sound behind him. He opened his eyes and turned, sword drawn.

Aoife gasped and dropped his shield, which thudded on the pebbles. Her eyes were wide, and she stared not at him, but at his sword, which was pointed directly at her throat. She gulped. Neither dared to breathe.

The sound of the oars paused.

He lowered the sword and Aoife sank down, huddling into the rocks, then she picked up his shield and handed it to him. Tormod hefted it, ready to fight.

When he turned back to look out across the water, a small boat had rounded the rocky headland and was only a stone's throw from the beach. He could hear low voices and catch most of what they were saying. One man wanted to go back, but the rest thought they should press on.

"The others are at the edge of the beach," Aoife whispered. "Björn is by the rocks at the other side. Ylva has gone back to the hall."

"Go," he murmured. "As quickly as you can. Go back to our room and bar the door. Arm yourself with a weapon and wait for me."

Aoife did not leave.

"Go." He gritted his teeth. "I do not wish to lose you so soon. And I cannot fight if I am thinking only of keeping you safe."

Another splash indicated just how close the boat was getting to their hiding place. Tormod tried to push Aoife into leaving, but she seemed frozen in place. He realised she was listening.

"So we're clear." The voice was low but carried across the dark water. "Destroy the livestock and anyone who tries to stand against us."

"What of Lady Aoife?"

"Cadell's orders were clear. No one is to be spared."

"But..."

"The Norsemen believe we will not attack for fear of harming her, but our orders were clear. She matters less than this land. Our land."

"But..."

It was the same voice again. Tormod smiled grimly. At least one of Cadell's men thought their behaviour wasn't right. He wasn't exactly surprised, just disappointed. And then a sense of rage began to build in him. He understood these men would not hesitate to kill him or any of his kin, but the fact they would also be willing to kill Aoife, one of their own, disgusted him.

"Lady Aoife is a traitor. She has proven it before. You know her father escaped from Alt Clut only because she was in league with the Norsemen and warned them away."

"That is ridiculous, Siward. If she were truly in league with the Norsemen, then why did she save her family? You know there have always been rumours that she was... touched."

There was a silence and then laughter. "Well, she's certainly been touched now — by that Norse scum. Now, once we round these rocks, there is a beach where they have built their settlement. Set fire to what you can, kill anyone who stands in your way - even the Lady Aoife herself, Godwin. She is as good as dead to her father. Now we must go the rest of the way in silence."

CHAPTER NINETEEN

BROTHERS
OF
THUNDER

TEARS SPRANG TO AOIFE'S eyes, but she would not let them fall. So, it was true. Her father really did not care whether she lived or died. She straightened and pushed against Tormod, but he held onto her.

"Where are you going?"

She frowned. "Back to the hall, like you said."

"Go to our room and bar the door," he said. "I will fight for you. I will keep you safe."

She stared at him for a second, then shook her head. "No, I will go to the main hall. Find Ragna and do what she tells me. Fight if I have to."

Tormod opened his mouth as if about to speak, then closed it.

She started to leave, but he pulled her back again.

"Did you know of this?" he asked. "Did you know that he would have you killed even as I thought your presence made us safe?"

She gulped, unsure what the right answer to this was. "No." She tried to pull away, but he held her firmly. "I didn't know. I thought that maybe Ula might have..." She tried to twist in his arms and this time he let her. She wasn't sure it helped. Now they were pressed against each other, his face close enough to hers that it seemed their breaths mingled and their bodies were almost as one. "I thought my father cared for me, that he would protect me, then..."

"Then he made you marry me."

"I wondered what his motives were, but I didn't think he would let me die. I knew Ula wanted me out of the way of her own daughters, but I thought my father... I fear that everything has changed since I lived at Car Cadell. I do not think my father is still... I cannot believe he is still in control, or that he would order them to kill me. I just can't." She tried to laugh, but it ended up as a choked sob.

"You are not disposable to me." His mouth closed over hers, hard. He sought to possess her, devour her, steal her will away from her.

She felt him harden against the softness of her stomach, then broke their kiss and blinked up at him in confusion. How could he be thinking of that when he was about to fight? She heard a noise and realised how much closer their attackers were. She had to leave him. Here she was a distraction—she must let him turn his passion to fighting. She took a step away from him. "I will be in the hall with the others. Come back to me."

"I will." He kissed her again and pushed her away towards the village.

Aoife crept back to the hall. Just as she reached the main door, she heard a boat scrape on the shore and many feet splash into the water. She had recognised at least one of the voices and the knowledge made her feel sick. How could her own kin turn on her like this?

Praying Elisedd was safe at Håkon's farm, she knocked on the door and Ragna opened it for her. Quickly she slid through the gap and helped to close the door and drop the bar in place. Near the fire, the youngest children lay sleeping. Everyone else was awake and armed. Even children. Ragna pressed a long-bladed knife into her hand and offered her a shield for the other.

As their eyes met, they heard shouting from the beach, followed by screaming. Aoife had never been so close to battle before. Her father and his men had fought with others many times, but it had always been at a distance. She had only heard these sounds before in her visions and she was finding it increasingly hard to separate out the real from the imaginary.

Everyone tensed when they heard screams of pain rather than of anger. The same worry was reflected on all their faces. Who had been injured or killed? Was it a father, a husband, a son, a kinsman... a lover? Ylva was standing next to her. She glared at Aoife.

"You have brought this upon us," Ylva said.

"No, Ylva," Ragna intervened. "You think they would not have come, anyway?"

"But she... Björn..."

"And who is the jarl's wife here?" Ragna demanded.

Ylva stared at Ragna before lowering her head.

Aoife knew she could let it pass, but the pain of what she had overheard earlier whipped through her. She turned to the villagers. "Ylva may be right." She was not sure if her Norse was good enough to say what she needed to, but she had to try. Ragna could translate when she ran out of words.

"These men may have attacked because of me, but not *only* because of me. They want this land back. They see it as theirs. They tried to trick Tormod by giving him me as a bride, knowing they would not hesitate to kill me, but I knew nothing of this. I am as much their enemy as you yourselves. They want me dead as much as they want you dead. And to that I say to you that the enemy of my enemy is my friend. I will stand with you. If you will allow me to."

Ylva took a step towards her.

Ragna stepped between them, but Aoife pushed her aside. "You do not need to protect me, Ragna, but I thank you. If Ylva has something to say, then she should say it."

Aoife's attention was drawn by a slight movement at Ylva's side. Her knife. But she did not raise it higher than her side.

"How do we know you are not a traitor?" Ylva said.

"You do not, not for sure. But if I were really going to betray you, why would I do it like this? Why not simply murder your jarl in his bed? In our bed." Aoife straightened and held her head high, her hair brushing her shoulders from under her headscarf.

Ylva frowned. "You were supposed to bring us safety. But Björn said he thought even your own people hated you. And I see now that it is true. If anything happens to either of them tonight—"

"Enough," said Ragna. "The battle will be won by the victors and if any die, then they will feast in Valhalla and be happy. You know that, Ylva. It will be a time for rejoicing."

Aoife tried to understand what Ragna was saying, but struggled with the concept. "They would be happy to die?"

"In battle, yes. A glorious death."

Ylva smiled at her—not a cruel smile, but one of superiority. "It is why our enemies rarely win. Even in death we are victorious."

Aoife was beginning to understand that the mindset of these people was entirely different from her own. And while she couldn't quite grasp it, it did make many things understandable.

She thought of Alt Clut. She had taken her family away, so they were not there for the fight. Did Tormod see her as a coward for that action? She regarded all the women in the hall; the children too. All armed, all ready to fight. Not bound by a society which kept them helpless and at the mercy of the most powerful men.

She took a step towards Ylva. "Tormod was ready to fight tonight. He will not fail any of you. I will not fail my husband. I will not fail this village."

Ylva did not take a step back but neither did she now seem aggressive towards her. Instead she smiled and put a hand on Aoife's shoulder. "No, he will not fail this village, and perhaps you will not either." Ylva patted her shoulder.

It was a better result than Aoife had hoped for.

The women and children turned and faced the door together.

CHAPTER TWENTY

O NCE THE BOAT HAD made landfall, the Britons seemed to hold position for a while. Perhaps they were securing it or simply waiting to see if their arrival had raised any alarms.

Tormod kept his eyes on the spot where he knew them to be, although the Britons had chosen their landing place well. Well enough that Tormod guessed at least one of them was a previous resident of the peninsula.

Three, four, five sets of feet splashed into the water, then a sixth. The men huddled for a moment, low voices no longer carrying. They didn't duck or head for the rocks, as they seemed certain no one was watching them.

Tormod froze when he heard movement from behind him and a seventh man made his way down the jagged rocks to join the others.

"Their guards are dead," this man said when he arrived at the group. "The villagers are mostly in the hall. It is a feast night. They celebrate Midsummer like the pagans they are. Oh, and I saw their jarl and the Lady Aoife outside, heading for near here I believe, but there is no sign of them now." The man laughed. "They did not seem happy with one another. If she is killed, it will be easy to blame the Norse for it. And we can use that to justify our actions in defence of her."

Tormod noticed one man did not laugh with the others and indeed stood a little way off to the side. The dissenter from the boat, perhaps.

"I waited north of here in case they found that the guards were dead. I was nearly caught by one of the scum rutting like a beast with a woman."

Björn and Ylva, no doubt. Tormod held his breath.

"It meant I couldn't watch the village, but they are still feasting, although it seems to have grown quieter in the last while. They are drunk most likely, in their hall, waiting for their dead guards to warn them."

Tormod clenched his fists at the mocking laughter.

"Now, start with the livestock and then burn the houses, quickly and quietly. Try not to let anyone raise the alarm. We are outnumbered and they fight like the very devil himself."

"And the Lady Aoife?" the man who stood to one side asked.

"We are to spare no one."

"But..."

"No one."

Much as Tormod detested this man, he could tell the idea of killing a kinswoman did not sit well with him. Finally he grunted in what Tormod took for agreement and the men set off towards the village.

He did not think their plan was a good one. Were they so confident they would win? It seemed a foolish thought, given that in less than a hundred years these people had lost more and more of their land to invaders from every direction. Perhaps this was why. It was likely each man carried a knife and a long sword with a shield that was heavy, far heavier than those used by the Norse. It made them slow and often the shields were useless as it took so long for them to get into place that Norse axes and swords had already done their job.

Tormod offered up a prayer to Thor, his namesake.

Even at this darkest point of the night, there was still a glimmer of light as dawn fought to pull its way over the mountains to the east. He could see the men still moving as a group. They would be completely surrounded once he moved into place between them and their boat. He waited just a moment longer, then moved quietly across the shingle, his own footsteps masked by those of his enemy.

One of them must have heard him and started to turn. Tormod crouched low to the ground, waiting. He was sure it was the one who had not wanted to harm Aoife but he couldn't be sure. When he turned back and followed the others, Tormod stood and took two heavy steps forward. Around the edge of the beach he saw Ulf, Björn and Arne and many other warriors. The group in the centre panicked, and with loud yells ran at the Norsemen. One even turned and saw him.

Tormod wondered why they did not hold their tight circle in the middle—it would have been a far more defensible position, but the fear in the eyes of the man who charged him answered that.

Raising his shield to block the man's sword, he swung his axe and cried out with the passion for fighting that had been bred into his people for generations, the thrill of battle emptying his mind of other concerns. At his cry, the Norsemen attacked. All ready to die and be assured of their place in Valhalla.

The battle, such as it was, did not rage long. Winning or losing was never the question for Tormod. He knew his people would win. This place was his. The Britons were too concerned with living and not concerned enough with winning. They fought as individuals, none truly willing to die.

He swung his axe once more at the man in front of him. Only the man's last-minute attempt to dodge saved him. The side of his head made contact with the shaft of Tormod's axe and he fell to the ground, not dead, merely unconscious. Tormod stepped over him to carry on fighting, but found that no other was left alive.

Björn moved to stand over the survivor, and Ulf placed his sword at his throat.

"Chain him!" Tormod ordered. He caught a glimpse of disappointment in Ulf's eye. Björn's expression was almost impossible to read. "He may have much to tell us."

"Very well," Ulf said, his tone not matching his words.

Chapter Twenty-one

BROTHERS
OF
THUNDER

L OCKED INSIDE THE HALL, Aoife jumped at every clang of weapon upon weapon, every thud of weapon upon wood. She cringed at every scream. She kept her eyes firmly on the door, her knuckles white around the handle of the axe she held. She was aware, however, of Ylva, sensed the other woman watching her, sensed her suspicion, but she ignored her. Her loyalty lay with Tormod, and she would prove it.

The sounds of the battle outside ceased after a while. Aoife had no idea how much time had passed, and they all jumped when someone banged on the door.

"Who's there?" called Ragna.

"Björn."

Ragna and Ylva hurried forward and unfastened the bar.

Björn strode in, his clothes soaked in blood, and with a wild look in his eye. He was smiling. Aoife couldn't move. What if the Norsemen had won, but at the expense of Tormod's life? What would happen to her then? She watched as warrior after warrior entered the hall, resisting the desire to rush forward to see where he was. When he walked through the door grinning from ear to ear, she didn't know whether to hug him or slap him.

"We have a prisoner," Tormod said. "But the others are dead." He was filthy, sweat soaked, and with sand clinging to him. His clothes were splashed with blood from head to toe and there were large areas where it had soaked in.

Aoife gulped at the sight, but she was happy to see him alive and ran towards him.

His eyes glowed with excitement, that same lust she'd seen in them earlier, magnified now from the frenzy of battle and the joy of victory. She pushed the thought from her mind that they had been her own people that had been killed, their conversation in the boat almost enough to convince her that she owed none of them any loyalty. Apart, perhaps, from the one who had hesitated about killing her — but she would have never wished any man dead.

Tormod grabbed her as she reached him and pulled her against him. He kissed her long and deep, then lifted his head and began shouting orders at the assembled group. She understood only a small amount of them, but there were to be more watchmen on the shore and a patrol out on the water. No one was to go anywhere unarmed or alone.

She noticed Ylva tending to Björn in a quieter corner of the hall, turned away when he pulled her down beside him and kissed her. There was little worry that the blood he had been covered in was his own, although he did have a nasty gash on one arm.

When she looked back at her husband, she realised he had noticed her watching the pair. She blushed as he laughed.

Tormod grabbed her hand and pulled her towards the back of the hall, then through the door leading to their room.

As soon as they were through it, he closed it and pushed her up against it. He kissed her urgently as one hand pulled up her skirts while the other fumbled with the fastenings of his breeks. She gasped when he lifted her and held her in place against the door. His fingers probed, testing her readiness, then he guided himself inside her and thrust deep, kissing her roughly, filling all of her senses. She could smell the sweat and the blood, sense his passion, his desperate need to bury himself in her and celebrate the fact he was alive. Briefly she wondered if any woman would have done, then she pushed the thought from her head and accepted that here, tonight, he had chosen her, and as his wife she could only hope he always would.

He cried out as he came, and her own release followed swiftly. He seemed in no hurry to withdraw, just held her there, panting, trying to catch his breath. Finally, he lifted his head. For a long moment, he stared at her.

An emotion stirred deep inside her, an emotion she didn't want to put a name to.

"I didn't mean to do that..." he said.

Her heart sank.

As soon as he had lowered her feet to the floor, he pulled away and hurried from the room. She blinked, wondering what had caused such a sudden change. Even if she asked him, he might not know himself.

She shook her head. Would it have been so hard to understand a husband from among the Britons? She drew in a breath. She couldn't imagine finding a husband among the Britons. Her father and Ula had probably tried before sending her to the abbey.

Tonight, however, Tormod had wanted her, truly wanted her. But had it been mere lust, the kind slaked with any woman or had it been about her? Perhaps her response was unworthy of a wife? And yet it had made her feel wanted. That when he had been fighting, it had somehow been for her, because of her. To keep her safe. After the battle, he had come to her, been so desperate for her that he hadn't even waited to bathe and...

Her hands flew to her mouth. She knew what he had done differently, knew what was bothering him. He had no withdrawn from her. She ran a hand over her stomach.

He had wanted to wait for a child, and now he may not get his wish. She looked towards the door, wondering whether she should follow him and speak to him, or wait for him to return. Then, remembering the sounds of the violent fight from outside, and with no real idea of where exactly Tormod had gone, she decided to stay where she was.

She removed her clothes, washed quickly in a basin of cold water, left from earlier then slipped into a clean sark. When curled up on the bed, she intended to stay awake until Tormod returned, but sleep soon claimed her.

Chapter Twenty-two

BROTHERS
of
THUNDER

Tormod strode through the hall. The thralls and other women scattered as he passed. Even Ragna took one look at him and left him alone.

Outside dawn was breaking. He leaned against the door. What had possessed him to do that? No, that at least was clear. The lust of battle had still been on him, the joy of victory. He had been careless, too overcome by lust to remember that he meant to wait, so that it would be clear to all the villagers any child Aoife birthed was his own. He couldn't even admit the reasons why it was significant without undermining his position as jarl. He sighed. The impact of Ingrid's deception was never ending, or so it often seemed. And he didn't want a child's life ruined because of his mistakes, no matter how much easier it would make his own to do so.

There was a chance now of a child, whether he wanted one yet or not. He tried to push from his thoughts the hurt on her face when he'd said he had made a mistake. How could he explain to her about Ingrid? About how he'd been taken for a fool? None of that was Aoife's fault, and yet... He could barely admit to himself what had happened in the past, so how could he explain it to her? He didn't want her to know how foolish he had been in the past. His poor judgment had nearly been the death of him, and those around him. All he had to do was look at Arne to remind him how important it was to trust the right people. The decisions he made as jarl were important — not just for himself, but for the villagers who depended on him. And especially for the other Brothers of Thunder.

He stopped short, realising with surprise that the reason he didn't want her to know how foolish he had been, was that he cared what she thought of him. Or was it was something else? Maybe he loved her and wanted her to love him in return?

No, he would never be such a fool as to love another woman. He shook his head. That was a thought he was not going to entertain. What was done was done and he would have to live with the consequences as he lived with the consequences of his marriage to Ingrid. He could only pray to the gods that this would be less catastrophic.

Tormod unbuckled his sword from his waist and hefted his axe in his hand. He headed out of the village. Once he reached the edge of the forest, he began to run. Earlier, he had allowed himself to be distracted. He needed to be alone, to run, to clear his mind and body of the anger and shame that filled him. Why could he not put this behind him? Perhaps he should have insisted Arne stayed at home, in the Norselands, but Ragna had begged him to allow her son to come. Told him that it would not help either of them to pretend nothing had happened.

He gripped the axe tightly, swinging it in front of him when branches got in his way. Otherwise, he pumped his arms back and forth, matching his steps. He could feel his heart racing, his blood beginning to burn. He ran and ran until he could run no more.

When he stopped, his breaths were loud, and his chest heaved. He was deep in the forest and on the crest of a small hill. As he calmed, he heard it. Snorting, and the footsteps of an animal. A boar most likely. He turned slowly in a circle, trying to see through the darkness of the trees. The glint of its eyes gave its position away. He dropped the axe from one hand to the other and back again, preparing himself for the fight he knew would come.

The boar stared at him, pawed the ground a time or two, but didn't move.

Tormod stared at it. It was a big beast, one of the largest he'd seen on these shores, and its tusks were sharp. They would make a fine trophy. He swung the axe around once, then again. The beast lowered its head to the ground, then attacked.

Everything outside of the fight ceased to exist. There was only the swing and miss or swing and hit of the axe. Each time it sank into flesh was a small victory on the way to final triumph, each time it glanced off the tough hide of the boar a time to recalculate, change the angle of the thrust, the speed of the blow. Screams from both man and beast surrounded them until finally there was only Tormod's breathing.

He dropped to his knees as the boar collapsed for a final time at his feet. He hung his axe on his belt and lifted the beast, staggering under its weight. His muscles shook with the effort, but he had won and he would return to the village with his spoils, no matter how heavy they were or how long it took.

Tormod had run much farther than he'd realised. It was nearly full light by the time he reached the village again and took the boar into the hall. He dumped the carcass beside Ragna, who said nothing, merely looked at him and jerked her head in the direction of the beach.

Tormod didn't even bother to undress, just strode out into the cold water and, once far enough out, ducked under it. He remained under the water, his body finally cooling while his breathing and heart rate slowed. His lungs began to burn, so he surfaced and took a deep breath. Water sluiced off him as he pulled off his bloodstained clothes and threw them towards the beach. Then he swam a little.

Reality began to seep in. The water was bitterly cold, and his arms were trembling from the exertion of carrying the boar so far. He closed his eyes and floated onto his back, rubbing at his hair and wishing he had some soap.

A soft splash beside him got him to open his eyes and drew his attention to Björn's presence on the beach. Realising what had made the noise, he scrabbled on the rocky seabed until he found the bar of rough soap his cousin had thrown towards him and quickly cleaned himself and his hair of the last traces of blood and sweat. Then he threw the bar back towards the beach. He exited the water, and as he strode up the beach, Björn handed him a fur that he wrapped around his shivering body.

"We will feast later," Björn said as they continued up the beach. "I hope seeing you again will be enough to calm that wife of yours, but I doubt it."

"She was worried?"

"We all were." Björn looked at him. "No shield, no sword, no armour, just gone. I have been looking for you."

"I had to get away," Tormod said. "I had my axe."

Björn put a hand on his shoulder and stopped him. "She thinks you are angry with her. You are punishing her for the sins of another. She is all alone here. If you turn on her..." Björn left the sentence hanging. Then he looked over towards the barn where Ulf and Arne stood guard over the prisoner. Arne looked away, but not before the sunlight highlighted the scars on his face. Scars from injuries that everyone had believed would kill him.

Tormod closed his eyes, remembering. None of them had thought Arne would survive the journey home, but he had, although he was delirious with fever and had lost a great deal of blood. There was little skin that had not felt the touch of their enemies' swords or axes - in an ambush meant for him.

Tormod opened his eyes and pulled the fur tighter around him against the chill of the morning air. Ulf approached them.

"The prisoner is chained. Do you wish to deal with him now?" Ulf asked.

"No, once I have dressed and eaten will be time enough," Tormod replied. "Let him start to truly fear us before we question him."

"Or it may give him a chance to escape," Ulf retorted.

Tormod stared at his cousin for a long moment. Ulf's gaze did not waver, and Tormod knew he had every right to doubt his judgment, but as jarl, Tormod could not let such doubt stand unchallenged. "Surely he will only escape if Björn has failed in his duty to chain him."

"I can assure you he is well secured," Björn said.

"We need to keep our heads clear and discover exactly what is going on. If Cadell has broken the terms of our alliance—then we shall respond in kind

Ulf held Tormod's gaze for a minute longer, then nodded. "Very well."

As he passed Ulf, however, his cousin put a hand on his shoulder, halting him.

"Did we not already hear enough? Lord Cadell has deceived us. His daughter is worthless. He doesn't care if she lives or dies. Her presence here does not protect us."

Tormod didn't look at Ulf. He clenched his fists, struggling to stop himself from lashing out at his cousin, making him withdraw his words. But he couldn't. Ulf was right. In one way.

Tormod turned to Ulf and met his gaze full on. "My wife is not worthless." He realised as he spoke the words that he truly believed them.

"Your wife..." Ulf left the words hanging for a moment, then dropped his hand from Tormod's shoulder. "Let us pray to the gods that you are right."

Tormod closed his eyes and took several deep breaths, trying to calm the red rage that had descended over him at Ulf's words. He tried to persuade himself that his cousin's words had not affected him as much as they had. And pushed away the thought that what he felt for Aoife went beyond mere convenience. He couldn't love Aoife. He wouldn't allow it. It was safer for everyone if he didn't.

Tormod opened his eyes and looked around at the small groups of warriors and villagers who were still discussing the battle's aftermath. All of them were armed, and Tormod sensed from many of them the dejection that the battle had not even reached them. The Britons had not made it past their first line of defence. Still, if this were a sign of what was to come, then it would not be long before the whole village was needed. By then, he needed to ensure that Aoife was seen as one of them, not as Cadell's daughter. If Aoife carried his child, their jarl's child, then she would be protected. At least working on that issue would not be a hardship.

"Ulf!" Tormod wasn't sure what to say. He rubbed a hand down his face. "You are right. We need to rethink our alliance with Lord Cadell."

Ulf's face held an equal mix of triumph and relief. "We have been fooled by Cadell. We need to plan our next move."

A chill ran through Tormod's veins. He knew his cousin had tried to take the edge off his criticism by saying 'we', when Tormod knew fine well that this was his fault. He had been fooled. And not for the first time.

"We need to decide what we do with the prisoner and..." Ulf broke off, holding Tormod's gaze.

"And my wife?" Tormod was torn between knowing that his cousin was right, and hating him for it. "My wife is innocent."

There was a lengthy pause before Ulf said, "You are sure?"

"Yes."

It was enough. It had to be enough. If Ulf was going to challenge him on this, then better that he should know now. He was relieved when his cousin nodded.

Tormod took a deep breath, remembering Elisedd's stories about life at Car Cadell and Aoife's sense that her father himself, might be in danger. "But if Lord Cadell needs our help, then we must also honour that," said Tormod. "I believe that may be why the maid sent her son here, sent Elisedd here. After all, who would send a child into an enemy camp unless what is at home is something far, far worse?"

Ulf frowned, but seemed to be seriously considering Tormod's words. "We have many questions to ask the prisoner. But Tormod, you need to deal with the prisoner in a way that reassures our people. Keep your wife away from the *Thing*."

"These men came to kill all of us. My wife included."

Silence. He couldn't tell whether Ulf believed him or not.

"I don't think we'll ever convince some of the villagers of that," Ulf said. That, at least, was one less thing to worry about. "Not unless you can get the prisoner to admit it. And then..." Ulf ran a finger across his throat.

Then the prisoner would be guilty of trying to murder the wife of a jarl and Tormod would have to have him executed. In one way, he had no objections. In another... He wondered how his wife would react. They had already killed five of her countrymen last night. Those countrymen who had attacked their village had done so with the intention of killing Aoife as well as the Norsemen. If things had gone differently, they might well have succeeded. He knew she had heard the men in the boat. She knew they had been ready to kill her themselves, but their prisoner was the one man who had queried that order. Killing him would achieve little.

Ulf marched off before Tormod could reply.

"Ulf is right," Björn said. "There are many who are worried."

"Worried?" Tormod bristled. Their suspicion of his wife was unwarranted, but not everyone would see it that way.

"You know what I mean. Worried that your loyalties are now divided."

"I am hardly the first jarl to marry the daughter of an enemy for the promise of peace."

Björn regarded him carefully. "I know that, and they know it, too. It is simply that here, with these people, everything is new and different. They don't understand."

"They choose not to understand."

"And you have to deal with that. You need to keep them all together. Us all together."

Tormod regarded Björn, concerned his cousin would not meet his eye. He expected this from Ulf. Ulf always challenged him, but Björn... Björn was solid, reliable. If Björn was worried, then Tormod really did need to take action.

"Find out what you can," he instructed Björn. "Then find me and we will speak. Bring Arne."

Björn nodded at him grimly.

Tormod headed for the hall, and through it to the room he and Aoife shared.

CHAPTER TWENTY-THREE

BROTHERS
OF
THUNDER

T ORMOD WASN'T SURPRISED TO find Aoife already washed and
dressed, but he *was* surprised to find she had piled her
clothes neatly on the bed and topped it with the small pouch of
her valuables that she had arrived with. "What are you doing?"

She jumped and turned to look at him, grabbing the pouch and
pressing it to her chest. She relaxed when she recognised him.
"You are alive."

"Would you have preferred it if I wasn't?" He threw the fur over
the end of the bed and strode to where a fresh set of clothes was
laid out for him.

"No. I was worried. I..." She turned away from him as he dressed,
and he wondered if the tears he had seen in her eyes were for him
or herself.

"What were you doing?" he asked gently.

"Preparing to leave. To see my father. I have to ask him why..."

"Don't."

She froze. "But..."

"Why do you think he will help you now?" Tormod asked. "Besides, there is no one here that I can spare to take you. No one that
I could be sure would come back to me from your father's lands
unharmed."

Aoife remained still, biting at her lip.

"You heard those men last night. If they are willing to kill you, then what worse fate awaits any of us... barbarians?"

"You are not barbarians! But you have come here, taken our lands and—"

"These lands were empty, my lady," said Tormod. "No one defended them. We only wished for a new place to call home."

The two of them stared at each other across the room. Then she dropped her gaze.

"I wish for nothing more than a home, also," she said quietly.

"Your home is here now, with us." He didn't examine why he felt the need to reassure her. How much easier it would be to simply let her go and find a wife from amongst his own people. And yet something about her called to him.

"I need to know why my father was willing to let me be killed. Something is not right at Car Cadell and I need to know what it is. Until I do, I don't think any of us are safe."

"I will keep you safe."

For a moment her face lit up with hope.

Then there was a knock at the door.

"Come!" he shouted.

Björn entered. "Tormod, the prisoner. You need to hear what he has to say."

"I will be there in a moment," Tormod replied.

Aoife gaped at her husband. "There are prisoners?"

"One," Björn said.

She turned away from him, shaking. "Is he to be killed?"

"Do you wish him to be?" Tormod asked.

"I don't know," she said after a long pause. "They came because of me. I heard them. They were going to kill me."

"They came because of us. You and this village."

Her face when she looked at him was a mask of anguish. "I can't believe that my father ordered it. I think there is something very wrong at Car Cadell."

Tormod couldn't decide whether she was right, or simply cling- ing to a last remnant of hope for her father's love. Although... he thought back to the way Cadell had looked to Ula during their negotiations and wondered if Aoife was, in fact, correct. Elisedd's arrival seemed to prove that there was something wrong, too.

"I think so too," he said. "Now we need to arrange a visit. But we will take the time to plan and prepare and be ready for whatever we find there."

Aoife breathed in deeply, then nodded.

Tormod strode towards her and encircled her in his arms. After only a moment's hesitation, she leaned into him. He closed his eyes, relaxing into her warmth. He was happy she was alive and sure that he was not willing to give her up.

CHAPTER TWENTY-FOUR

BROTHERS
OF
THUNDER

AOIFE OPENED THE DOOR a short while later to Björn, Ulf, and Arne and ushered them inside. She had offered to leave them to talk in peace, but Tormod had insisted she stay. Now, she looked at Tormod, surrounded by his cousins. They were a formidable group—she pitied anyone who had to fight against them.

When questioned, the prisoner had admitted that they had, indeed, attacked the village on Lord Cadell's orders and that he had not specified that Aoife be spared.

"She doesn't deserve to die," the prisoner had said. "It was not her choice to marry you, she should not suffer further for it."

After he had said this, it had been decided that his life would be spared, for now at least. Arne had suggested that keeping him alive in case they needed proof of Cadell's duplicity might make him more valuable in the long run and Tormod had agreed.

"We should send Lord Cadell a message," Ulf said.

Aoife started. She should have been listening, but somehow... somehow she simply didn't want to deal with the reality of the situation and was unsure why Tormod had asked her to be here.

"The bodies of his dead will be a start," said Ulf.

Aoife looked at Ulf. Of all the group, he had changed the most since the fight. She had always sensed that he was a warrior first, but now she saw few signs of the man she had come to know since her arrival. He refused to meet her eye for a start, and she feared that he was blinded by thoughts of revenge.

"If you do that," she said, "then my people will see it as a threat. And it will only help to prove that you are indeed their enemy."

"We are," Ulf said. He started to stand, but Tormod pushed him back down. Ulf continued, regardless. "They have attacked us twice now, tricked us into accepting you as our jarl's wife with promises of safety. Those promises have been broken."

Aoife tilted her head to one side and looked at him. "From their perspective, it is you who are the aggressors."

Ulf laughed. "This land was deserted before we arrived. And if your people are not strong enough to hold it, then they don't deserve it. That is the way of the world. The strongest survive."

"Your people captured and murdered our king," Aoife pointed out.

"King Artgal was killed at the bidding of another. Anyway, why should we listen to you?" Ulf demanded. "You came to us as a promise of peace. A promise that has proved to be false."

"Ulf," Tormod warned.

Aoife smoothed her skirts. It was time to take a stand, even if it was a small one. "That is one way to look at it. But a wise man might see things differently. I am married to your jarl, which makes me one of you. My father's kin showed they do not want me. Last night they did not come only to attack the village." Aoife stopped, took a breath. "They wouldn't have hesitated to kill me, then they would have blamed you for my death. I heard them. If they want me dead, then they are nothing to me."

With that, she stood and strode from the room out into the main hall. She ignored Ragna's query as to whether everything was all right and headed outside. Once there, she leaned against the wall, trying to get her pounding heart to slow. She was deep in thought, numb—truly cast adrift. She had no idea what the future held for her now. Would the Norse turn on her, also believing her to have no further value? Would Tormod divorce her, or would they simply have her killed?

Then she remembered the way Elisedd had been treated. An inconvenient child, a suspected saboteur, and yet he had not been killed at first sight. He had had a trial. Perhaps she would be granted that. She blinked back tears. Her father would not have troubled himself with such details. If he thought he had found a traitor, then they would be killed with no such trivialisations as a proper hearing, let alone a trial. Ula would have insisted upon it.

As her heart stopped pounding in her ears, she heard Tormod and the others shouting. In Norse, so she could only understand odd words here and there. She wished none of this had ever happened. Wished she were back in the abbey...

No, whether she lived or died here, it was better than being in the abbey. These last few weeks, she had had more freedom and affection than ever before. It was hard not to feel grateful.

The voices quieted, and she sensed the group had fallen back into their usual harmony. Perhaps a quick decision had been made about her and her future.

The door to the hall banged open and the four of them strode out towards the barn. She shrank back into the shadows so they didn't see her. She wasn't ready to face her future quite yet.

She made her way back to their room and sat on the edge of the bed. Exhaustion swept through her. She ran her hand over her still flat stomach. What if she was with child after last night? How would that change her life? Would Tormod be angry? He did not want her to have a child yet, he'd made that clear. So what would he do if she became pregnant?

She would lie down for a minute. Just until she was feeling better. By then she would be ready to face whatever decision had been made about her. She closed her eyes and drifted into an uneasy sleep.

Once again she dreamed. In those dreams she saw the bear and the wolf and the hawk, heard the rumble of thunder and felt its presence within her. A queasy sensation indicated she was on a boat. She tasted the spray on her tongue. Fresh water, not salt. And yet she was on a longship, could see the proud head of the dragon in front of her and feel the flapping of the sail behind her. She turned and saw many men hunched over their oars. There were other boats on the water.

A cry made her turn. In front of her she saw her father's fort, in total darkness.

Then she was at the gates, then running into the courtyard. An unearthly silence blanketed the place. Death hung in the air. She looked around. There were bodies everywhere. She ran and ran, but couldn't reach the end of the staircase. Lightning flashed, blinding her.

She woke with a start.

Tormod stood beside her, axe in hand. They had decided to kill her, after all. She screamed and pushed herself back on the bed, curling up as far from him as possible. She steeled herself for the blow, then heard the axe clatter on the floor. Instead, his arms came around her, his body covering hers, strong and solid.

He stroked her hair and kissed her forehead. "What is it?"

"Nothing."

"More than nothing," he said, pulling away from her. He placed a finger on her chin and tilted her face to make her look up at him. "You were screaming. I thought someone had come to kill you."

So, he had come to save her, not kill her. "I-it was... It was just a dream."

She swallowed, fearful he would press her for more details.

"They will not take you from me," he growled.

She clung to him, grateful for the support, but unsure how or why he had become so protective. "What... what did you decide?"

"About your father?"

"Yes, and about me and the prisoner."

"There is nothing to decide about you. You are my wife."

"But Ulf is right. This marriage was supposed to protect you, protect the village. And now you know my father is willing to have me killed. I am no help in protecting anyone."

She felt Tormod laugh before she heard him. "It was supposed to be a marriage which cemented an alliance, yes, but I do not need you to protect me. I would never rely on only one thing for safety. Particularly if that was a woman. That is not what the problem is."

"Then what is the problem?" She pushed at him and sat up. "Ulf thinks I am a traitor."

"No, he does not. He thinks you are a victim."

"But he said—"

"He often speaks in anger before he has time to catch up with his own thoughts. That is why he is not jarl."

"I see." Aoife took some time to digest this. Tormod's arms around her were a comfort. "But the other villagers…"

"The whole situation is uneasy. We knew it would be before we came here. We must deal with it and learn to live here, whether that is in peace or not." Tormod let go of her, kissed her lightly on the head and then stood. "We will visit your father next month."

She gulped.

"Why not sooner?"

"We are waiting for another group of settlers to arrive. As there is always safety in numbers, we will wait until they have arrived to give us a stronger force to take with us and a stronger force to leave here. Then we will sail to Car Cadell."

"Do you plan to confront my father directly about these attacks?" Aoife asked. "Or pretend the alliance still holds?"

"Directly," Tormod said. "And we must assume that there will be other attempts on us before then. But he is going to see that his plan has failed. That you are very much alive and the village is not theirs for the taking. We will leave as soon as we are ready to face him and take the prisoner with us. If he refuses to tell the truth about the attack in front of your father then he will be executed."

"What will you say about our marriage, about the alliance?"

"There is nothing to say. I have a wife who understands these lands better than we do and who I am willing to fight to the death for."

Aoife's heart lifted when she heard his words.

"It may take a week or two before we are ready," said Tormod

She saw the earnestness in his face and knew he spoke the truth. "And what about the others?"

"The others?"

"Björn and Ulf and Arne."

"Any of them will fight for you."

"Are you sure?"

"Yes." Tormod grabbed her hand and held it tightly. "Even if they will not do it for you, they will do it for me. Your father may think he has tricked me into this marriage, but even if the alliance is worthless, I still have you."

"But what am I worth?"

"You are still his daughter, and he will still have to see you in the arms of the enemy."

She pulled her hand from his, uncomfortable with what he was saying. She had thought perhaps he cared for her, but now it seemed she was merely a way for him to win against her father. "So, because you have me in your bed, that is punishment enough for him? My stepmother will be happy to see I am being bedded by a barbarian." Her hand flew to her mouth.

"Is that what I am?" His measured tone gave away little of his feelings, but she had felt him tense.

"It is how my stepmother sees you, yes." She couldn't make herself look at him. What had possessed her to say such a thing?

She didn't think of him that way at all, but she knew her kinsfolk did.

"And is it how you see me?"

She shook her head, but closed her eyes and turned away from him.

He sat down beside her and she turned back to him. He took her into his arms. "Are you sure?"

"Yes," she managed to breathe out before his mouth closed over hers. The kiss was not at all gentle. There was a dark, possessive power underneath it which made her want to cling to him forever.

All too soon he broke the kiss, but stayed close to her and whispered in her ear. "Then how do you see me?"

"As my husband," she whispered. "You have never hurt me, not the way I was hurt or punished before—and even though you know you have been wronged, you are still not punishing me for it. My father would not be so forgiving."

Tormod's hand slid beneath her skirts and she shuddered as his fingers ran along her bare skin. When he touched her like this, it was easy to think he wanted her, needed her. Abruptly, he lay down, taking her with him. He kissed her again, then kissed around the edge of her face, her neck, while his fingers sought to loosen all the fastenings on her clothes he could reach. He soon gave up and pushed her skirts up, loosened his own breeks and entered her. He pulled one knee up and used it to angle himself inside her, his eyes on hers as he sought to maintain a steady rhythm.

Aoife raised her head and kissed him, pleased when he responded. Somehow, it seemed so much more intimate than their other connections. His arms slid around her back, hauling her up against him and changing his angle of entry. Soon, his steady thrusting was hitting just the right parts of her. She gasped and shuddered through an intense climax but, and this time he stayed inside her as he came. Then he abruptly stood and fastened his breeks.

Aoife hastily pulled her own skirts back down and sat up, frustrated by his changes of mood and her inability to understand him. "Last night. What did I do wrong?"

"Nothing. You did nothing wrong. When I said I made a mistake, it was only because..." He hesitated and looked at the ground. "It is important we don't have a child. Not yet. Last night... Last night lust clouded my mind. It will not happen again."

"What other purpose do I have here? I don't understand."

"There is nothing to understand." He looked back at her, frowning.

She found that hard to believe.

For a moment she thought Tormod would leave, but then he closed his eyes and took a deep breath. "You asked me last night whether there was a child. There is. My first wife's son. He will be sent over. Probably he is with the settlers we are expecting. Now that I am married, my father will have sent him."

"And I will care for him? We will be a family?"

Tormod did not answer right away. "Perhaps. This can be decided when he arrives. For now, let us just be together as man and wife. Am I not enough for you?"

"Yes, of course. I just thought that... Nothing." After all, what else could she say? At least she no longer worried that she had displeased him. And then the impact of his words hit her. "Your wife's son?"

"Yes."

"Not... not yours."

"No. But to admit that would be to admit that I had made a terrible mistake," Tormod said.

She smiled cautiously at him. "You would not be the first man to marry a woman who already carried another man's child. Could you not have divorced her? Your people do not seem averse to divorce."

"It was not only the child." Tormod hung his head. "It is more complicated. By the time I realised, I didn't want to admit that she had fooled me. Not only was the child not mine, but she only wanted me because she thought I was more likely to become jarl than her lover."

"Who was he?"

Tormod frowned at her. "I don't know. She would never tell me but we agreed to stay together and she promised to be faithful in the future."

"But she wasn't?"

"No, she started sneaking away from the village to meet him." Tormod sighed. "Maybe if I tell you what happened you will understand." He sat for a long moment before he spoke again. "I thought we had met by chance in the woods one day when I was out hunting. For a few weeks we met in secret at an abandoned hut deep in the woods between her father's village and my own. I thought she loved me and persuaded her to run away from home to marry me."

"You did not go to her father to ask?"

"No, my father and hers did not get along. They often fought over land, accused each other of stealing cattle." He shrugged. "I thought I was being so clever, stealing his daughter away from him without his knowledge."

"You married her, though?"

"After a month or so, she told me she was pregnant." He stared at his hands, purposefully not looking at Aoife.

"When I told my cousins, I thought they would be pleased, but they were not."

"They did not believe her?"

"No," he said, then made a wry face. "They had been away for a few weeks. Their father's death had caused many problems for the family. I suppose it is one of the reasons I was hunting alone when I met Ingrid."

"They weren't happy about the marriage?"

"Ulf was especially outspoken," Tormod said. "But I don't know if that was better or worse than Arne not speaking to me for months."

Aoife smiled. "It is nice to know it is not just Britons Ulf is suspicious of."

"And it was just as well they did not trust her. I was too willing to believe everything she told me. They kept an eye on her, Arne and Ulf in particular."

Aoife tilted her head to one side, considering his words. "Why?"

"They didn't trust her and told me she was lying to me but I refused to see it. Ulf had seen her leaving the village more than once and had followed her back to the hut we had met in. When I confronted her, she said it was because it reminded her of when we had first met."

"But it wasn't?"

"No, she told me that she was worried no one in the village trusted her, said my cousins were trying to poison me against her." He stopped and put his head in his hands. Then he shook his head and sat up. "Later, I learned she was meeting her lover there. But I believed her and did not listen to my cousins as I should have. What sort of a jarl does that make me if I cannot see through the lies of my own wife?"

Aoife bit her lip and tried to push aside her own guilt. She wasn't betraying Tormod. Not like that.

"But you were not jarl then?"

Aoife swallowed when he shook his head. She was not being entirely honest with him either, and struggled to work out what to say to him that would not reinforce his negative view. "She, too, paid a high price."

Tormod frowned. "She did. It was a terrible way to die."

Abruptly, he left the room, leaving her with more of an under-standing of his reluctance to have a child. The knowledge was a relief in so many ways although if it were only over the child, she wasn't sure why Tormod seemed so distressed. She was sure there was more to the story that he was not willing to share with her. Perhaps one day he would trust her enough for that.

CHAPTER TWENTY-FIVE

W EEKS PASSED WITH NO further attacks on the village. Then one morning they were woken by the shouts of a watch-man.

"They are coming! They are coming!"

Tormod hurried from his bed into the hall where he met the guard. He had brought his axe, but the man shook his head and grabbed his shoulders, his expression joyful.

"No, not the Britons. Our own people. My wife may be amongst them. They are already part of the way up the firth and the winds are strong. They will be here soon!"

Tormod acknowledged his words, then let the watchman go to spread the news to the others. He returned to his room to find Aoife almost dressed. The uncertainty on her face made his heart twist. It seemed like every time their life together settled, something happened to disrupt it. Although at least in this case, it was a positive rather than a negative event.

"What is it?" She put her hands over her mouth, then took a deep breath and clenched her fists at her side. "Is it my father?"

"No." Tormod smiled, pleased more of his people were arriving. He should have asked how many boats but had been too relieved that they were not under attack to ask. Aoife swept her hair to the side and began to braid it as he watched. "You must have been used to having someone do that for you."

"At one time. But not for a while. In the abbey..." She swallowed. "It is strange also to have my head covered only by a scarf, but Ragna has been teaching me ways to plait my hair and... And I am sure you do not need to hear about such things. How many people are arriving? Are there homes for them all?"

"I must go and find out," he replied, moving close behind her and drawing her back against him. He laid his chin on her shoulder and sighed. She twisted her head around and kissed him. Soon he turned her to face him, his body pressing into hers, their kisses making him want more.

Shouts from the beach reminded him that he had new arrivals to greet and, despite the news from the guard, he must ensure that they were ready for foe as well as friend.

He set Aoife away from him. "Later," he whispered, and smiled when she blushed.

"What will they think of me?" she asked just as he reached the door.

"They will think you are their jarl's wife."

She studied his face and pursed her lips. "I hope so." She returned to plaiting her hair. "I will join you when I am ready."

He paused, realising that it might make it easier for her to be accepted by the new arrivals if the two of them presented a united front from the outset. "I will wait for you."

"Then do not distract me."

His heart lifted when she laughed.

When they arrived on the beach, Tormod counted seven boats moving up the firth and into the sea-loch. The shield designs on the foremost boat he recognised as from his father. Even so, the warriors led by Björn, Ulf and Arne were ready in case the visit was not a friendly one. Everyone who waited was armed and, although there was excitement in the air, there was also a ripple of tension. At a far-flung outpost such as this one, news of changes of power back home was often slow to reach them, so even folk they had left as friends could have changed allegiances.

Tormod shook his head, trying to dispel the thoughts. Living amongst a foreign enemy was affecting him and he saw intrigue everywhere. The boats were likely little more than settlers arriving, as they were expecting. As they waited, people from the farms all over the peninsula joined them.

When it drew close enough to shore, Tormod took one look at the man at the prow of the foremost boat and hurried towards it, tugging Aoife along behind him.

"Who is it?" she asked him.

"My brother, Anders," he replied, not looking at her. He waved at his brother, then stopped when he saw the small figure beside him and dropped his hand. "And my son."

"Your son?" Aoife asked.

"Yes." Tormod stood stock still, staring. For the first time, he admitted to himself that while he had been expecting the boy in one way, in another, he had hoped his father would keep him, perhaps forever. But why should he? The boy was no more his grandson than he was Tormod's son.

"Tormod?" Aoife said. He looked at her. She closed her eyes and swayed a little. "I don't feel well."

He helped her sit on the rocks. She put her head down and he touched her hair gently with his fingertips.

"Better?" he asked when she looked up at him a few minutes later. Some of the colour had returned to her cheeks.

"Yes, thank you. Go, greet your son." She smiled wanly at him. "Do you think he will like me?"

Tormod stared down at her. "Does it matter?"

She looked at the boy on the boat, then at Tormod. "I don't... I thought if I am to look after him that it would be better if we were friends."

Tormod said nothing for a moment. "So long as he obeys you, there is no need for him to like you."

"I thought you would prefer it if..." She frowned and looked towards the shore. "The boats are nearly in. You should go—they are waiting for you."

"Will you be all right?"

"Yes. I will sit here for a few minutes before I come and join you."

Tormod started to walk towards his brother Anders' boat, his steps becoming quicker as he grew closer. Anders leapt ashore and ran towards him. When they met, the two men embraced, and Tormod felt a sudden pang of longing for the home he had not seen for more than two years. He shook off the thought. This was home now.

"It is good to see you, brother," Anders said. "And look who I have brought."

"Hello, Father," Einar said, stepping forward.

Tormod looked down at the boy. He had grown since he had last seen him. He must be eight now. Around the same age as Elisedd. Tormod grasped the boy's shoulder and felt him trembling. He peered into eyes matching his first wife's. Eyes which had hidden a lie Tormod could never forgive. He snatched his hand back and turned away.

"Tormod!"

He stopped at Anders' shout.

"Your son has been looking forward to seeing you. Will you not take him and show him his new home?"

Tormod stared at Anders, then blinked and looked at Einar. How had he thought the boy could stay with him and Aoife? He was a constant reminder of Tormod's past. He should start his family anew, with his wife.

"Hello." Aoife's voice startled him. She had come over without him noticing. She knelt down beside Einar and took his hands. "I am Aoife. Your father's new wife." Tormod would have congratulated her at how good her Norse was in such a short time, but he was too shocked to say anything. "Tell him I will find somewhere for him to stay, and I will look after him as if he were my own," she added in Brythonic.

But Tormod said nothing.

After a moment, Anders cleared his throat and translated what Aoife had not been able to say in Norse for the boy. The boy smiled at Aoife, but his eyes were wide.

"Are you not going to introduce me to your new wife?" his brother said. "And then we can talk while she finds a bed for your son. I am unable to stay and must leave as soon as the boats are ready to return."

Tormod made the introductions, then Aoife led the boy towards the hall. He was sure Ragna would find somewhere appropriate for the boy to stay, for the time being at least. Tormod would resolve the matter soon. As he turned to help unload the boats, he saw many of the villagers watching the boy, nudging their neighbours to look over at him as he entered the hall with Aoife. They quickly looked away when they noticed Tormod staring at them.

Chapter Twenty-six

BROTHERS
OF
THUNDER

T HE BOY'S HAND WAS warm against her own. Einar. His name was Einar. She couldn't understand Tormod's reaction. He was a fine boy, hale and strong, although it was clear that there were few similarities between them. Even Tormod's own brother had been shocked by his dismissal of the child. No, not shocked, Aoife realised. It seemed Anders had been ready for Tormod's reaction and prepared to step in. Whether he was Tormod's natural born son or not, Tormod had indicated that it was necessary to act as if he was and yet it was Tormod who was not doing so.

The other villagers appeared content to maintain the pretence and Aoife was determined to care for the boy, as she would wish a child of her own to be cared for. She had been around the same age when her own father had remarried and she was going to be a better stepmother than Ula had been to her.

Another wave of dizziness hit her and she staggered.

"What is wrong?" Einar asked.

"Nothing," she assured him. "It will pass." But the boy gripped her hand even more tightly as they made their way towards the door of the hall. As they passed the hearth, Aoife looked down at where a thrall was finishing skinning a rabbit, ready to put it in the soapstone bowl to cook on the fire. It was a sight she had seen many times and the smell of the blood and fur a familiar one, and yet today it had her clasping at her stomach and hurrying past.

She pushed open the door to their room and stepped inside, then quickly pulled it closed as soon as the boy had followed her.

She sat on the bed, then took huge, gasping breaths of the fresher air in an attempt to stave off the nausea.

The boy watched her from near the door, his eyes large and frightened. "Are you going to die, too?" he whispered.

"No," Aoife replied. She shook her head, but that proved to be the final straw. She grabbed at an empty bowl on the table and was violently sick. Her stomach continued to rebel for the next few minutes and somehow she was not surprised when she felt a cooling cloth placed on her forehead and the bowl removed from her and an empty one put in its place. She sat mumbling, concentrating on breathing in and out, in and out. A mug of water was held to her lips. She sipped.

"Thank you," she managed to croak at Ragna, who smiled grimly at her. The older woman passed the bowl to a thrall who left with it.

A small hand touched her own. She jumped at first and Einar pulled back, but she smiled at him and reached for his hand.

"My mamma died," he said. Aoife didn't understand the next bit, but assumed it was a question.

Ragna answered hurriedly, then shooed the boy out. Aoife tried to protest, but wasn't up to it. Ragna smiled at her. "Rest, Aoife. You will feel better soon. I will bring you something to drink that will help."

She frowned at the older woman. "I am sure I will be fine tomorrow."

"I think it may be a few weeks or more until you are yourself again," Ragna said. "Your husband said he did not want a child so soon, but he should have known better than to try to control that."

"A child? Tormod said there would be no—"

Ragna laughed. "Aye, men often do." She closed the door behind her.

Aoife closed her eyes but her mind was racing so fast she thought she would never sleep, but she must have because she awoke a while later. The room was empty, but she had the sense someone had just left. Perhaps that was what had woken her. Gingerly, she sat up and put her feet on the floor. She still felt a little lightheaded, but the nausea had passed. A steaming herbal drink sat beside her bed. Ragna must have brought it for her.

Outside she could hear the noise of everyday life, but it seemed as if there was more joy in it today after the arrival of the new-comers.

As the jarl's wife, she should have welcomed the new arrivals earlier, but she had been too bound up in Tormod's poor treat-ment of his son.

She ran her hand over her stomach. Could she be with child? Tormod had seemed so sure he could avoid a child for now, although on the night of the battle he had made a mistake. She tried to work out when her monthly courses had last come and realised it had been weeks now.

The door opened and her husband stepped in. Guiltily, she let her hand drop to her side. They regarded one another, Aoife wondering what to say.

Eventually she asked, "Where is Einar?"

She knew it was the wrong thing to have said when Tormod's face clouded over. "Ragna has found a bed for him in the hall."

"That is good news," Aoife said.

"You are feeling better?" His expression was wary.

"Yes, Ragna has brought me a drink."

Tormod inclined his head, then crossed to the other side of the room and pulled his shirt off. As he looked for a clean one, Aoife indicated her sewing basket. "There is a new one I made for you," she said.

"Thank you," he said, holding it up and admiring it.

"Are the new arrivals settled in?"

"Almost. I am going to the bathhouse. Will you join me?"

"Is that allowed?"

"Of course. You are my wife. Unless of course there is someone else you would prefer to be looking after."

"There is only you, Tormod. Although I thought you would wish me to make your son welcome."

He laughed a bitter laugh. "Yes, Ingrid preferred his company to mine, as well."

"You are being ridiculous," she said. "You told me you needed to keep up the appearance that he is your son. And..."

"And?"

"I know what it is like to have a new stepmother. I would prefer not to treat Einar the way I was treated. Is that so unreasonable?"

The silence stretched between them, and then another bout of dizziness rushed through her. She cried out as her head spun, then realised it was a vision overwhelming her.

She was in Håkon's field again. She heard the crackle of the fire and wondered why her vision was of the past and not the future. Then she realised this was different. She turned slowly, feeling the presence of death all around her. A cow fell to its knees, then crumpled onto its side.

The fire was no out-of-control blaze, but one tended by Håkon. She smelled burning flesh. This was no cooking fire—it was a pyre of dead beasts. She screamed at the sight of empty eyes and tongues lolling out of heads.

"The animals," she murmured. "In Håkon's field, the animals are dying."

A raven croaked high above. She looked up, trying to see it through the thick, black smoke. Suddenly, it cleared, and she could see the raven flying with its partner over the fortifications of a keep. Then she was flying with them, looking down on the world. She spread her wings and soared, sure now it was Car Cadell below her.

She landed on grass outside the palisade and looked towards the fort. The rays of the dying sun illuminated the familiar stone structure. Around it were the walls of the courtyard and beyond that the wooden palisade, stained dark in places. She reached out a hand to touch the stain. Ravens croaked overhead, and when she drew back her hand, it was red with blood. She screamed.

She grabbed onto something solid beside her, then slowly she realised it was Tormod. She was cradled tightly in his arms, but they were no longer alone. Björn, Ulf and Arne were all crowded into the room as well, and when she heard a noise in the doorway, she saw Ragna ushering Einar outside.

"Well," Björn said, clearly shaken. "If you are not murdering your wife, then we will leave you in peace." He and Arne stepped back towards the door. Ulf didn't move, but watched as Tormod laid her down on the bed.

"It was a bad dream," she said, swallowing. She reached for the drink Ragna had brought her earlier, cold now, but it helped calm her. "That was all."

Tormod and Ulf stared at each other, then Ulf turned and strode purposefully out the door. "You should sleep," Tormod said, running a hand over her forehead. For a moment, she almost told him the truth about her dreams and visions, but fatigue swept over her. What had Ragna put in her drink? Her eyes drifted shut.

CHAPTER TWENTY-SEVEN

BROTHERS
OF
THUNDER

T HERE WAS A KNOCK at the door. Tormod went over and opened it but blocked the way into the room. Ragna took a step backwards into the hallway and he followed her, pulling the door closed behind him.

"How is she?" Ragna whispered.

"Sleeping." Tormod frowned at his aunt. "What do you think is wrong with her?"

"Tormod." Ragna sighed and smiled. "It is likely she carries your child."

"But I have been—"

"Careful? Tormod, I have birthed nine children. Four of whom were conceived when my husband was 'careful.'" She placed a hand on his arm. "And have you always been as careful as you should? Lust has a way of making us forget, which is how it should be between a man and his wife. Anything less and you are cheating each other. She is not a passing fancy or a concubine, Tormod. She is your wife."

Tormod stepped away from Ragna. "No, it is too soon."

"It is not, she has been here more than two months." Ragna smiled slyly at him. "And Midsummer Eve is a popular time for babes to make their way into their mother's bellies."

Tormod thought back to their coupling after the short battle on the beach at Midsummer and knew he had no defence.

"She is nothing like your first wife, Tormod. No one will be concerned to know your new wife is now with child." Ragna shook her head. "Perhaps you have been surrounded by enemies for so long you are seeing them everywhere."

"I have had my enemy in my bed before." He looked at the ground.

"Tormod." Ragna waited until he looked up at her. "That was not the same and you know it. Einar's mother *was* your enemy, and you should have seen that, but she was a clever and deceitful woman who fooled all of us."

"My cousins were not deceived by her."

"And that is fortunate for all of us, but my sons are suspicious of everyone and are particularly overprotective of you."

"Then they shouldn't be. It is I who is responsible for them."

Ragna laughed. "I'm not sure that they see it that way. My sons follow you because you are a good leader, the right man to lead this village. They would not do so if they did not believe in you."

Tormod heard her words but struggled to allow himself to believe them. "Every time I look at Arne... Every time I see Einar... I am reminded of how I allowed myself to be deceived and the consequences it nearly had."

"But you have learned," Ragna assured him. "You will not make the same mistake again. I do not believe you have."

"And if I have? Who will die this time? All of us?"

"Aside from those who attacked us in the Norselands, the only one who died last time was Ingrid."

"Arne almost died." Tormod was unable to meet his aunt's gaze. "You nearly lost your son because I refused to believe him when he told me she did not love me."

"But I did not. And if I had, it would have been Ingrid who was to blame," Ragna said firmly. "It was not you who lay in wait for him at that hut. Ingrid knew her lover and his friends were waiting there to attack whoever followed her."

"It should have been me."

"Arne may have nearly died in your place that day, Tormod, but he would do it again. He would be happy to give his life if it meant keeping you alive. You are his jarl and he considers it an honour to protect you."

Tormod swallowed. Ragna's words were shifting things in his mind.

"And besides," Ragna said firmly, "this is no longer relevant. Ingrid deceived us all, but that does not mean Aoife is the same."

"But what if she is?" Tormod asked. "I forgave Ingrid for lying to me about the child. Let her live even after her family attacked us and Arne—"

"That was a long time ago and in another land," Ragna said.

"My father told me back then that I did not deserve to be jarl. What if he was right? How can I be jarl when I am so easily deceived? Maybe I do not deserve to rule."

Ragna smiled and gently squeezed his arm. "You do deserve to be jarl. Never doubt it. Everyone in this village followed you here because they believe in you."

Tormod frowned. "Perhaps if she is with child, it is the lesser of two evils."

"Two evils?"

"She spoke of the animals dying," Tormod said. "Of fire and more death."

"How odd." Ragna pursed her lips. "Our animals are well. Perhaps it is nothing more than a bad dream. Pregnancy plays funny tricks on a woman at times."

"She dreamed about the fire in Håkon's field as it happened. What if she dreamed about it because she already knew it was going to happen?"

"Tormod. She is not like Ingrid. I am sure of it. You must speak to her and ask her. If she is innocent, she will answer you with no hesitation. Think about how you would make a judgment if it was for another instead of for yourself. Perhaps you will see it more clearly then. But do not base your judgment on the actions of another. Look to the future."

"I have more than just myself to keep safe," Tormod said. "I have the whole village to think of, the other settlers who will follow."

"I know, but I am sure you will come to see the truth as it should be seen. Perhaps your wife can help you. She is carrying your child. Do not let the past cloud your decisions."

Tormod watched as Ragna went back into the hall, then he went into his room. Aoife was asleep, her face more relaxed than he had seen it before. His stomach clenched at the thought that she might be lying to him, but as he watched her sleep, her features relaxed and she appeared even more beautiful than when she was awake. He sat beside her and stroked her face. She smiled in her sleep and moved towards his touch.

Then he pulled off his clothes and slid into the bed beside her. Tomorrow he would confront her and she would answer him without hesitation and put all his fears to rest. After that, he would put his past with Ingrid behind him and look only to the future.

The next morning he was woken by someone hammering on his bedroom door. He yanked open the door to find his three cousins on the other side. "What is it?" Their expressions were dark.

Ulf pushed his way past him into the bedroom and stood in front of Aoife, his arms folded. "Elisedd came to the village this morning. Håkon's animals are dying," he announced, eyeing Aoife. "Just as Lady Aoife said last night."

"Out!" Tormod grabbed Ulf by the shoulder and marched him towards the door. "I need time to speak to my wife. Wait for me in the hall. Do nothing until I come." Ulf opened his mouth to argue but Tormod slammed the door on him and leaned against it. He watched Aoife's face carefully as she pushed herself to an upright position then he sat down beside her, causing the mattress to shift. She groaned and hugged her knees, trembling. "How are you feeling?"

Her eyes closed for a moment, then opened again. "I've been better."

"What will you do with me?" Her voice was small and tired. She sniffed, then held herself stiff and straight and reached for the drink before taking small sips.

Tormod stood and paced to the small chink in the wall. Outside the fire crackled in the centre of the village. A number of people stood around it drinking, but there was tension in every one of them as their gazes were regularly drawn towards the hall.

"I am sorry," she said at last.

"What for?"

"For whatever I have done to displease you."

"What do you know of the animals dying?"

There was a long silence while he continued to stare outside. He had hoped his marriage would mark the start of better fortunes, but everything seemed to keep going wrong. He looked at his wife to find her watching him.

"Only what Ulf told us."

"Last night. How did you know?"

"I told you, I dreamt about it. I saw cattle falling to their knees and dying." She shivered. "A huge pile of them, burning."

"You have been out at Håkon's farm every day."

"At your suggestion. Do you think I am to blame for this?"

"You were sick yesterday and now the cattle are sick today. Perhaps those things are linked?"

"If they are, then did you consider that maybe I am not to blame, that perhaps I am also a victim?"

Tormod frowned, then grunted in acknowledgement.

"I have visited Håkon's farm at your bidding, tried to do everything you asked. I have worked with Magda, taught her my language, and tried to learn yours. Every day I have walked over there." She stopped and waited until he looked at her. "I have looked after Elisedd, I said I would care for your son, I have willingly shared your bed, but it's not enough, is it? I am sorry I am ill, perhaps for being with child when you don't want another child... at least not with me."

He searched her face for any trace of deception and found none. "That is not—"

"Tormod!" Ulf shouted from the corridor. When there was a loud banging on the door Tormod tutted, then stood up and strode towards it. "One moment," he shouted, then leaned against the door and turned to face her. "Whatever you know, you must tell me now."

"I don't know anything!"

"What is killing the animals? Is that why you are sick or—"

"Ragna thinks it is because I am with child."

"And you?"

The pause before she spoke told him that there was more to be said. What was she not telling him? Why was she hiding some of the truth from him? Despite Ragna's words, he felt a leaden weight gathering in his belly at the thought he'd been deceived again.

"How would I know? I am newly married, I have never—" She looked at the ground.

"Why were you beaten?"

"What?"

"Why were you beaten? Why were you sent to the abbey?"

"I told you why." She met his gaze once more and sounded sincere, but still his suspicion lingered.

"You said that you became ill at Alt Clut and that was why your family left."

"Yes."

"And now you are sick again when something strange is happening. And there are the dreams as well." Tormod stared at her.

"Why would your family have you beaten for warning them and saving their lives? Why? Why won't you tell me?"

Aoife put her head on her knees and sobbed. "I-I... I'm sorry."

Tormod punched the door behind him and turned his back on her.

Tormod had no idea whether he blamed Aoife for the problem or not. He pulled open the door, unsurprised to find his cousins waiting there.

"Well?" Ulf asked, coming into the room and staring at Aoife. "What does she know?"

"My wife says that she knows nothing."

Ulf scoffed.

"I will go and see for myself," said Tormod. "And then I will decide who is to blame."

"Let me come," Aoife said.

"But..."

"You should bring her," Arne said from the doorway. "She knows more about the plants and animals here than any of us."

Ulf whirled around. "And what if she is the cause?"

Arne shook his head and rolled his eyes. "She is not the cause, Ulf."

"I have done nothing!" Aoife said, pushing herself unsteadily to her feet. "You blame me and accuse me and yet refuse to believe me when I speak the truth."

"Aoife..." Tormod began.

"No! I dreamed of the animals; I don't know why. Can you control your dreams? I have done nothing wrong. Why won't you believe me?"

"I believe you." Arne's voice made them both jump.

"Leave us," hissed Tormod. "This is between me and my wife."

"No, it is not. This affects us all," Ulf said.

"Aoife has knowledge none of the rest of us yet have and I, for one, am not willing to ignore that just because of your pride," Arne interjected. "If you don't wish Aoife to go, then I will take her. We will leave as soon as you are able."

Taken aback, Tormod faced his wife. "I believe what you have told me," he said after a moment. Her head shot up and he saw the surprise on her face. "But I don't believe you have told me everything. Tell me the truth. All of it."

She pursed her lips and shook her head.

"Why can you not tell me the truth?"

"I am afraid."

"Afraid of what? Me? I will not harm you for telling me the truth."

"Can you promise that?" Aoife asked. "Can Ulf?"

Tormod frowned. "Yes."

Ulf's expression remained blank.

She almost smiled, then the fear returned. "You don't know what the truth is yet."

There was silence for a long moment. He could see it in her eyes, in the way her mouth started to move, there was more to be said.

"I know nothing about why the animals are sick," she said.

Ulf scoffed.

Tormod's heart sank and a coldness descended over him.

CHAPTER TWENTY-EIGHT

AOIFE LOOKED FROM TORMOD to Ulf. The same distrust was visible on both their faces. Should she tell them her secret? Did she have any other choice? She swallowed, unsure whether she was doing the right thing or not. Was everyone in her life destined to turn against her? She was indeed cursed. Cursed if she told the truth, cursed if she didn't. It was true she didn't know why the animals were sick, but as Håkon's farm was the most easily accessible from her father's land, it was only reasonable the Norsemen were making the assumptions they were. Either she had done something to cause the sickness, or she knew that her father had planned to do so. It didn't matter that neither was true.

Her father had sacrificed her for the sake of Ula and her children. She should have let them die at Alt Clut. She pushed the uncharitable thought aside. No, she would never behave as badly as Ula. Though perhaps Ula would have preferred to die than to suffer the dishonour and suspicion that had followed them ever since the night of the feast. Aoife realised now there was simply no way to fix the problem. The only things she could do were tell Tormod, trust him, and hope.

"I will come with you to Håkon's farm," she said to Tormod. "And then I will tell you everything. But only to you. I will accept whatever decision you make then, but first let me see if I can help."

She glanced from one man to the other. Tormod looked confused, while Ulf's expression gave nothing away.

"Can you ride?" Arne asked her and she was grateful for his presence as he seemed to believe in her innocence. "Or will I hitch the cart?"

"I would prefer the cart."

"I can look after my own wife, Arne," Tormod said.

"Just be sure you do," Arne said as he headed for the door.

"And make sure it is not one of us who suffers this time if you are wrong," Ulf added.

"I will make sure you do not suffer, Ulf," Tormod said as his cousin left the room.

Aoife tried to work out what was going on, but there was something she did not yet know, some piece of the puzzle she did not yet understand. "What happened with your first wife? Her death was not the problem, was it?" Aoife asked.

"If you are not ready to share your secrets, then I am not ready to share mine," he said and turned away. "Come, we must go. We can talk of this later after we have been to the farm."

As the cart trundled into the farm, Aoife wished she had simply stayed in bed. While her feeling of sickness had not been so bad this morning, the odour of the farm and the beasts affected her. At the edge of the field, just where the beach met the land, there was a pile of animal carcasses, their tongues lolling out as she had seen in her vision.

"*Herre.*" Håkon's voice was urgent. "I fed them early this morning and then I heard the cries and came out to see them dying. All in this field are sick."

The farmer caught sight of Aoife and his face fell. He pointed a bony finger at her. "Why is she here? Perhaps she is the cause of this sickness. She has been here almost every day. Or told the boy to do it."

A chill slid down Aoife's spine at Håkon not using Elisedd's name. "I am not the cause."

"She might be able to help," Arne said, stepping between Håkon and the cart.

Aoife alighted and headed towards the animals' feed trough. It was mostly empty, but she raked through it and withdrew a slender, white tuber. "Where did you get these roots?"

"They were grown last winter to feed the herd."

"You grew these?" She waved it—it was a longer, narrower one than most of the others.

"It's a parsnip, so?"

"It looks similar, but these are poisonous," she said. "Did you put these in here?"

Håkon looked at them carefully. "No, you are right. Those are different. No."

"I will check the barn," Björn said. "Show me where you keep the animal feed," he instructed Håkon. The two hurried off towards the barn and returned a few minutes later with a handful of the poisonous roots.

"They have been mixed through with the others," Björn said. "It is definitely deliberate."

"We all know your people do not want us here," said Håkon to Aoife.

"I am not my people. And besides, why would I tell you about the roots? I could have said nothing and continued to let you feed them to your animals."

Tormod stepped up to Håkon. "Do you dare to accuse my wife?"

"Wife? And are you sure that is how she sees it? She is not here merely as a spy, to ensure we fail? I heard she was sickly yesterday and now today the animals have also sickened. Her people say she is cursed. Everyone has heard the rumour. And the rumours she betrayed them, too."

"And where did you hear this? Who spreads these lies about my wife?" Tormod rushed over to Håkon, loomed over him. The farmer took a step back.

Aoife grabbed Tormod's arm, anxious to stop him doing something he might regret. She did not want Tormod damaging his status with his people for her sake. Not when it was not a lie.

"T-there were traders just the other day, Britons. And the boy—" Håkon gulped and took a step back. "I... I asked Elisedd and he told me it was true."

"And I say my wife is not responsible for this," said Tormod. "Do you wish to challenge me?"

"No." Håkon looked at Tormod, then at Aoife. "But nor do I wish to be made a fool of. Again."

Håkon started to turn away towards his fields, but Tormod pulled him around to face him. "What do you mean by that?"

Now Aoife could see real fear in Håkon's face.

"Nothing, *herre*. Just that the Britons may have tricked... us." Håkon blanched and lowered his gaze.

Tormod let him go and stood for a moment, anger playing across his face.

Aoife was surprised when Arne stepped forward. "No one has been tricked. It is just a coincidence that the animals became sick so soon after Lady Aoife. Besides, she has already shown how useful she is to us. You did not recognise the native plant as a poison, Håkon, but Aoife did."

"And my wife's sickness has nothing to do with your animals and everything to do with me," Tormod said. "She is expecting a child. Now check your animal feed. Set a better watch on your barn and your fields. Our new arrivals may have some amongst them eager for such work."

Håkon looked at Ulf, who shrugged. "You are the closest farm to Cadell's lands," Ulf pointed out. "The easiest target, but we will ride around, check the other farms."

"Very well," Tormod said.

They watched as the cousins rode off. Then Håkon took his leave, promising to mount a guard at all times. Aoife turned to her husband, and he offered her his arm. She took it, and they started to walk away. She felt a little unsteady and was grateful for the support and that Arne had intervened when he had.

For a long moment, Tormod said nothing. Then, "Håkon was right, though. I have been deceived again. I am not fit to be jarl."

Aoife stopped walking. "What? How can you even think that? You just said—"

"If Håkon has no respect for me, then I have no right to lead. And what I say to my people is not the same as I will say in private, to my wife." He walked away from her.

"But you do," she said, hurrying after him. "You have every right to lead. Your people are happy to follow you."

"Then tell me what it is you are keeping from me." They stopped and faced each other.

She stared at him. Once she told him, would he spare her life until he knew whether she carried his child or not? Or perhaps he would simply kill her, having no wish to have any child of his own be the spawn of a foreign devil.

"Your dreams," he prompted. "The field, the fire, the animals dying... You knew about all of it."

She took a step back. She couldn't speak, couldn't swallow, could barely breathe. Light-headedness overtook her and she swayed.

He reached out and gripped her arm, then pulled her body firmly against his own. "Look at me." It was a demand she had no choice but to obey. "You knew all of it before you were told." A sudden screech made them both look up to see the two ravens circling above. Could they be the same ones? "Tell me."

"Tell you what?"

"About your dreams, about what you see, what you know," Tormod said urgently, then let her go and stared up at the birds. "The ravens... they are with you. Why?"

"I... I see things," she said, taking a deep breath. "In dreams. In visions. I had a vision of the attack at Alt Clut and warned my family. They didn't believe me, but were embarrassed because I had acted strangely at the king's feast. We were the only ones who escaped before the siege. Afterwards, the others claimed we were in league with the Norsemen."

Tormod stared at her.

"And so your parents blamed you when the other nobles voiced their suspicions?"

"Yes. And it was my fault."

"Because you had a vision?"

"Yes, like this morning and just now. Sometimes it happens in a dream, a very vivid dream, where I can smell and taste the scene as if I am truly there. Other times the visions come upon me when I am awake. Sometimes I faint."

"You see the future?"

"Only rarely. Sometimes it is the present, but in another place. I don't know what I'm seeing. I can't help it. What will you do to me?"

He didn't answer her. "Is this true?" He shook her gently.

"Yes." She tried to pull away, fearful he was going to break his promise not to hurt her and was shocked when instead, he leaned forward and kissed her.

"A seer!" he said, laughing. "I can't believe it. Why did you think I would punish you for that?"

Her heart pounded. "You... you don't think I'm evil?"

"Evil?"

"The Church, the priests, everyone. They whispered I was evil. The spawn of the devil. Had it not been for my father, I think Ula would have had me killed."

"But this is a gift. A skill few possess. And your people see it as evil?"

"Maybe not in the past, but the Church... well, the Church sees things differently."

"Yes, I am aware of that, but I didn't realise they would reject one of their own because of it. This is why you were beaten at the abbey?"

"Yes."

"Your father must have welcomed handing you over to a Norseman to marry. Punishment for you and justice in the eyes of the Britons."

"I can only assume that is how he is regarding it," she said. "Or rather, how Ula sees it."

Tormod laughed. His grip on her loosened, but he still held her close to him. "Your father has no idea what he has given away. And I am indeed a fortunate man. A seer. Now, tell me what else you have seen."

She frowned, still not quite believing his reaction. "Over the last two winters, most of my dreams were of darkness and storms and..." She stopped and laughed. "It is foolish."

"Tell me."

"It is nothing. A simple nightmare born of fear of a strange place. Thunder and bears, wolves and birds. The two ravens leading me to a circle of light, where I knew the bear and the wolf and the hawk waited for me. But I know there is a fourth presence. A man."

Tormod smiled at her. Then he threw back his head and laughed again, then kissed her soundly.

Thankful his mood had lifted and he no longer seemed so angry, she kissed him back. His hands ran down her spine, letting her feel just how she affected him.

He broke their kiss, smirking. "This man — you have seen him?"

"No, never. I just know he is there. I feel him more than see him. I think he is the storm coming for me. The thunder. I can feel it in my bones. It engulfs me. And I don't know whether to be afraid or not. I'm sorry," she said, turning away. "As your wife, I should not be thinking about another man."

He turned her back around and stared into her eyes. "Good answer," he said, smiling. "But you are not dreaming of another man. I am the thunder. Tormod, thunder. You have been dreaming of us all along. The bear, the wolf and the hawk. They are Björn, Ulf and Arne. That's what their names mean."

Should she tell him now what she had seen? The Brothers of Thunder walking through her father's fort, across the bodies of her people. And of her father lying dead. The sound of screaming and the cold fear of betrayal.

"Then you must not go to Car Cadell," she whispered.

"Why not?"

"I saw you there," she said. "There was blood, so much blood and so many bodies. My father was one of them."

CHAPTER TWENTY-NINE

BROTHERS
OF
THUNDER

T ORMOD DROVE THE CART back to the village in silence. It didn't matter that they didn't speak as Tormod knew they had reached a new understanding of one another. The way Aoife held firmly to his hand proved it.

Tormod hadn't replied to her request not to visit her father's fort. Saying he would not go was a promise he could not keep. Sooner or later, he must, and he knew it would be sooner. He wanted to ask her more about her visions, but decided she had had enough for the day. Once they were well rested and well fed, he would ask her.

A seer? It explained so much. He was relieved that was all she had been hiding from him. He could almost understand why, especially having seen the bruises on her body when she first arrived. One fist clenched around the reins at the memory. Perhaps he should ridden to the abbey and confronted whoever had done that to Aoife. One day he would, but the time had not yet been right.

Tormod squeezed Aoife's hand as they crested the hill and the village came into sight. She smiled at him. He smiled back, noting the colour had returned to her cheeks and there was no sign of her earlier weakness. In fact, she appeared healthier than she had in the time she'd been there. It was strange. The weeks seemed to have both passed quickly and to have lasted a lifetime, as if he had known her for far longer than the time spent with her. His heart clenched as he looked at her. No matter what, he felt the gods had had a hand in leading him here, bringing Aoife to him. She was a passionate and vibrant woman and he was glad he had saved her from her fate of being left in the abbey, forgotten and uncared for. He wondered if she felt the same, or if she would rather have stayed there—with her own people.

"Are you sorry you are here?" he asked suddenly.

"What do you mean?"

"I mean, you are away from your family, your home, your people."

"I have not been a part of those things since my mother died," she said. "And since my curse was discovered, I have been treated with suspicion."

"It must still be strange and unsettling to be amongst people so different from your own."

She shrugged. "It is certainly comforting to know that Elisedd is nearby. I remember when he was born. It was a stormy night. Rhiannon had helped me to bed and was brushing my hair when she bent double, screaming. I was scared. I was too young to be there when my sisters were born, but Ula said I could be at Rhiannon's birthing. I called for help and took her to her room. She could hardly walk there and we had to stop. Her labour went on all night. I held her hand. I will never forget the pain and fear in her eyes when she looked at me and then..." She stopped. "It was a relief when he was finally born."

Tormod brushed a tear from her cheek and pulled her against him. A knot of tension within him began to build. "It is not always easy to bear a child," he said as he stroked her hair.

She pulled away a little. "But I remember her face after he was born, the joy on it. It seemed to make it all worthwhile, and then..."

"Then?" he prompted, dreading what came next even though he knew Rhiannon had survived. Memories of Ingrid, how pale she had been, how pale and cold their child. She had lived only long enough to know their son had been stillborn, that her efforts and pain were for nothing. A wave of sorrow swept over him, strange given that at the time it had been the one emotion he'd been unable to feel.

"She kept bleeding. The midwife tried everything she knew, and finally it stopped. But it took a long time for her to recover. I would have helped with Elisedd, but of course, Ula would not allow it. Rhiannon was, after all, my maid. She has never had any more children." Aoife sighed. "She must be so worried about Elisedd."

"I'm sorry," Tormod said. And he realised he really was.

Emotions whirled within him. Aoife had seen a terrible side of childbirth. He had seen it, too, had already lost one wife that way. A sense of guilt tormented him when he remembered at the time thinking it was justice for what had happened to Arne. It was not unreasonable to think he might lose another wife and child. The thought made him realise how much he didn't want that and hoped Ragna was wrong about Aoife already being with child.

"I'm sorry, you lost Ingrid when Einar was born. I shouldn't have..."

Tormod pulled away from her. "Einar?"

"He is a fine boy. It is sad that he never knew his mother. That she never got to know her son."

Tormod's heart began to pound. He let go of Aoife's hand. Did she not realise? He swallowed.

"Was this another reason why you were so reluctant for me to conceive? In case I die in childbirth?"

He wondered what to say. Perhaps he should just be honest with her now. After all, Håkon's comments earlier must have been confusing for her. There was no point in trying to pretend any longer. And yet, it made him feel weak, and weakness was something a jarl could not afford.

"It is part of it," he said finally, then sighed. "It is complicated..."
Just then, they rounded the final turn before the village. Tormod
drove down to near the stables and a couple of boys ran out to
deal with the horse and cart. Aoife smiled at them and Tormod
thanked them.

As they headed for the main hall, he noticed Aoife watching
Einar sitting next to the fire with Elisedd. Arne must have thought
it better for Elisedd to remain in the village rather than return to
the farm amidst the sickness. The two boys had a game board out
in front of them. Aoife clapped her hands in delight. "Listen."

Tormod listened to the two boys playing the game. They
stopped often for Einar to explain rules and tactics when Elisedd
made a mistake, giving him a chance to correct it.

"Einar is a kind boy. He is helping Elisedd to win," Aoife said to
him.

Just then Einar caught sight of Tormod and after only a handful
of moves had beaten Elisedd.

Elisedd sighed and stared sadly at the board. "Again?"

"This time I am not going to help you," Einar said. There was a
nasty tone in his voice that had not been there before. The Norse
boy straightened and cleared the board, preparing to play again.

Elisedd frowned at him.

Tormod walked forward and clasped Einar's shoulder. "It is
good you are showing Elisedd how to play."

"I can beat him easily," Einar boasted, puffing his chest out. "He
does not know the rules. I have had to teach him and—"

"Einar!" Tormod snapped. He closed his eyes and took a deep
breath. "I am glad you were showing Elisedd how to play. It does
not matter whether you are the victor or not when you are training
someone. There is little glory in defeating an enemy who does not
know how to fight. Do you think our warriors in Valhalla boast of
easy victories or of the ones that were a challenge?"

Einar frowned. "I thought you would want me to win! After all, one day I will follow in your footsteps and be jarl here."

Around them there was a sudden moment of silence, as if collectively everyone held their breath. Villagers working nearby and the women at the fire all turned to watch. Most knew the truth of Einar's birth, although none would dare say it out loud. Accepting him as their future jarl was, however, a different matter entirely and one, Tormod realised, must be addressed.

Elisedd remained focussed on the game board and seemed oblivious, but Einar and Aoife had both picked up on the fact that something was amiss.

"Father?" Einar said.

Tormod kept his gaze on Einar, ignoring the others round him. Now that Einar was here, he needed to know the truth. The villagers would never accept him as jarl as things stood, and Einar had to be told. But this moment was too public to tell the boy something so personal, something that would change his life forever. He cleared his throat.

"Sometimes situations are more complicated than we realise," he said. "We do not always have to be the one on top. Teaching others is an important skill as well. And encouraging others to improve their skills is nothing to be ashamed of. It is what makes a warrior a good leader as well. Not everyone is destined to be a leader, though, and we do not all become jarls."

Einar looked from his father to Elisedd and back again, confused.

"I thought you were my friend," said Elisedd.

Before Einar could answer, Tormod said, "He is. You are one of us now, Elisedd. Einar will continue to teach you to play and train to fight with you." He turned to Einar. "I hope you have continued your training in the time since I left."

"Yes, Father."

"Then you and Elisedd will make good sparring partners and you will make sure he learns as much as you do. I am entrusting this task to you." Tormod squeezed his shoulder.

Einar glanced over at Elisedd and a slow smile spread across his face. "Yes, Father. But am I allowed to win?"

"You are allowed to try," Tormod replied. "Never underestimate your enemy." Tormod caught sight of Elisedd's face falling. "Or your friends."

Einar got to his feet. Both boys were smiling now. "Come. I will teach you what I know and we can be the best pair of fighters ever!"

Einar ran off towards the barn where the wooden swords were kept, but Elisedd didn't move, just stared at Tormod. "Is Håkon still angry?"

"No, not with you," Tormod said. "Or Lady Aoife," he added when the boy's eyes darted to his wife.

Elisedd nodded and followed Einar into the barn. A few minutes later the two ran back over with helmets on and wooden swords in their hands. Any villagers who had been watching them had thought that the scene was now over and all had returned to their work.

"Perhaps I should stay... advise them," said Tormod.

"I will do it," said Arne, coming up behind them.

"Did you find any problems on the other farms?"

"No," said Arne. "I heard what Einar said. You must deal with the situation somehow. The sooner he understands, the better."

"Understands what?" Aoife asked.

Arne put a hand on Tormod's shoulder. When their gazes met, they held. Thoughts whirled in Tormod's head. It was a challenge, Tormod knew, but he also knew that perhaps it was time to let this particular challenge stand.

"I will teach the boys," Arne said. "Both of them. I would like to foster Einar. It will go some way to you repaying the debt you seem to believe you owe me."

"Father?" asked Einar uncertainly. "I thought..."

"I will tell him why," Arne said. "Later."

For a moment Tormod did nothing, said nothing. Then he turned to Einar. "Arne will teach you. You are privileged to learn from a warrior as brave as Arne. To be taken in, fostered and trained by a warrior such as him is a great honour."

Einar nodded, despite looking confused.

"You will always have a place here. But it might not be the place you thought," Tormod said. Einar frowned and opened his mouth to speak, but Arne picked up a wooden sword himself and started to go through various moves, and both boys were distracted.

Tormod's shoulders slumped as he and Aoife walked towards the hall. She glanced back a few times at the boys before stopping next to the fire. "Why did that seem... as if you were giving Einar away?"

"I'm not. He is not mine to give," he said, then he pulled himself to his full height. "And it is all in the past."

"Please, I need to understand." She put a hand on his arm, but he shook it off. He didn't want to have this conversation just now. He glanced back at Einar, taking in the shape of his face, the uplift of his mouth, the line of his nose. The boy had the pale blond hair of his mother. The rest of his features he must have inherited from his natural father. Whoever he was. Ingrid had taken that secret to her grave. A grave into which Arne had also nearly fallen. He strode away from her, towards the shore.

Chapter Thirty

A OIFE NEEDED TO KNOW about the past so she could understand the present, whether her husband agreed or not.

Tormod was clearly upset—the tension in his shoulders was clear as she struggled to keep up with him as he strode along the beach. She wasn't going to let him just disappear, though. She was tired of all these secrets and half-truths. How could he just give away his son like that? Fostering was common practice, but this seemed somehow more permanent. And what debt?

"Tormod!" she called. He ignored her and kept walking. "Tormod!"

This time he paused and looked at her over his shoulder, then shook his head and strode onwards. His boots were stronger and more able to deal with the stony beach, while her shoes let her feel every stone beneath her feet and she winced whenever the sharp edges dug into her skin.

He was past the bathhouse now and the shingle was becoming larger stones and rocks. He barely paused when he reached the rocks and continued to walk as if they were of as much concern as the shingle had been. It was not nearly so easy for Aoife, who had to stop often to choose the best route. More than once she had to turn back to avoid pools of water or large patches of mud she daren't risk stepping into and discovering they were deeper than she had thought. She did her best to keep up with him, but feared that by the time she made it to the top of the rocks he would be far from her sight.

He wasn't. He had stopped at the far side of the next cove and was staring north up the sea-loch. A wave of light-headedness passed through her that she put down to relief. She started to make her way down the slope towards him.

He was a solitary figure standing at the edge of the water, the waves lapping at the tips of his boots. She could understand why there was something amiss about his relationship with the boy. She had seen the distance between them before, although she did not want it for her own children. It was the distance between her and Ula and, while Tormod did not seem to hate Einar the way Ula hated her, there was still something very wrong. Even more wrong was the idea of Einar living with Arne permanently. She sensed a deep sadness in the decision for both men. More than just an acknowledgment that the boy was not Tormod's natural son. He had not wanted her to keep secrets, and yet he was keeping many of his own.

"Tormod?" He didn't turn or acknowledge her presence, so she guessed he had known she had followed him the whole time. Her fists clenched. He had known and had not slowed down or better yet stopped. Perhaps it was a test to see how much she cared. She would soon find out if she had passed. "Tormod?"

She placed a hand on his shoulder and was surprised when he spun around and grabbed her by the waist. He took a long look at her face, then closed his mouth hungrily over hers.

Eventually, he wrenched his mouth from hers and leaned his head against the side of hers, panting. Her thoughts whirled. She had been correct; her husband's emotions were as disturbed as her own. Arne fostering Einar did not account for the pain she saw in his face, the desperation she had felt in his kiss.

"What is going on? Why does it seem like Arne is going to bring up Einar?"

"The villagers are willing to accept him, say nothing about his parentage, especially about his mother, but he cannot become jarl."

"I understand, but..." Aoife pulled back from him. "What is it you are not telling me? There is something more, isn't there?"

Tormod's head bowed, and he took a deep breath. "Ingrid did not die when Einar was born."

"Oh," she said. "I thought..."

"No." Tormod sighed. "Ingrid birthed Einar—another man's child—no problem at all."

"I don't understand," she said. "I thought..."

"It was my child that killed her."

"Yours? But..." She stared at him, she couldn't make her mouth form words. She was struggling to understand what he was saying.

"You do not need to love me..." He paused, a frown crossing his face. "But I do not wish to lose you."

"Oh, Tormod." So he feared her dying? He had wanted to wait to have children because he believed it had been his fault Ingrid had died. A knot of tension inside her loosened, and she reached for him. He kissed her again, his kisses more desperate than passionate, but she returned them, cupping the side of his face, trying to reassure him.

He lifted her and carried her up the beach to the edge of the woods, where he laid her down on a patch of grass before joining her. He swept her skirts up her legs and fumbled with his breeks. He used his fingers to touch her intimately, teasing her until she began to tremble with anticipation. His fingers moved from that sweet spot and she could feel how wet she was when he slid two fingers inside her. Then, with little ceremony, he moved over her, shoving her legs apart with his own, and pushed inside.

She welcomed the desperation she felt in him, the need to be one with her, to join with her. Unlike after the battle on the beach, however, this time he was looking at her and she knew he was seeing her, Aoife, and not just any woman. His thrusts were deep and reached right to her very soul. He changed his angle, and she responded to the contact on her most sensitive part. She clung to him, soundless words escaping her until she cried out in ecstasy, losing touch with the reality around her as she felt him reach his own peak and spill himself deep inside her.

He collapsed on top of her, panting. She was too disoriented to care. When finally he sat up, he pulled her skirts higher, baring her stomach, and ran his hands over the smooth skin. She shuddered and looked down at his hand covering the gentle swell of her stomach.

"I am sorry." He kissed her there, then peered up at her. "If you are with child, then I will welcome it. We will be a real family."

She reached for him, touching the edges of his hair, and kissed him. Just then, a twig snapped nearby. Tormod looked around and settled her skirts back down, but did not rush to move. She started to pull away but he stopped her.

"Stay," he said. "Everyone knows we are married. This is hardly a clandestine tryst in the woods." He moved to lie beside her, smoothing her skirts fully into place as he did so. She shuddered when his hand grazed her nipple through her dress. She looked up to see the two ravens watching them from the branches above and smiled at them. She heard the cry of a baby on the wind, felt a ghostly presence at her breast, then a contented gurgle, and she knew that all would be well with their child.

She smiled at her husband. "The child will be fine," she said, indicating the ravens.

"You have seen this?" He asked, sounding awed.

"I have felt it," she assured him. He smiled at her.

"I was rough with you," he said. "I'm sorry."

She looked away, unable to tell him that while he had been rough, she had liked it. Had liked the feeling he wanted her so much he couldn't even wait until they were in bed. That he had to have her there and then and also that he seemed to finally be seeing her as the future mother of his children. The only thing Ula had told her she would be of use as.

Tormod put his fingers on her chin and turned her to face him. "It will not happen again." He rolled away from her and started to stand up, but she reached for him and tugged at his hand.

"I hope it will," she said.

They exchanged a long, silent look, then he smiled and settled back down beside her. She leaned over and placed her lips gently on his. It was a sweet kiss, but she could tell he was keeping it that way, holding himself back. In part, she wished he wouldn't, that he would let go of his emotions again. Another twig snapped, and she looked up to see the ravens fly off together.

"You are the only one who has ever wanted me," she said, turning her attention back to him.

He glanced at her. "I will always want you."

"I was worried that you didn't. That it was the reason you didn't want to have a child with me."

He tensed. "I will welcome all the children we have together." He smiled again and her heart lightened just a little.

"You do not need to send Einar away because of me."

There was a long pause, and she thought for a moment he hadn't heard her.

"I'm not," he said finally.

"But, I thought... you said."

"I'm not. Arne will look after Einar well. He does not... resent him the way I do." Tormod laughed bitterly. "Perhaps he should. He has more reason to. Come, we will speak more of this later."

She knew he wouldn't tell her any more of the story. Not now, anyway. She let him help her to her feet, and they walked side by side, hand in hand, along the forest path back to the village. When they reached it, Einar and Elisedd were still sparring, although Arne had stopped teaching the boys and was sitting with Ulf and

Björn next to the fire. All had horns of mead in their hands and were laughing together. Aoife smiled at the sight.

As they approached, however, Ulf drained his horn and stood. Tormod stiffened.

"Arne says Einar is to live with him now, that he will train both him and the Briton as warriors," Ulf said.

"That's right," Tormod replied.

"Is this an admission the boy is not yours?" Ulf took a step closer to Tormod. There was a pause, and it was as if for a moment the world stopped, for it seemed to Aoife no birds sang, the waves stilled and around them everything held its breath, waiting for Tormod's response.

"No, it is not," Tormod said. "But Arne has offered him a future as a warrior, rather than as jarl and I have decided that Einar will accept this. It is the best solution for all concerned."

Ulf snorted. Tormod grabbed him by the kirtle and yanked him towards him. For a few seconds, Ulf struggled, then Arne stepped in and pulled them apart.

"Enough!" Arne turned to the two boys, who had stopped sparring. Einar's face was deathly pale and Aoife worried he was going to faint. "None of this is the boy's fault. I will not see him suffer any more for his parents' sins. I will train both Einar and Elisedd as warriors, and that will be the end of it. What happened in the past is over. Finished. It is time for us all to move on."

Ulf started to open his mouth, but an angry glance from Arne stopped him. He looked his brother in the eye.

"What happened was no one's fault, but those who betrayed us," Arne said. "I do not want you to argue over this again. Tormod is our jarl, and you will either accept this or leave."

"And if I choose to leave?" Ulf asked. "Would you really choose the man whose foolishness caused you such harm over your brother?"

"Tormod has led us wisely ever since. I will not hold one decision against him," Arne replied. "After all, if I did that, then perhaps you would not fare so well, Ulf. You have not always made the wisest of choices yourself."

"But I am not jarl."

"No, you are not. And before you say anything else, consider who those words will harm the most."

Ulf glanced over to where the two boys stood watching the confrontation. "And what of the problems now? Do you not see the same thing happening again? Tormod allows strangers to live amongst us, strangers who may wish us harm."

Tormod started to speak, but Aoife interrupted him. "Neither Elisedd nor myself wish you harm. Elisedd has already stood trial under your own laws and been proved innocent. Do you not accept the rulings of your own people?"

"You have not faced something similar, though," Ulf replied. "And Tormod's choice of wife in the past nearly killed my brother."

Aoife frowned, trying to work out how that could be true. "When my father's men attacked the village, they were instructed not to hesitate to kill me. What loyalty do you think I owe them after that?"

Ulf glared at her, then marched off towards the hall. Tormod moved to follow him, but Arne put a hand on his arm.

"Let him go," Arne said. "He will come around. He is torn between wanting to avenge me and wanting to remain loyal to you. Perhaps in defending this village, defending your wife, he will be reconciled with the past."

CHAPTER THIRTY-ONE

BROTHERS
OF
THUNDER

AOIFE WALKED WITH TORMOD back to their room. They entered, then stared at one another. She tried to gauge his mood, difficult when he just stood there leaning against the door.

He was lost in thought, but at least he didn't appear to be angry.

"So, the village will accept Einar even though he is not your son, so long as he does not become jarl?"

Tormod walked over and sat down heavily on the bed.

"Yes," Tormod replied. "I have always acknowledged him. Perhaps that was a mistake. But after what happened to Arne, and his mother's death... well, he was young. He had done nothing wrong. Even if his mother had betrayed us all."

"All of you?" Aoife asked, frowning. "But I thought it was Arne..."

The silence in the room grew heavy. Twice Tormod started to speak, but no words came out. Then his shoulders slumped, and he began.

"When I first met Ingrid... I thought she was the most beautiful woman I had ever met," he finally said. "I was young, eager to prove myself a mighty warrior, to go and seek out my fortune in other lands, but Ingrid... Ingrid obsessed me." He sighed and moved back to sit on the edge of the bed. Aoife joined him and tried to put an arm around him. He shook it off. "I do not deserve your sympathy. And I do not want your pity."

"It hurts you to tell me this story. I only want to comfort you," she said, placing a palm on the side of his face. "No sympathy, certainly no pity. You don't seem to be a man who needs pity, Tormod."

"Arne is the one who deserves pity. He is the one who..." Tormod looked at her, then took her hands in his. His touch was cold, and she wished she could warm him.

"Ingrid's father lived across the fjord. Her family were not well-liked, always ready to accuse their neighbours of stealing or raiding in difficult times," Tormod said. "We knew better than to trust them, but I thought she was different. As I told you before, it was only after we were married that I realised there had been someone else before me. I don't know who he was or why she left him but when she met me, she needed a father for her child. I liked to boast about how I would be a jarl one day and she was an ambitious woman."

"Or maybe she did care for you?"

Tormod shrugged. "After Einar was born she seemed obsessed. Spent all her time fretting about him and whether he was safe in the village or not. She told me she was worried her father would find her and asked me often about how safe the village was."

This wasn't really answering her question. "Arne's scars?" She frowned. "How did he get them?"

"One day Arne saw her leaving the village and followed her. She returned to the hut where we had met in the summer. When he confronted her there, she said that she was lonely and wanted only to return to the place where we had first met and been happy."

"And Arne believed her?"

"No. But I did. A few days later, Ulf followed her." He stopped, took a breath. "This time he saw her meeting someone at the hut."

"Einar's father?"

"I can only assume so," Tormod said. "When Ulf told me, I refused to believe them. That night the village was attacked by Ingrid's family."

"And Einar's father?"

"Ingrid's father and his warriors, certainly. She knew the attack was coming and sneaked out but my cousins had set a watch on her. Arne was watching her that night, and followed her." Tormod closed his eyes and rubbed his forehead. Then he looked back at her, a deep sadness in his expression. "Ingrid's lover was waiting at the hut for her to come to him. He was going to marry her once I was dead."

"She didn't take Einar?"

"No, which is strange because after when I asked her why not she said she had wanted him to be with his father." Tormod shrugged.

"You don't think he was among the people who attacked the village?"

"No, but he and Ingrid's father had planned the whole thing together. He wanted Ingrid and her father wanted our village."

Tormod stood up and paced to the door. "In the end it was Arne and not me who nearly paid the price."

"But the attack did not succeed?"

"No." For the first time in a while, Tormod smiled. "They had not counted on my cousins." Tormod stopped speaking.

"When Arne reached the hut, they were waiting for him. They attacked him, thinking he was me. Ingrid didn't tell them any differently. Just stood and watched what they did to him. They tied him up, then tortured him. Hundreds of shallow cuts on every patch of bare skin, not enough to kill quickly. They wanted him to die a slow, painful death."

Aoife put her arms around Tormod. He laid his head on her breast and she thought that he might weep, wondered what she would do if he did. He lay against her for a while, then he sat up, gripping her arms.

"We thought he would die." His voice was barely more than a whisper. "When I first saw him... there was barely any of his skin

215

that didn't bleed. It was horrific. Not the way for a warrior to die. Slow, painful. I wondered if I should kill him myself, but I couldn't, even though it was my fault. He lay in a fever dream for weeks."

"How did you find him?"

He paused for a while and she knew this was getting harder for him to talk about. "When the village was attacked, they got in quickly, did a lot of damage, got through all of our defences. But we had more men and in the end they were simply outnumbered. They had divided their men by leaving too many at the hut to wait for me." He indicated a particularly nasty scar. Aoife laid her lips gently on it and he shuddered. "He paid for that challenge with his life."

"But you found Arne in time, how?"

"We killed them quickly and when we realised both Arne and Ingrid were missing, the hut was the first place we went." Tormod refused to meet her gaze, staring instead at a spot on the wall.

"So, you saved him?"

"Yes."

"Her lover didn't take her with him?"

"No one except Ingrid and Arne left the hut that night, alive." Tormod smiled grimly. "We took Ingrid back to face punishment for her crimes. She had told her father all the weakest points of the village, and planned to marry her lover once I was dead."

"You had thought she cared for you?"

"They had not heard the way she spoke to me, experienced the way she was with me." He stopped abruptly and pursed his lips then continued.

"But you weren't killed. And neither was Arne."

"Somehow Arne survived the night, and then a day and a week and a month."

"And he recovered."

"Eventually. Although the scars will never fade." Tormod smiled sadly. "It was my fault. If I had not met and married Ingrid, her father would not have attacked the village."

"I doubt that is true," said Aoife. "And besides, their attack was not successful."

"Not ultimately, no, but we still lost good warriors that night." Tormod hung his head. "And villagers, wives, children."

Aoife nodded and held his hands. She understood now, why Tormod was so ashamed of the past. He had trusted the wrong person, shared information with her that she had used against them. Then she frowned.

"If she was a prisoner, how did she come to have your child?"

"When Arne survived, my father freed her," Tormod said. "He considered banishing her but I... I..." He stopped and looked down at his hands. "As I said, I refused to believe them. She was still my wife."

"But," Aoife began and then stopped. "You took her back as your wife? After what she had done."

"After she was freed, she had nowhere else to go. She begged me for another chance, and I thought that Einar should have a mother." He put his head back and sighed. "We agreed that she would provide me with a son of my own and then we would divorce."

"But she died?"

"Yes, the child came early and neither of them survived. Having my child killed her."

Aoife frowned at him. "You being the father would not have been the deciding factor in whether she lived or died."

"No, but... I had wished her dead so many times."

"And you know for sure that you are not Einar's father?"

"He was born soon after Yule," Tormod said. "We had only met in late summer."

"Children can come early."

He grimaced. "No, the babe was full-grown. It is one thing to not disown him as my son. It is another to allow him to someday inherit everything I have worked for, especially if I have children of my own. And I cannot love Einar as a father should because I am not his father."

Aoife was silent. The fact that Tormod was unable to love Einar no matter how wonderful the boy was, just because of who his parents were, hurt her. "Why can't you love him?" she asked quietly. "He is naught but a child, innocent of the sins of his parents—"

"Ingrid deceived me. It nearly cost Arne his life. It nearly cost the lives of everyone in the village."

Aoife thought back to when Ragna told her that the way Tormod saw the past was not the way others did. "But it didn't," she said. "Are you sure that is what people think?"

"What else could they think?"

"That you spared a child and brought him up as your own, even though his mother had betrayed the village. It was not Einar's fault, after all."

"It was my fault. I should have seen through her. I should have…"

Aoife saw the expression of shame that crossed his face. Suddenly, she understood the root of his anger. "You loved her. You thought she loved you."

"She lied to me, so she would be safe. Fooled me not once, but twice, and everyone knew it."

Aoife started to speak and then stopped. How could Tormod think like this? The villagers did not feel this way about him, she was sure of it. Why would they have come with him across the sea if they thought he was a weak leader? The blame for all of this lay with Ingrid, her family, and her lover. She frowned. Tormod had loved Ingrid, and she had betrayed him—a betrayal that had nearly killed his cousin. That must have hurt his pride, but surely he was making it worse than it really was? "But her people, they might have attacked you, anyway. And you would not have become jarl if your people had not believed in you."

"Yes, they could have tried," Tormod admitted reluctantly. "But she must have told them where the weak spots in our defences were. Without that knowledge, they could never have got so close. Certainly not as quickly as they did."

"How did she know the weak spots in your defences? If she only lived there a few months before the attack, then..." she trailed off, a sense of dread in the pit of her stomach.

Tormod sat, silent, tense.

"You told her?"

He looked at her, his eyes hard. "I told you, I was a fool. She said she wanted to know so she would feel safer. Said she was afraid of them attacking the village, but all along she was telling her father how to defeat us."

Aoife placed her hand lightly on his arm and squeezed it in reassurance. "Your wife is dead, but you must tell Einar the truth. He deserves to know."

"Arne has promised to do this. But this is not something I can admit publicly," Tormod said. "If I do, then the village will know I am not fit to be jarl."

"I thought you said they already knew about the boy."

"They whisper it behind their hands. None dare say it to my face."

"Perhaps it does not matter."

"It should. A man so easily deceived does not deserve to be jarl. And now there is you."

A cold shiver trailed down her spine. Was he comparing Ingrid's betrayal of him to her? "Me? I have not betrayed you."

"Your father fooled me as she did. Making me believe he was willing to form an alliance with us. And yet, it is clear it is your father's men who have attacked us. He has made a fool of me once again. The villagers may not forgive me twice."

She couldn't make her mouth work to say anything. How could she deny it? What he said was true, and she should have told him her suspicions as they rode to the village that first day. Ulf had been right.

She buried her face in her hands. "I am sorry. I believe my stepmother has poisoned my father against me. They would be happier if I were dead if you killed me." She pulled her knees up to her chest and put her head down on her knees.

He said nothing. Eventually she had to lift her head to see if he was even still in the room. He was so silent.

"Aoife."

She looked at him.

"You have done nothing wrong. It was I who should have seen through your father's tricks, not you."

He was blaming himself for the situation, and she knew he should not.

"You said before you were not relying on my father keeping his word," she said slowly, as she realised the way he was thinking of the situation made no sense.

"True." He frowned at her.

"If it is true, then you have not really been tricked, have you?" She could see him considering it, testing the idea in his mind.

"That is not, however, what I led the villagers to believe," he said, then he smiled, just a little, and pulled her against him.

"They trusted you to try to keep them safe. Despite knowing what had happened before."

"And I have kept them safe," he agreed. Then he tensed again. "It is not only about them, though. From the moment I saw you, I didn't care whether it was a trick or not. I wanted you." He didn't look at her as he spoke, and she could tell it cost him to say this aloud. She smiled as his words warmed her heart. "I was happy to have you as my wife, no matter what happened with the rest of the bargain. My people can defend themselves. Allies are useful but not necessary."

It took her a long moment to fully digest what he was saying. "Then you do not hate me for it?"

"No."

She opened her mouth to speak but was interrupted by a knock at the door.

"Come," Tormod said, standing and moving away from her.

The door opened and Arne stepped in. "More boats are coming. Not from Cadell's lands, but from south of the river."

Aoife frowned. "Ula's brother, Lord Marcant, rules those lands south of the river. He petitioned the new king for my father's lands after Alt Clut. Called my father a traitor because we left the feast. King Rhun refused, but said he would consider it over time, so there is always the possibility that... Do you think my visions showed the truth? Do you think my father has been killed?"

"It is certainly possible. But for now, we must deal with this attack. We should try to burn the boats before they land."

"A good plan. I will gather the archers," said Arne.

"Stay here and stay safe," Tormod said to her, then kissed her forehead.

"Let me come," she said, gripping his hands tightly in her own.

He shook his head. "Not yet. I will send for you. Or I will come back here for you."

He ducked out the door and left with Arne.

Chapter Thirty-two

BROTHERS
OF
THUNDER

Tormod followed Arne in silence. They made their way stealthily onto the headland, taking care not to be visible from the water. The summer nights were darker than at home, but even weeks after the solstice there was little full dark here. From their lookout point, they could see south across the river and observe where the mouth of the sea-loch opened into the firth. As he had expected, he could see no sign of his men until he reached them. Ulf and Björn had a large group of warriors with them. They were poised, watching and ready to move to where the boats tried to land.

"Well, *herre*," Arne said after Tormod had had enough time to assess the situation. "Do we wait for them and catch them unsuspecting, or do we attack with fire arrows?"

"They are not with Cadell," Tormod stated.

"How can you be sure?" Ulf asked. "Did your wife tell you this, or did you merely decide it for yourself?"

Tormod glared at Ulf, who gazed back unflinchingly. Tormod sensed the rest of the warriors holding their breath. He, however, had no wish to fight any of his cousins. Not when this new threat approached. Although, pieces were fitting together, that before had not seemed related.

"My wife told me." Tormod waited for Ulf to argue and was surprised when he did not. "Her stepmother's brother holds the lands to the south. I think Lord Marcant wants Cadell's lands. This is not our fight. I believe this is a fight between Britons and we are being made scapegoats. The situation begins to make sense now I know of these things. She does not lie to me, to us. Of this, I am sure."

He stared at Ulf as he spoke, daring his cousin to challenge him, knowing if both Ulf and Arne accepted his position, the whole village would be fully behind him.

Ulf looked at Arne, who hadn't taken his eyes off Tormod.

Arne turned to his brother. "If these men had knowledge of Cadell's failed attack, then why do they sail for the same point? Not a single man returned from the attack, which makes them either very foolish or—"

"Or they are not in league with Cadell," finished Ulf. He frowned and gazed out at the boats. Then he seemed to come to an acceptance of the situation. "Should we wait?"

"No," said Tormod. "We should let them know we are ready to fight them, let them know we are not here for them to attack with impunity."

Ulf smiled and gripped his axe more tightly.

A knot of tension unfurled in Tormod's belly. He knew Björn had his back, he had made his peace with Arne—or as close to it as he would come in this lifetime—and Ulf was now ready to accept him as jarl. Until he left for a village of his own. A slight pang of regret hit him as he realised that was something that might happen in the foreseeable future. He could not expect his cousins to remain with him forever. "Quickly, ready the arrows and fire as soon as the boats are within reach."

Staying low and thanking the gods for a rock face behind which the fire could burn, Tormod waited for the archers to be ready. Each had a boy helping with the arrows. Each volley would take time to light and fire, and the rest of them needed to keep their distance, but they would do it. They would see off these invaders and hold their land. They had done more with it than it seemed anyone had in the past, and if these Britons could not see the value in what they had held, then they did not deserve to hold it. Besides, his future sons would be half-Briton through their mother and have as much right as any other to the land. He smiled as he realised that he was beginning to see a future in which Aoife survived birthing his children.

Within mere moments the fire burned strong. They must be quick before the plume of dark smoke gave their position away. The archers looked at Tormod. He signalled to them to begin, and the night was filled with the twang of bows and the sound of arrows flying true through the air.

There were shouts on the water and then a single scream cut off quickly. Tormod watched as four of the arrows struck their targets. One killed a man instantly, and the others landed on the boats. The sailors shouted and cursed, trying to douse the flames and pull the arrows out. They managed it with one, but the others must have embedded deeply enough in the wood they could not extract them.

Another volley. And another. One of the boats was burning now, those aboard trying desperately to put it out and then giving up and jumping into the dark, deep water and swimming for the other boats. One boat started to turn, but it was shown no mercy. Arrows rained upon it as fast as Tormod's archers could fire. Another turned, and soon the three remaining boats were heading back across to the south side of the river, two smouldering and the third burning.

The Norsemen stood and watched the attackers flee. No need now to lie in wait. Tormod felt a strange mix of emotions; glee at seeing their enemies turn tail, but also a soul-deep disappointment the prospective battle had come to naught. Tormod was satisfied with the victory, but this could not go on.

"Tomorrow we will hold a *Thing*. Let every villager know. Send riders out to the farms in the morning. No part of our land is more than a few hours' ride. All who wish to attend should be able to make it and we will decide what to do about this."

"No more deals with Lord Cadell," Ulf stated.

"No," Tormod replied, holding Ulf's gaze.

"And what of his daughter?"

"My wife will have her part to play in our decisions, as all members of this village will."

Ulf nodded and Tormod strode off back to his rooms more secure in the knowledge Aoife would be seen as one of them.

CHAPTER THIRTY-THREE

BROTHERS
OF
THUNDER

A N HOUR INTO THE *Thing* and Tormod had made up his mind
about how to go forward. Aoife stood near him but on the
outer edge of the circle and every so often he saw her tense when
her people were spoken of. The first time, he had smiled over at
her just to reassure her that simply because he must listen to every
accusation, did not mean he must believe it — and he certainly did
not believe any of it reflected on her.

"And what does the Lady Aoife have to say about all of this?" Ulf
asked. Again. Why was his cousin insisting on emphasising that his
wife was a Briton?

Tormod ran his hand over his face. What was his cousin up to?
He had hoped their victory would have put Ulf's fears to rest but
apparently not. "How can you expect my wife to know what her
father, whom she has not seen for two years, plans to do?"

"These are her people who attack us."

"They *were* her people, Ulf. As you are kin to the other Norsemen. Do you know what Ivarr the Boneless has planned for today?
Tomorrow? Next summer?"

"No..."

Aoife chose that moment to move around to the causeway and
when Tormod nodded, she crossed it. A hush fell around the
circle.

"*Herre*," began Ulf. "Surely we cannot—"

"All have a right to speak and be heard, Ulf. That is the law of our people."

Ulf folded his arms, and Tormod fought to unclench his fists. He was sure they had resolved this last night. What was Ulf up to?

"I know nothing of the plans of my father," Aoife stated clearly, in slow but accurate Norse. "But if I did, I would tell my husband. The men who tried to attack last night were not my father's men." She paused for a moment and Tormod could see her swallowing as if trying to work out what exactly to say next. "I believe the men who attacked from the south are kinsfolk of my stepmother, Lady Ula. Before their marriage, Ula's brother, Marcant, had tried to take my father's lands by force. I am worried they may have tried to do so again. Perhaps they already have. Perhaps it is not my father who has betrayed you."

Ulf stood facing her. "My lady, how do we know you are telling us the truth? You may have simply tricked our jarl into believing you to leave us vulnerable, leave our village open to attack. It would not be the first time you have been fooled by a pretty face, Tormod."

Tormod pushed himself to his feet, incensed that Ulf had the gall to challenge him and insult Aoife. Ulf winked at him and he frowned. Realisation dawned. Ulf was forcing him to address the fears of the village in public. "Aye, Ulf, you are right. Who among us has not?" And with that, Tormod laughed. When he stopped, all around the circle stood in silence watching him.

"Husband?" Aoife put a hand on his shoulder and looked at him, worry in her eyes.

Tormod looked around at the assembled villagers, desperately trying to work out how to say this in the most effective way without admitting just how much of a fool he had been in the past. "Cousins, friends, villagers. Ulf is right. I was deceived in the past. It nearly cost my cousin his life and led to an attack on my father's village in the Norselands. I was young, and foolish. But

I have learned since then. Grown older and wiser and I will not make the same mistakes again. Although I may make others. I am only human, after all."

He paused for a moment and met Arne's eye. His cousin acknowledged him.

"Lady Aoife is merely a pawn in her father's scheme. Her father's—or whoever is controlling him—which I suspect is the real truth of the situation. Everyone makes mistakes, and we pay for those mistakes, but let me assure each and every one of you I went into this marriage in the full knowledge Cadell may well have been deceiving us. It did not matter. We hold this land and we are strong enough to keep it without Cadell as an ally, and even with Cadell as an enemy. Whatever mistakes I made with my first wife were not repeated with my second. An alliance with Lord Cadell was a luxury, not a requirement. Ingrid's son Einar will live and train with Arne, allowing any children Lady Aoife and I have together to take over these lands in the future. It is only right that lands which we hold due in part to her presence, pass to her children. Hopefully far into the future."

"Tormod," Aoife said, but he shook his head.

"The past is behind us. Cadell's intentions no longer matter. All that matters is Lady Aoife is my wife, head woman of this village. Her knowledge will help us settle here. There is nothing for me to regret in this marriage, nothing for me to hide."

Aoife covered her mouth with her hands and gasped. He put out a hand and took hers, holding it firmly, pleased at the shy smile creeping across her face. He pulled her to him and kissed her. There were mutterings from all around the circle which sounded positive.

Tormod held Aoife at his side and faced the villagers. "Now, I suggest we consider how to respond to these attacks. First, we should approach Lord Cadell. Then we will look for enemies further afield."

"I agree," said Björn.

"And I," added Arne.

There were general mutterings of assent from around the circle.

Tormod looked at Ulf, waiting for his response.

"And I," Ulf said loudly, grinning at him.

Tormod smiled.

Chapter Thirty-four

BROTHERS
OF
THUNDER

T WO DAYS LATER, THEY set off in the longships. Tormod had not wanted to leave the village under-protected, so a large group of warriors had been left behind.

They sailed north up the sea-loch, rather than south and around the tip of the peninsula. Tormod planned to portage the ships through the isthmus at Tairmbert, at the top of the sea-loch, and from there, sail into Loch Llumonwy and approach Car Cadell from the north.

The thought made Aoife smile. Her father would not expect Norsemen from this direction. Gaels, maybe, but not the Norse. Any in the past had used the entry from the River Clut into the River Llumon and arrived from the south.

In the longships, the rhythm of the waves made her feel queasy again. With each passing day she became more convinced she did, indeed, carry Tormod's child, although they never spoke of it.

The croak of a bird came from above. The ravens were back. Watching her. Warning her. She was so absorbed by them she didn't even sense the vision descending over her until her sight became obscured as if by blood and her knees buckled. "Tormod!" A shudder ran through her as she called out his name, and he grabbed hold of her before she fell.

She closed her eyes and ran her hands across them, trying to rub away the blood. Blood everywhere, pooling between the cobbles in the courtyard, splashed on walls, matted onto horses' coats, seeping from the bodies of the fallen. Below her, she could see the hawk flying about the fort wall. She was part of the thunder rolling above, and far beneath on the flagstones. The bear and the wolf prowled around the dead. They were not attacking, and were not responsible for the bloodshed, but she could feel the thirst for blood, for revenge, in each of them.

"They're dead," she whispered as she came back to the present and opened her eyes. "All of them. Blood is running down the walls. My father... We should go back. It's not safe there."

"Tell me what you saw," Tormod said, ignoring the curious glances of those around them.

She told him as coherently as she could, but as with many of her visions, what she had seen became less clear when she tried to put it into words.

"Be extra vigilant," Tormod ordered the warriors. "I will keep you safe," Tormod assured her.

She clung to him. A deep sorrow welled up from inside her, but she refused to let the tears fall. Not over a dream. She heard a now familiar croak and looked up. "The ravens," she said, gesturing towards the mast where they sat.

"If only they could talk," Tormod replied. "Or maybe it is they who speak through you."

"Perhaps." She made her way to the prow of the boat and grabbed on to the side, staring at the place where they would land. It would be hard work pulling the boats across even though it wasn't far, but it would be worth it. Before, she had worried about how she would react to her father and stepmother, but now a much greater danger faced them. An enemy waited for them. An enemy far more powerful than her father. She was sure of it. As sure of it as she was sure her father was dead.

She closed her eyes, trying to make sense of all her visions. The bear and the wolf and the hawk. The sound of thunder. That sound filled her, reverberated through her very being. It wasn't fear it made her feel, but peace. She smiled to herself. All along it had been Tormod. Why were her visions so slippery? Why could they not just be clear? Or perhaps it was the lack of clarity that mattered. She didn't actually see the future, since the future could always be changed by her actions, the actions of others. Nothing was set in stone. Yet.

For a moment, she nurtured an ember of hope her father still lived. Then it sputtered and died. She knew in her heart he was dead. Betrayed.

The boat's prow scraped against shingle. She opened her eyes as Tormod picked her up and lifted her onto the shore. When he put her down, he didn't let go straight away, but held onto her and kissed her thoroughly until Björn nudged him.

"Just because you have a woman," his cousin grumbled.

Tormod let her go and laughed. "You have Ylva."

Björn gave him a dark look. "No one has Ylva. Ylva does what she pleases."

"Then maybe it is time someone tried harder to please her," Tormod said.

Björn's expression grew darker, and he turned away.

Aoife crossed to where the few other women who had accompanied them waited, ready to assist if necessary. As a group, they made their way across the narrow stretch of land separating the two lochs at the isthmus. The men dragged the boats up a narrow stream and then finally across bare land, using tree trunks hewn for the purpose where necessary, until they reached the edge of Loch Llumonwy.

"My lady," Tormod said as he lifted her again. He splashed through the shallow water with her in his arms and set her down in the longship, then climbed aboard himself.

"I could have walked," she said.

"I know. But I don't want your father to think you have become a barbarian. You should arrive looking like a lady."

Aoife said nothing. She felt little need to turn up looking for anyone's approval. She stared down the loch, seeing the familiar landscape, albeit from a different angle. Once this had been her home, and yet it had been a long, long time since the word had meant what she believed it should.

"How does it feel to be going home?" Tormod asked.

"I was just thinking..." She stopped, looked up at him and tried to smile. "Car Cadell has not felt like home for a very long time, not since my mother died. And yet..."

"And yet?"

"And yet in so many ways it is home. Or was."

"Was?"

"My home is with you now," she explained, frowning at him.

He stared at her for a moment, then reached for her hands and held them in his own. A simple gesture and yet it made tears spring to her eyes. "We will be there soon. And once things are settled, we will go home, together."

They stood side by side as they journeyed down the loch. The winds were with them and it would take less than an hour to get there. Aoife wondered how long it would be until they saw movement on the shore.

When they were more than halfway to the fort and had seen no signs of life, she turned to Tormod. "Do you not think it is odd?"

"The stillness?"

She nodded. There was barely even a sound of nature beyond their boats.

"Silence!" Tormod ordered.

All noise on the boats ceased, bar the creak of the mast. Everyone looked around, puzzled expressions on their faces. They rounded a headland and Car Cadell lay in front of them, set back a little from the shore on a craggy hillock. Dark rocks lay between it and the water's edge.

"There's no smoke," said Aoife.

She stared at the coast of her father's lands, frowning as they got closer to the fort and the first of the guard towers appeared. She watched it carefully but saw no sign of movement, no sign anyone had noticed their approach and sent a message. Perhaps a boy on foot ran through the woods? But no birds flew up, and the woods seemed silent and still.

Tormod must have noticed her focus, because he placed his hand on her waist and gave her a querying look.

"The guard towers are empty," she said.

"Are you sure? You don't think they are expecting us and lying in wait? That they are just hiding?"

"No." She shook her head. "They are not there. There are no fires or anything."

"Do you think your vision was true?"

Aoife stared at the fort, at the palisade, at its gates, at the surrounding land. Little by little, she began to see differences. Then, although she could see the scene in front of her, it was as if a second image had appeared in front of it. She closed her eyes, and the vision grew stronger. She could smell roasting meats, hear the clanks of cutlery and crockery. The meal began, but she could feel the tension in the room. Ula stood apart from her father. She saw her father stare at his wife, his eyes questioning. Ula and her daughters left the hall. Cadell stood, confused, and then chaos ensued.

Aoife pressed her fists against her eyes, but nothing could block out the vision of the short swords and axes pulled from beneath cloaks and tables, and used to slaughter first her father and then any man, woman or child who had gone to his defence.

There was a deathly silence and the vision was gone. Tormod's arms were around her, holding her, his voice reassuring her. "What did you see?"

"They're dead," she said and opened her tear-filled eyes. "They're all dead."

"All of them? The whole fort?"

Aoife took a few deep breaths, aware of the scrutiny of the warriors around her. "No," she whispered, "not all of them. Only the ones loyal to my father. And... my father." She felt Tormod's arms tighten around her in response to the news.

"Who did this?"

"I don't know. My father's men, some of them. They were sitting down to eat and then Ula and her daughters left the room. Then they used short swords and axes and..." She stopped and looked up at Tormod, then at his cousins and the other Norsemen surrounding them. Some of them were staring at her, but as she looked at them, really looked at them, it was with an expression of awe rather than fear.

"This may not be what happened," she said. "At least not exactly. Sometimes it is an interpretation, rather than fact. Like the bear and the wolf and the hawk surrounded by the sound of thunder that haunts my dreams. So you might not want to take it all too literally."

Tormod smiled at his cousins. "It seems my wife is a seer of sorts." Then he squeezed her arms and laughed. "She has been seeing us in her visions for some time now."

"If only you could fly like your namesake, Arne," Ulf said. "As a hawk, you could fly above the fort and come back and tell us whether an army waits for us in there."

Aoife smiled, relieved he had finally accepted her.

"What do we do in your dreams?" Björn asked with a grin. "I mean, if you are dreaming of me..." He stopped as Tormod frowned at him.

"The thunder is only the beginning of the storm," she said. All of them stared uneasily at the fort ahead of them.

Chapter Thirty-five

T HE SOUND OF THE longships crunching against the shingle beach was loud in the eerie silence surrounding Car Cadell. Tormod and his men had waited and watched from just off shore for more than an hour, but the silence had remained unbroken. Aoife had stared at her former home all that time, not a single word passing her lips. The two ravens perched on the ship's mast stared at the same place. It was the Lord Odin keeping watch over them, he was sure of it. It also reassured him of her loyalty. After all, who was he to second guess Odin?

"It is time to move," he said. "There may be more trickery. Or survivors. Be alert."

The warriors headed up towards the fort walls in three groups led by Ulf, Björn and Arne. Tormod remained on the shore with Aoife and the fourth group of warriors, all wary and ready to head quickly for any one scene where trouble might erupt. The gates in the wooden palisade that surrounded the fort and its farms lay wide open, although that was not unusual. More unusual was the lack of activity on the farms, the animals simply wandering.

It was Ulf's group who approached the gates in the stone walls of the fort directly. When they reached them, they knocked. Any enemy would already be aware of their presence if they were watching. The sound echoed off the buildings and walls. There was no response and barely even a whisper of breeze. Ulf pushed the high wooden gate. It swung easily inwards. The warriors positioned themselves, but nothing happened.

Ulf turned to Tormod, his face serious. "There has been a massacre," he shouted. "I can smell blood, and there are rats, so many rats."

Ulf and his men entered, but it was not long before they returned to the gate, ashen-faced. Ulf returned to the longships to speak to Tormod.

"I do not think there is anyone left alive," Ulf said. "Although, as the fort has not been burned, I would assume the victor plans to come back. There are not so many bodies. Perhaps some were taken as prisoners."

"Perhaps some were complicit," Tormod said. "Lord Cadell?"

Ulf shook his head. "Dead."

Tormod reached for Aoife's hand. It was stone cold. "And what of the rest of his family?"

"There is no sign of his wife or any of his daughters. In fact, we found few women. But it looks like the bodies of many of the fort's inhabitants lie in the great hall, as the Lady Aoife saw. They have been there for at least..." Ulf made a face. "I would say about four days. No more."

"So, before the boats attacked us."

"Yes, perhaps they thought..."

Tormod waited for Ulf to speak, but his friend was deep in thought. He eventually continued, "It is possible the other Britons thought Cadell was in league with you."

"It was supposed to be an alliance," Tormod acknowledged. "Perhaps the other Britons resented it."

"You thought Cadell had tricked you."

"And you think maybe he did not?"

"Given that he now lies dead, I'd say it is a possibility."

"I must see for myself." Aoife was pale but looked determined. "I must see for myself," she repeated to Ulf, then turned to Tormod. "Please."

"You will only find it distressing," Ulf said.

She looked at the gates, then back at him. "It is better to know than to imagine. Or to dream."

"Very well," said Tormod.

"I will go back," Ulf said. "Continue to search for anything that might prove who is responsible."

Tormod saw conflicting emotions play across her face and when she took a step towards the gates regardless, he let her. His whole being relaxed when she stopped and turned back to him.

"If they only found my father's body, then Ula is responsible for this."

Tormod stared at her. "You think so?" he finally said. "You do not think she and your sisters have been taken captive?"

Aoife closed her eyes, then shook her head. "No, in my vision, she stood and left the room with her daughters. That seemed to be the signal to attack my father. I think Ula would do whatever she thought was necessary to survive."

Ulf laughed bitterly. "I knew a woman like that once."

"Ulf, lay out Lord Cadell's body for my wife to say her farewells," Tormod said. "You may see him then, but not before."

Aoife opened her eyes, tilting her head up towards the sky, her lips moving in prayer.

"I'm sure he sits in Valhalla," Tormod said, placing his hand on her shoulder.

"Thank you," she whispered, then laughed through her tears. "Although I'm not sure that's where he will be or would want to be." She squeezed Tormod's fingers in acknowledgment of his kindness. "I would like to go to my old room, if that is all right?"

"I will take you myself," Tormod said.

"Will you bury the dead?" Aoife asked him.

Tormod rubbed a hand across his forehead. "We will try," he promised. "We will have to do something. It seems likely whoever invaded this place did not intend to occupy it immediately. Otherwise they would not have left so many bodies—"

"So many? But there are no birds, no signs..."

"Do not look around," Tormod said, putting a hand out to stop her when she began to do just that. "If they have not dealt with the dead yet, then they are leaving them there for a reason."

"In my visions, when my father and his men were attacked, it was Norse swords and axes that were used. Not the long swords favoured by the Britons."

"They may be waiting, watching. Ready to catch us in the act, so to speak."

"You really think they are here, waiting?" Now there was genuine fear on her face.

"Where is the priest?" Aoife asked suddenly. "Father Bricius. Even if it was other Britons who did this, they would not kill the priest."

"We will search for him. Any that are not among the dead must be considered traitors to your father."

"It is not hard to believe that Father Bricius would betray my father. Nor Rhydderch. Both were more loyal to Ula than to my father." She sighed. "I almost pity him living amongst so many who would not hesitate to betray him. You are fortunate to have the loyalty and respect of those you lead."

"I am, indeed. Now, let us go."

"And Rhiannon. Elisedd's mother," she added at Tormod's confused expression.

"We will look for her."

Ulf went in front of them as they walked through the gates and into the courtyard, then crossed to the door that opened into a circular tower attached to the largest building. When they went through the door, it clanged shut behind them. Tormod stopped.

"I'm sorry," he said, holding her body tightly against his own and kissing her gently on the lips.

"This is not your doing," she said, leaning into him.

He revelled in the thought she trusted him. Her arms tightened around him and he smiled.

He held her for a moment longer, then pushed her to arm's length. "There is little we can do for now. We must take this to Doomster Hill upriver in time and present it before your king, but for now, we will visit where you wish and then search for Elisedd's mother. Just to be sure."

"Thank you."

They went up the stairs curving inside the thick walls, Tormod with his sword drawn and his axe at the ready. Aoife had a knife in her hand and kept a safe distance behind her husband. Although he sensed the tower was empty. There was a stillness simply not felt in a building with any life in it.

On the first floor, she gestured for him to push open the door.

Inside the room were four narrow beds made up, empty, but otherwise nothing. Just an ordinary bedchamber.

Aoife was staring at a space where a bed once stood. Hers, he presumed. "There is nothing left," she whispered.

"What do you mean?" He looked around at the bare walls, the empty surfaces and bare cupboards.

"My sisters knew what was coming," Aoife said. "They have taken all their trinkets with them. Everything that was precious to them."

He watched as she ran her hands over every surface and looked around each bed and on the floor and thought of how little she had brought with her. "Are you looking for something?"

"I had a pendant of my mother's with a cut amethyst at its centre."

"An amethyst pendant? Was it a cross engraved with knotwork?"

"Yes... how did you know what the pendant looked like?"

He was silent for a long moment, not wanting to either hurt her, nor lie to her. "I saw your stepmother wearing one like it."

She said nothing, but her expression hardened and her fists clenched. She turned and headed for the stairs.

"Wait!" But she was gone. He hurried after her, finally catching her as she reached the bottom of the stairs. Ulf waited for them there.

"What is it?" Tormod asked him.

"We have searched everywhere. There are no signs of the priest, Lady Ula, or the daughters. Or at least none of the dead women... well." Ulf swallowed and ran a hand down his face. "We have only found three dead women, and all appear to be servants."

"Rhiannon?" Aoife said, but Ulf shrugged. She straightened. "These were my family's servants The least I can do is look upon the faces of the dead. They died in my family's service. And I should look for Rhiannon." Aoife took a deep breath. "What will I tell Elisedd if I find her?"

"We will tell him the truth, together," Tormod promised her. "Just as soon as we know what it is."

She looked at him. Tears glinted in her eyes, tears she refused to allow to fall. Then she smiled. "Thank you."

Chapter Thirty-six

BROTHERS
OF
THUNDER

T HE STENCH OF DEATH was heavy in the air. The coppery smell of blood had intensified until she pushed open the door to the great hall, when it was replaced by the stench of putrefaction and rot. All of Tormod's men in the hall when she entered stopped what they were doing and waited out of respect as she looked around the hall. Then they resumed chasing away the rats and moving bodies outside.

"You must burn the dead," Aoife stated.

"Not bury them?" Tormod asked.

"No," she said, after thinking about it. "It is too late for that. It would be better to burn the bodies. The rats are already here, and to bury so many in these circumstances... it's not practical."

Tormod looked closely at her. "If you are sure. The Church..."

"The Church, or the priest, is either amongst the dead or has run away. My mother was a Pict and they are not afraid to burn their dead. The people of this fort loved her; they would have carried out her wishes. It was only after Ula arrived that things changed. And now she is gone too." Aoife peered around the courtyard.

"We have not found her body."

"All the more reason to not consider what she would have done," said Aoife, frowning. She blinked, then took a deep breath. "We will set the fort to rights, and then we must go to the king to see who will inherit."

"You have no brothers?" Tormod asked.

"None that lived."

"So, who would inherit the fort?"

She shrugged. "Perhaps if I had a son, I could petition the king for him to inherit. And my father had a brother. He died at Alt Clut and my cousin, Cenydd, and his mother returned to live with her family after that. Further south. Near the old wall and Car Luel. He would have a rightful claim, as well."

"What of Lady Ula and your sisters?"

"Do you think they're still alive?"

"Yes. I think they have escaped along with the priest." Tormod took her hand and held it tight in his own. "Do you think there might have been something between Lady Ula and Bricius?"

Aoife snatched her hand away from him. Her mouth opened and shut like a fish. "He's a priest. There are rules, basic decency..."

"The way you were treated was not very decent."

"That was different," she returned quickly, wondering why she was defending them. "They saw me as sinful. Cursed. They said they were trying to help me. To save my soul."

It was what she had always been told. How the beatings and other punishments had always been justified, and yet... The words rang hollow in her ears even as she said them. How could she be guilty of something she did not control? She looked into her husband's face, unsure if he believed her or not. He took her by the elbows and pulled her against him.

"They were wrong to do so," he said, then kissed her. "You are not cursed. The gods made you the way you are. Who are they to deny you your gifts?"

For a moment, she looked at him, wanting to believe. Then she tried to pull back, shame sweeping through her. She shook her head. "The devil made me the way I am."

"No," Tormod said, his arms going around her. "You have helped us, saved us. You saved your family, and still they treated you badly. The Church treated you badly and perhaps it was because..."

"Because?"

"Did they say you were cursed when your mother was alive?"

"No, although I have always had dreams and visions," Aoife replied. "But I was so young then, no one would have—"

"So, it was only once your stepmother was here?" Tormod asked. "And Father Bricius?"

"Yes. The two of them always sided against me. They were the ones who went most often to my father. It was Father Bricius who suggested they send me to the abbey after Alt Clut."

"Did you ever see them together?"

"Ula and Bricius? Yes, but he was her priest, her confessor."

"And your confessor, too?"

"Yes." She gulped. She had been such a fool. She had told Bricius everything she feared and... Now lots of small memories flowed through her mind.

A sense of dread began to steal over her. She closed her eyes. Fragments of overheard conversations, the way they had been so close sometimes when Aoife and the girls had entered the room, the way Father Bricius had looked at Ula. Perhaps Tormod was right. Except that would mean... She opened her eyes and looked at Tormod.

"Father Bricius came to Car Cadell with Ula," she said. "You think they have been working together?"

He was silent for a long moment. "It's a possibility. It's always a possibility. I am sure she betrayed you, and the timing..." His gaze shifted off hers. "You said Lady Ula's brother owns the land to the south? The one whose ships attacked us?"

"Lord Marcant. Yes."

"Is it possible he was also responsible for this? That he wants this place for himself? And our village?"

"Lord Marcant is a greedy man," Aoife said. "It would not surprise me if he was behind this." Aoife looked around her and shuddered. "Who would want this place now? It's cursed. The unconsecrated dead have lain here for days."

Then she shuddered again, a sudden sensation of excruciating pain in every limb, her eyes, her ears. She must have screamed, although she didn't remember doing so, as when she came back to her senses, Tormod had a hand over her mouth. One or two of the warriors had stopped to watch them, but at a signal from Tormod, they resumed their clearing-up duties.

"Shh, you are safe," he said. "My men will think I am murdering you. Or worse, that someone else is."

"I'm sorry. I felt them being tortured." Aoife took a deep breath and pushed away from the comfort of her husband. There was no reason to stand here. She sensed Tormod behind her and knew she was safe with him defending her. She walked into the courtyard and then kept on walking towards the gates. Away from the past, away from all the pain, fear, and death.

She made it all the way to the side of the loch before she had to stop and be sick. She knelt down and retched more than once and was grateful when she felt Tormod's arm around her and a cool cloth wipe her forehead and her mouth. And then she felt it. A small flutter in her belly. She ran her hands across her stomach and looked up at Tormod.

"The child," she said, smiling at him. "I felt it move."

"Even in this place of death, hope for the future is with us," Tormod said, leaning close to her and kissing her forehead. "Come, I will take you to see your father's body, see if Rhiannon is amongst the dead, and then we will leave this place. Forever. There is nothing for you here now."

"No, there is not." She put her hand out and cupped his face. "But there is everything for me with you."

"Come, let us do that and leave." Tormod smiled and kissed her. Then he took her hand.

After taking one last look over the loch and a deep breath to clear her mind and settle her stomach, she turned and walked hand in hand with him towards the fort.

"They have laid your father out on the table," Arne informed them as they reached the doorway to the great hall.

Tormod's hand tightened on her own and she steeled herself to see her father for the last time. She took another breath of fresh, clean air and stepped through the doorway.

The hall should have felt familiar—she had lived for almost twenty years going in and out of it on a daily basis—and yet it felt like a foreign place. She breathed through her mouth, although nothing could stop the stench of death from reaching her. Her attention was drawn immediately to the top table where a body lay, covered in a cloth. The closer she got, the more her steps slowed. But she didn't stop. She needed to do this. She needed to see with her own eyes and know for sure.

Blood pools, dark and sticky on the floor, indicated where bodies had already been taken away from around the table.

"The women are here," Arne said, gesturing to a group of three bodies. Aoife steeled herself and looked at them, breathing out a relieved breath when none of them were Rhiannon. Then she turned back to the body on the table.

"Where was my father found?" she asked.

Tormod looked at Arne, who indicated a spot close by.

Aoife nodded. That was where he had fallen in her vision. She gripped the edges of the cloth covering her father's face. She was prepared for what she would see beneath it, and for the first time she prayed the sight would trigger a vision. Something to tell her how and why this had happened. A vision that would settle the future for her.

She pulled back the cloth, a loud sob escaping her throat as her father was revealed. She wasn't sure what she had expected. His face almost looked peaceful. She went to pull the cloth further down, but Tormod stepped forward and stopped her. Her eyes were filled with tears, and she allowed them to fall.

A second later, her prayers were answered. She leaned against her husband, closed her eyes, and let the vision slide over her.

Car Cadell. Twilight. Four nights previously. Her father sat at the top table, Lady Ula beside him and her brother on his other side. Father Bricius was also present. A messenger arrived.

"My lords, there are sightings of the Norsemen. The guard towers in the north have seen them. You must send a war party to stop them," the messenger reported in great, gulping breaths.

"You heard the man," Cadell yelled at Rhydderch. "Send a war party. Our fastest riders. Take them by surprise. I knew they could not be trusted."

Rhydderch stood and bowed to Cadell. Aoife saw the glance he exchanged with Lord Marcant and her fists clenched. Her father had been betrayed not just by his wife, but by his priest and his steward. What chance did he have against all of them?

Then she was aloft, a bird flying over Car Cadell. The war party was about to ride out. On the other side of the wall, a large group of soldiers lay in wait. And the gate didn't close behind the war party.

Back inside the hall, Ula and her daughters were walking out of the room as the guests attacked their hosts. Father Bricius moved towards her father.

Her eyes flew open. There was no need to see any more. She could fill in any remaining gaps. But the vision would not let her go.

She closed her eyes again, gripping tightly to Tormod as she tried to push the vision away, to no avail. Slowly, she realised the details were different.

Once more, she flew high above Car Cadell. This time there were soldiers still outside the fort walls. Not Norse warriors. Britons, moving in from the south. Already she could see the aftermath of battle, the bloodstains in the courtyard, just as it had looked a short while ago. With a sickening realisation, she spotted the longships pulled up on the shore just to the north and there... there were Ulf and his men on the shore.

Her heart pounded. It was daylight in this vision. This was not four nights ago. This was now. Her eyes shot open. "It's a trap! They're here!"

Aoife wasn't sure what she expected her husband's reaction to be, but a small grin was not it. She looked around. There were a few men in the great hall.

"Come," he said, taking her hand. "We have a family matter to clear up."

They stepped out into the courtyard. From there, they faced the gateway. A small group of soldiers, Britons, approached. Aoife recognised one or two as her father's men and clenched her fists at the thought of their treachery.

"Don't worry. We are ready to fight," Tormod whispered to her, then kissed her. "Come."

They watched the soldiers enter. The men split into two groups, each moving to one side of the courtyard. Four riders came in and paused side by side, facing them.

Aoife stared at them, anger soon replacing surprise.

"Lady Ula, my condolences on your recent loss. I hope those responsible will be punished appropriately," Tormod said. Ula glared at him and said nothing. Beside her, Father Bricius and Steward Rhydderch shifted nervously in their saddles. Tormod turned his attention to the fourth rider. "Lord Marcant, I presume. I am acquainted with some of your men, I believe. Not, however, with yourself. What a shame you did not arrive in time to prevent this slaughter."

CHAPTER THIRTY-SEVEN

T ORMOD WAS READY FOR them. His warriors were ready for them. The Britons just didn't realise it yet. They had obviously thought to surprise them and perhaps besiege them in the fort, but if there was one thing Tormod had learned to expect in his life, it was deceit.

"Lady Aoife!" Lord Marcant shouted. "I am delighted to see you. I had been informed there were none of Cadell's people left alive within these walls after a terrible slaughter wrought by your Norsemen. How fortunate to discover you are still alive. Although, I am not sure you truly count as one of Cadell's people anymore, do you? Especially if you and your husband are the ones to have betrayed him."

"I have betrayed no one," retorted Aoife.

Tormod took her hand. "There is no need for you to speak to him. You do not need his approval. It would be worth nothing to you."

Aoife turned to him, her face clearly troubled. "You are right. Although perhaps they are right as well. Perhaps I *am* a traitor, for I no longer see myself as one of them."

Tormod gave her a tight smile. "It is possible to stand in two worlds. You do not have to choose one over the other."

Aoife put her head on one side, considering his words, then turned back to Lord Marcant. "But I am not as much a traitor to my people as the ones who murdered my father. Or the ones who plotted against him. Against their lord. Against their husbands. That is a far, far worse betrayal."

"None of that matters," Marcant said, waving his hand as if the whole idea was inconsequential. "No one else will ever know. Within the hour you will be the only one of the Norse warband that invaded left alive. The poor, unfortunate daughter your somewhat misguided father married off to thieving Norse scum in exchange for the illusion of safety. However, I will rescue you from his evil clutches, from the clutches of the man who had your father murdered in an attempt to gain all his land, not just the small area on which your pathetic excuse for a village stands."

Tormod noticed Rhydderch and Father Bricius exchange puzzled glances. Now, that was interesting. Perhaps the Britons were not united in their plan. Perhaps Lady Ula and her loyal followers were about to be betrayed as they had betrayed Cadell. Tormod stifled a grin at the thought.

"Marcant—" Ula began.

Marcant gestured for her to be quiet and she obeyed, confusion etched on her face.

"Now, Lady Aoife, if you come towards me now, I will take you from this place. You and I will go to the king and claim all of these lands to hold in trust for our sons," Marcant said.

Ula stared at her brother while Rhydderch and Father Bricius tried to argue with him but he did not even seem to be listening.

"Your plan had its merits, sister," Marcant said. "But this is far easier. And arguably legal. She is, after all, the eldest of Cadell's daughters, and with a strong husband to take control I am sure Rhun will be happy to grant us these lands to rule together."

"I will never marry the man who murdered my father," Aoife retorted.

"Ah," replied Marcant. "That particular honour fell to Father Bricius, so you have no worries there. And soon, Lady Aoife, I will take revenge on your behalf on the man who not only stole your virtue but will bear the blame for the murder of your father and most of his household."

"How can you do this?"

"The only weapons we will find here will be Norse swords and axes. They came by ship in the night and hacked to pieces all they found within the fort. My sister and her priest were visiting me at the time and, of course, I had to come and seek justice. You witnessed the carnage and it confused you, left you accusing your own stepmother of treachery and it was just as well that I arrived to save you all. You will marry me, and all these lands as well as my own south of the river will be ours. We will become the most powerful family in Strath Clut."

"That was not part of the deal," Ula shrieked. "I was to rule here, with Bricius. We would marry my daughters to your allies and their sons would inherit one day, far in the future. You cannot marry her, she is part Pict and has been defiled by this, this... Look at her. She is no longer even modest and—"

"Lady Ula... sister," Marcant began. "You seem to forget I am in control here. Not you. The Lady Aoife provides me with a link to the Pictish kingdom, not to mention as Cadell's oldest child, she has the right to petition the king for these lands on behalf of any sons she bears."

"No!" Ula shouted.

"You can't be serious," said Father Bricius.

"Very serious." Marcant laughed. "I'm sorry, sister. Did you really think I did all of this for you? No, I will destroy the Norsemen and go to the king at Doomster Hill with the sad news all of Cadell's family and household are dead, apart from you and your daughters, murdered by the Norsemen. I will marry his daughter and destroy his murderers and will, therefore, have won the right to rule these lands, as well as my own. And now I have located Lady Aoife, it's time to move things along."

"I carry the Norseman's child already," Aoife said.

"Then it will be stillborn," promised Lord Marcant. "A minor inconvenience. Just like the two of you." The comment was aimed at Father Bricius and Rhydderch.

"But Marcant," Ula began as the priest stared at Marcant and then at Ula. Marcant smiled at them, then nodded to one of his soldiers. As the soldier drew his sword, Rhydderch turned his horse and, with a swift kick of his legs, was through the gates. Bricius opened his mouth as if to speak to Ula, then he too rode out through the gates. Ula covered her face with her hands as the sound of fighting outside the palisade could be heard. Then Marcant shouted an order, and the noise was drowned out by the fighting in the courtyard.

All was chaos.

Tormod thrust Aoife behind him and fought off a soldier who had headed straight for him. Then Arne came from the hall behind them and Tormod pushed her into his arms. "Get her out of here! Take her to the longship and out onto the loch."

Aoife waited only for a moment, then allowed herself to be hurried by Arne towards the rear of the great hall. She knew where he was taking her, and was surprised only at the fact the Norsemen had found the secret passage so quickly. She should have realised—her vision had shown Arne and his men at the loch-side end of the passage. Down through the wine cellar they headed and then along the dank, narrow passage through the rocks.

"Elisedd mentioned it," Arne offered by way of explanation. "And when we saw the Britons approach, we looked for it in earnest. It is a sensible precaution. And we would have never found the exit from the outside. We must hurry so I can return to the fight."

"But what if there are soldiers coming through the passage?" asked Aoife.

"There is someone guarding the other end, don't worry," Arne assured her.

CHAPTER THIRTY-EIGHT

BROTHERS OF THUNDER

TORMOD'S MEN FOUGHT WELL. They pushed the Britons out of the courtyard and as they passed through the gates of the palisade, it was easier to separate them out and pick them off. The archers' vantage point in the fort was another key to their success and soon the Britons were on the run.

Occasionally he caught a glimpse of Arne fighting and knew that meant Aoife had taken refuge in the longship now a distance from shore. He hoped the Britons had not noticed it and she was safely on board.

Finally, he reached Ulf outside the gates. He had Lord Marcant at the end of his sword, Ula beside him.

"Chain them!" ordered Tormod.

Ulf and some of his men set to work and when they were finished, he asked, "What will you do with them?"

Tormod shrugged. "Take them to their king for judgment. As an act of faith in the alliance he has with the Norse." He signalled for the longship to come in to shore.

"You will regret this," Marcant shouted.

"Not as much as you will, I suspect," retorted Tormod. "And at least I will live."

"Aoife is not worth this," said Ula. "Not worth any of this."

"She is."

"These lands are ours!"

"These lands belong to whoever can keep them," said Tormod. "And my children will be part Briton. However, I think, given the situation, it is important you are made to answer for your crimes against Lord Cadell. Your own household, Lady Ula. Your own husband. Your own people. And you had them killed."

"Cadell was a traitor. I should have seen it before I married him. His first wife... and then to be willing to honour an alliance with Norsemen." She spat on the ground.

The longship was now close enough to shore for him to see Aoife, apparently unharmed, standing on the deck.

He turned back to Ula. "You have let your own husband be murdered, and for what?"

"For this land. Land that belongs to my people. As does the land that you claim is yours."

"Not anymore," Tormod replied, shaking his head. "The lands belong to me and mine. One day they will belong to my child. By blood through his mother. And by might through me."

"Any child of hers will be the devil's spawn." Ula laughed cruelly.

"Aoife has a gift. Not a curse. Her sons will be mighty warriors. Destined to dine in the halls of Valhalla with heroes. While you... you are a traitor and a coward." Tormod signalled to Ulf. "We will take her to Doomster Hill for judgment."

Björn and his men appeared from outside the palisade. "There is no sign of the priest or the steward," said Björn.

"Where would they go? Where is the man who murdered your husband for you?" Tormod asked Ula, who merely laughed.

"You have no proof," Ula said, although she looked wary. "You will not find him, and besides, who do you think King Rhun will believe?"

"We will see," said Tormod. "Prepare to transport them upriver to their king."

Ulf did as he was bid.

Tormod waited while they were led away and then started to wade through the water towards Aoife's longship.

CHAPTER THIRTY-NINE

BROTHERS OF THUNDER

A OIFE HAD BEEN UNABLE to watch the fight. The Norsemen had fought well, as had the Britons. There had been losses on both sides and at times she had been unsure who would be victorious. She hadn't seen Rhydderch or Father Bricius anywhere. By now they must either be dead or have escaped. When the fighting was over, she saw that both Lord Marcant and Ula had been captured and was relieved that at least those behind her father's murder would not escape justice.

It was a great relief when she finally saw Tormod join his cousin. The fighting seemed to be over at that point. She watched as Tormod faced Marcant and her stepmother. Ula shouted at him, and Aoife saw her struggle in Ulf's grip, but there was no way she would escape from the much stronger man. She didn't know whether she could stand to watch what happened next. Then she saw Ula and Marcant being chained, and felt some sense of relief that Tormod hadn't had them killed. There had been enough death already and more than anything now, she wanted answers.

Aoife sank down onto the deck in relief until the sound of someone splashing through the water to reach the boat reached her ears. Before she managed to push herself to her feet, Tormod hauled himself on board.

"What will happen now?" she asked him, standing and staring at the sight of Ula and Marcant being led in chains towards one of the other boats.

"I am merely going to deliver them to King Rhun. He can pass judgment for the murder of your father and his household."

"She... she had my father killed."

Tormod said nothing.

"How could she?"

"Greed, ambition, who knows?"

"Where is Bricius?"

Tormod's gaze shifted uneasily towards Car Cadell and then back to her. "I'm sorry. Rhydderch and Bricius escaped. The warriors I sent after them returned empty-handed. They did, however, kill the soldiers Marcant sent after them."

"How is that possible?"

Tormod shook his head and shrugged. "I fear there may have been some sorcery at work."

"Bricius is a priest!"

"They have vanished." Tormod took her hands. "I am sorry. Bricius deserved to die for killing your father and for the way he treated you." His grip tightened on her hands, and he pulled her closer to him. "Nothing would make me turn against you."

Tears welled in her eyes, her emotions a conflicted mixture of grief and anger, but also of gratitude and love for her husband. Her father had made his choice, choosing Ula over her. That did not mean that he deserved this, however.

"Come, we will go to Doomster Hill and ask King Rhun to call a *Thing*."

"They don't call it a *Thing*."

Tormod shrugged. "It doesn't matter what they call it. They have built a place of judgment upriver in Gorfaen and we will take Ula and Marcant there."

"You think Rhun will listen to you?"

"Yes."

He sounded so sure that she almost believed he would be successful.

"After all," he said. "I am married to Cadell's daughter. It is my right to ask for his death to be avenged."

"I don't think that really means much to them. To any of them."

"It does to me. And besides, your king needs to maintain a relationship with my people. After what happened to his father... However, that is not our fight." Tormod ran his hands up and down her back, then set his mouth to hers. After only a moment's hesitation, she kissed him back. It wasn't the kiss that made her happy. It was the knowledge behind it that he saw them as being together. A family. She broke off the kiss.

"You are mine, as I am yours. We are family." He placed a hand carefully on her stomach. "All of us."

She smiled at him. A hope that she'd hardly dared to feel blossomed in her chest. She laughed, then stopped and looked back at her father's fort. "It doesn't matter."

"What doesn't?"

"King Rhun's justice. I know the truth. I know that I did nothing wrong, nothing to deserve this."

"And your father?"

"My father made his own decisions and died because of them. He fell in love with the wrong person. It's tragic, although he's hardly the first man to do so."

"Or the last." Tormod grinned wryly. "It is a fate that can befall any man. Even when he is determined not to."

He fell silent, staring at her. Then he kissed her again, smiled and ran his hand down the side of her face.

"Determined not to what?" she asked.

"Love you. I couldn't help it. Told myself that you were trying to make a fool of me as Ingrid had. That I might miss your true intentions if I allowed myself to love you."

She smiled at that, then her hand flew to her mouth. "Rhiannon! How could I forget? Have you found her?"

Tormod frowned. "I do not know what she looks like. All we can do is check the bodies."

They returned to the fort and checked every woman's body that they found. Aoife wept for the loss of those familiar to her, but when there was no sign of Rhiannon she held onto a small flicker of hope that she might still be alive.

"Perhaps they have taken her to Lord Marcant's household. I presume that's where your sisters are."

"I hope so," she said, and whispered a silent prayer for her friend.

"I will leave Björn and some warriors here to look after the fort. And after we have seen the king, we will return home, together."

She smiled. Home. One in which she was both accepted and loved. "Thank you. For giving me a home."

"Thank you," he replied. "For giving me one, and for being a wife that I can love."

"Even one who is cursed?"

"Your curse has saved our lives more than once. I am grateful for it."

EPILOGUE

BROTHERS
OF
THUNDER

A MONTH LATER, AOIFE stood on the shore, staring across the firth in the last of the evening's light. She heard her husband behind her. Delicious shivers flitted down her spine as he kissed her neck and ran his hands over her swelling belly.

She leaned against him, content. The king had banished Ula just the week before and she and her daughters had been sent to Car Luel. Marcant had been sentenced to death for the murder of Cadell, a sentence which was to be carried out upon the arrival of Cadell's heir. It seemed that Tormod had been correct. The system of justice adopted by King Rhun did indeed resemble the Norse system and judgment had taken place at Doomster Hill, a large mound of earth on the south side of the river within sight of the palace which was being constructed at Perthawc.

Tormod was content with King Rhun's ruling of Cadell's nephew inheriting the land, which was better than any other alternative. He was due to arrive soon.

Aoife worried about seeing her cousin again. She hoped that that distance was at least in part due to Ula's presence and not the rumours about her involvement at Alt Clut. She hoped that they may one day find common ground.

"This is for you," Tormod said as he moved her hair away from her neck. She realised he was putting a necklace on her and when she touched it, she smiled. A quick look affirmed her hope.

"Ula gave it back," she said as she stared down at her amethyst cross.

"Not willingly," Tormod said. "But I told Rhun that it did not belong to her and he forced her to surrender it."

"Thank you." She turned and kissed him. With their arms around each other, they looked down the river.

Above their heads, in the deepening darkness, two ravens flew, watching, waiting.

ALSO BY MAIRIBETH MACMILLAN

The Viking's Cursed Bride

Aoife has been an outsider most of her life. Half Briton, half Pict, she's been rejected by her father's new wife, despite saving them all from the Norse raid on Alt Clut two years previously. Rescued from a life of misery as a nun, she is forced to marry one of the Norse invaders to ensure her family's safety—ridding them of a cursed daughter, while putting her own life at risk.

Jarl Tormod intends to settle on the River Clut and a high-born bride from amongst the Britons ought to ensure the safety and prosperity of the Norse settlement. But as attacks on the settlement increase, Tormod realises the Britons have deceived him and is determined to take revenge.

All Aoife wants is a place to belong, but traitors are everywhere, and finding those responsible might mean losing those they hold most dear.

The Viking's Warrior Bride
Fighting for their future

Determined to redeem her father's name as a warrior, Ylva has no desire to be a mother. On the eve of returning home to the Norselands to find a foster family for her child, she is injured in an attack by a group of mercenaries. When Björn discovers her secret, everything changes. He has never wanted a family, but is anything else truly worth fighting for?

After a series of attacks on the fort they have been guarding, they disguise themselves as traders and travel up the River Clut to gather information, but the situation grows stranger with every village they visit. The Britons are unhappy with their king and his choice of allies, and someone is fanning the flames of dissent. Everywhere, villagers are missing and who is the mysterious bard living in the abandoned royal residence at Alt Clut? When a woman and her son stow away on the trade boat, all their lives are placed in danger and they are forced to make a stand. But how much are they willing to sacrifice for their future?

The Viking's Princess Bride
Kidnapped by Britons. Rescued by Vikings!

Princess Maithgemm of the Strathclyde Britons is hiding in the Norse settlement at Kirkjaster. Every day she looks across the River Clut to the lands that rightfully belong to her son, but claiming them might put both of their lives at risk. Staying with the Norsemen, however, is becoming intolerable thanks to one man — Arne Olafsson. He sees her not as a victim, but as an enemy. When she learns that even the other Britons fear that her presence compromises their safety, she takes her son and flees — straight into a snowstorm.

Brutally tortured and left for dead years ago, Arne Olafsson has a reputation as a fierce warrior but is recognised by his scars — scars that cover almost his entire body. Betrayed by a former lover, he avoids relationships. After all, who needs a woman who might kill you? When he follows the princess onto the moors, he fears she's leading him into an ambush.

Instead, they find themselves stranded in a snowstorm on the moors. Just as a tentative trust develops, the past returns to drive a wedge between them.

Do their lives, or deaths, lie together or alone?

THE VIKING'S WARRIOR BRIDE

BROTHERS
OF
THUNDER

CHAPTER ONE

KINGDOM OF STRATH CLUT. Late Autumn 872 CE.

The longship slid through the still waters of the loch as dawn broke. They had portaged from Loch Long to Loch Llumonwy the evening before and camped on the western shore of the latter overnight. Ylva Ivarrsdatter stood at the prow, ostensibly watching for her first sight of Car Cadell even though she knew the fort would not come into view until they had rounded the next headland. Instead, she closed her eyes and took a deep breath of the fresh morning air, desperate to subdue the nausea now plaguing her daily.

"Here, eat this," Elisedd's small hand pressed a chunk of bread into hers. She broke off a piece and chewed it before swallowing tentatively. It seemed to help. She ate another and then another. Then the boy handed her a skin of fresh water.

"Sip it slowly. Too much will make you sick," he said.

"Thank you." As she looked at his concerned expression, guilt tightened her chest. His concern for her was real, and yet when they had first met, she had seen only the face of a Briton, an enemy, and been ready to see him pay for a crime he had not committed. Perhaps it was a sort of penance that had made her agree to accompany him back to his former home in Car Cadell.

It certainly had the potential to complicate her own life if she was not careful. She looked down at him and ruffled his hair.

"Are you looking forward to seeing your mother?"

Elisedd nodded, but kept his gaze straight ahead over the prow of the boat. She was not the only one, then, who was worried about what would happen when they arrived.

"Ulf said..." Elisedd stopped and took a deep breath. "Ulf said I must be kind to her. She was not well treated by Lord Marcant's men."

"She went with Lady Aoife's half-sisters?"

"Yes, she became their lady's maid after Lady Aoife was sent to the convent."

"Surely they will have looked after her?"

He shrugged. His mother, Rhiannon, had been one of the Britons taken to Lord Marcant's lands south of the River Clut. Most as prisoners, but Ylva had thought that as lady's maid to his nieces Marcant would not have imprisoned Rhiannon. She shuddered. Men could be cruel to women they had power over. At least with Lord Marcant now himself a prisoner of King Rhun of Strath Clut, all his captives had been freed. There hadn't been many. Few had survived the massacre at Car Cadell, and Ylva had heard rumours the captives had been mistreated. She hoped Rhiannon was one of the luckier ones.

The longship lurched, and Ylva grabbed hold of the side. She closed her eyes and focused on breathing slowly in and out as her stomach roiled.

Elisedd slid his hand into hers and gave it a reassuring squeeze.

"It will pass in a few weeks."

Ylva jerked her hand away and stared at him. How could this boy — a boy too young for arm rings — have realised something she had only just admitted to herself?

"How... how did you know?"

Elisedd shrugged. "You are like this every morning," he said solemnly. "My mother told me when a woman is going to have a—"

"Don't say it!" Ylva said urgently.

"But—" Elisedd stopped.

"I am not yet sure." She tried to smile at him, but was unsure how successful she was.

Ylva had run through many scenarios in her head over the past few days when it had become clear there really would be a child this time. She did not intend to ever be a mother, had never wanted the complications and expectations motherhood would bring. She was a warrior born and bred, her dead father's only legacy. *Ivarr Djarfr*, Ivarr the Valiant. He had been renowned far and wide for his fighting skill, and she was determined to prove that his death had not been in vain. A child would hamper that.

Some warrior women simply left the babes to die on the rocks, but she knew she could never do that. Maybe Magda, the Norse woman who had fostered Elisedd these past few months, would take the babe and raise him for her. Him. She was sure it was a boy. But if Björn returned to Kirkjaster, then he would realise the child was his. She was worried he would ask her to marry him and then expect her to give up her warrior's lifestyle to care for the child, while he changed nothing about his own life. Life was not fair.

No, if she were going to have the child, she would have to leave Strath Clut. Perhaps she could go back home to the Norselands, but if she were going to do that, she would need to go soon before the winter storms set in. There were always the *Northreyar* or *Suthreyar* islands off the coast of this land, where many Norse people had now settled.

"Have you told him yet?" Elisedd's voice startled her. She had been so lost in her own thoughts that she had almost forgotten he was there.

"Him?"

"Björn." Then Elisedd frowned. "It is Björn who—"

"Yes." Ylva smiled to herself. Björn was the only man she had ever wanted, one of only two she had ever lain with, but the boy did not need to know that. Nor did Björn.

"Ah!" Elisedd nodded at her. "You wanted him to be the first to know. I understand." He pressed his lips together to show that he would not tell.

Ylva ruffled the boy's dark hair and did not correct his misapprehension. "How did you get to be so wise?"

Elisedd shrugged. "Is that why you came with me?"

Ylva sighed. "I came because Lady Aoife asked me to, and I didn't want to refuse a request from the jarl's wife. Plus, I wanted to make sure you kept out of trouble on the way here. When we arrive, your mother can take over, and I will go back."

Elisedd didn't smile at her feeble attempt at humour.

"But..." He tilted his head to one side and eyed her curiously. "But Björn is here. I thought that... you would be staying."

Ylva looked back at Car Cadell. "I came only to take you back to your mother. Once I have done that, I will return to Kirkjaster. We need to ensure that our own lands are defended."

"Will Björn return with you?"

"No, not until Lord Cadell's heir arrives," Ylva said. "And perhaps not even for a while after that. Car Cadell also needs good men to defend it and to help Lord Cenydd establish control over his lands."

"But surely you will need to be together?"

"No, we don't." Ylva squeezed Elisedd's hand. "Please, say nothing of this to anyone, I beg you."

"But..."

"Elisedd, it is complicated."

"But... you will tell him?"

"I don't know... Björn has always been clear that... that there is no future for us."

"But why?"

"We are both warriors, not suited for domestic life," she said. "He does not wish for a home and family. I will sort this myself. It is for me to deal with, truly."

"I would give anything to be able to see my father," Elisedd said, staring down the loch towards Car Cadell. The boy dashed a tear from his eye and straightened. She smiled at him. It was important for him to be seen as strong. She put a hand on the side of his face and brushed the last remnants of the tear away with her thumb.

"Some things are not meant to be. We must accept them and not fight against our fate. Be happy that you are going to see your mother and please, Elisedd, do not tell anyone."

The boy looked distressed, but he nodded. "I will do as you ask."

"Do I have your word as a warrior?"

Elisedd looked up at her, and a grin spread across his face and he puffed his chest out with pride at her words.

"My word as a warrior," he said firmly. "Does this mean I will get my arm rings soon?"

"I will mention it to Björn as soon as we arrive and ask him to speak to Arne," she promised, smiling. "But you are still young and have much to learn. Do not rush into a situation when you are not ready."

Elisedd nodded and leaned against the prow of the ship. The fort was visible now, and she could sense his excitement. An excitement that she couldn't share. This was not her home, even if the man she... the man she what? She and Björn were kindred spirits. Their relationship was one of convenience, nothing else. Love was not a part of that. Neither of them was born to love — only to fight.

Ylva had missed Björn more than she'd expected. Not all the time, but sometimes in the evenings and especially now as the nights grew longer. With each one that passed, she found herself wishing she could talk to him, hear his laughter, and in the deepest darkness, she often wished he was beside her, sharing his body. She missed the way he made her feel. She ran a hand over her gently rounded stomach. She had been fortunate in the past, but not this time. Perhaps it was merely the fact that over the summer, she and Björn had been in the same place at the same time for longer than they ever had before. Or perhaps it was because she had been training and fighting less often recently as she helped to finish the settlement.

She sighed. Would she tell Björn about the child? It would be much simpler if she made the decision herself, wouldn't it? She glanced at Elisedd and wondered what her child would be like at his age. The thought of never knowing made her frown. But Björn had always been insistent that he would never marry, never have a family. Björn was a warrior before anything else. It was what he was trained to be, and the only thing that he genuinely loved doing. She understood that. She, too, was a warrior. But unlike him, if they had a child, she could not be both a warrior and a parent—certainly not alone.

For a moment, she wondered if he might change his mind. Perhaps living in this new land, his view of the future would be different, and he would want a more permanent arrangement now. She shook off the thought. That was not for either of them, and they knew it. How could she tell him? Despite what she had said to Elisedd, she had not planned to. She had tried to persuade herself that she would when it became a certainty, but as the days passed, she grew less and less convinced that she wanted to tell him at all. Once he knew, she was sure he would want nothing to do with either her or the child. He would retreat into silence as he had done after his father's death. Of that, she was sure. He had always been clear that he would never be a father. Or else he would expect her to stay at home as a wife and mother while he lived the life she wanted for herself. She could not agree to that — not for anyone.

A strong breeze propelled them across the loch's surface, with no need for anyone to row and all too soon the boat grounded on the beach. She looked up at Car Cadell. The last time she had been here, there had been only silence and a fort full of the dead. Briefly she thought she could still smell the dead burning — over fifty men and boys and some women, too. Her stomach twisted again. She pushed herself to her feet, gathered her things together and climbed from the ship before splashing through the shallow water and onto the mixed sand and shingle of the shore.

As soon as they were on the beach, Elisedd raced towards a woman standing just outside the palisade. Ylva smiled as she watched mother and son unite joyfully. Whatever had happened to Rhiannon, she was still alive and eager to see her son. Tears sprang to Ylva's eyes at the sight, and she ducked her head so no one would notice.

The sensation of dry land played havoc with her sense of balance. The queasiness threatened to overwhelm her and, not wanting Björn to see her in this state, she hurried to the edge of the woods. As soon as she was hidden by the forest, she sat down and put her spinning head between her knees. She drew in deep breaths through her nose, determined not to give in to the whims of her body. She had learned to fight on through the pain of strained muscles and torn flesh — she could learn to ignore the discomforts of impending motherhood.

It wasn't as easy as she'd thought, however. She wished she had some more of the dry bread Elisedd had given her earlier — she would need to make sure she carried some with her at all times — but a soft gurgling alerted her to a small stream nearby and she stood and made her way slowly over to it. She washed her hands and face and took a few sips of the cool, clear water before heading towards the path that led alongside the beach to the fort.

She heard a faint sound in the woods behind her and turned. Nothing. Still, she headed towards the beach. She could hear someone walking along the shingle towards her. She leant against the trunk of a tree and tried to keep her breathing steady. She peered around the trunk and closed her hand over the handle of her sword. She shifted the bundle of her belongings towards the centre of her back and stepped out, sword pointed towards the figure that stood at the edge of the beach.

In front of her stood Björn, grinning. She kept her sword up for longer than necessary, then lowered it and smiled back despite herself. She had forgotten how much his physical presence affected her. The way he looked at her with a mixture of desire and laughter had always appealed. She sheathed her sword, and he took a step towards her. She breathed in the familiar scent of his leather armour and the man inside sending her senses reeling as it always did.

"Miss me?" he asked.

"No," she lied. "Why? Did you miss me? Is that why you came looking for me?" She mustn't let him know she had thought of him almost every waking minute - especially over the past few weeks. She wondered if he had another woman here, although the fact that he had purposefully sought her out would seem to suggest he didn't.

"You didn't arrive with the others off the ship, and yet Elisedd told me you were anxious to see me."

"Did he now?"

"I thought you'd be in more of a hurry to see me."

"You thought it was me who was in a hurry to see you?" Ylva's gaze slid lower to where the bulge in his breeks suggested it was his own lust that made him anxious to see her.

"The nights here have been cold and empty." Björn took a step towards her, drew her towards him, and lowered his mouth. He paused, his lips almost, but not quite, touching hers, and she knew he was waiting for her to kiss him. She slid her sword back into its scabbard and waited. What if he was able to tell? That was ridiculous. She had hardly known herself. And it wasn't as if anything they did together now would make the situation worse. Even if his desire for her was only physical, she shared those same desires. Everything was about to change. For now, she wanted to pretend things between them were as they had always been. Simple and purely physical. She leaned forward and kissed him. She couldn't get any more pregnant.

Continue Reading

About Mairibeth MacMillan

Mairibeth MacMillan lives on the shores of Loch Long on the edge of Argyll and Bute. While very picturesque, living there involves a keen understanding of logistics to ensure that her family get to the right places at the right times and hopefully with the right equipment! In her spare time, she enjoys wild-swimming in Loch Long, embroidery and candle-making. She was a drama teacher for many years until, during a career break, she decided to rekindle a childhood love of creative writing and playwriting. Over the years she has been successful with short stories and flash fiction in various competitions, magazines and anthologies. In 2014 she was shortlisted for the New Writer's Award at the Festival of Romance. Inspired by the discovery of a Viking fort marked on the Ordnance Survey map nearby, she started working on a series of Viking Romances set in the Kingdom of Strathclyde at the end of the Ninth century.

Find me on my website at mairibethmacmillan.com, or on Facebook at Mairibeth MacMillan—Author, and on Twitter @MairibethM.

Printed in Great Britain
by Amazon

37347933R00169